MW01170835

Justice Justice

Novels by Henry S. Maxfield

Legacy of a Spy
Another Spring

To: Jerry Hunter
the "2007" Jury Forman of the Year!

All the Best
Henry S Maxfield

JUSTICE JUSTICE

published by Southwick House
www.SouthwickHouse.com
15 Hickory Road Wolfeboro NH 03894
FIRST EDITION
Library of Congress copyright
September 5 2006 TXu1 – 318 – 279
TXUOO1319279

Justice Justice

Henry S. Maxfield

Southwick House Publisher
SouthwickHouse.com

FOREWORD

Trial by combat is a very old idea. Placidus discussed it in the 6th Century. It was referred to as Quasi duorum bellum, physical combat between two, the purpose of which was to settle disputes considered beyond the reach of human wisdom, the presumption being that God would intervene on the side of justice.

Our present adversarial system, based on the assumption that justice is an unachievable abstract, is the modern version of trial by combat. The results are just as haphazard. It is unlikely that opposing counsel are relying on divine interference for justice, if indeed, justice plays any role in the courtroom process.

What follows is true with that special validity unique to fiction.

DEDICATION

To My Wife, Elizabeth Burchenal Maxfield, who believes in the sterling qualities of lawyers – or most lawyers – and to those of us who wish that were true.

QUOTES

"I don't do justice, I do the law."
Oliver Wendell Holmes

"The law cannot think. The law accepts no responsibility. The law does not care.
Can the Law alone ever be an adequate substitute for justice??"

Henry Southwick Maxfield

Power tends to corrupt; absolute power corrupts absolutely
An observation that a person's sense of morality lessons as his or her power increases.
Lord Acton a British Historian

CHAPTER ONE

The cherry blossoms were in bloom along the Potomac. The sky was a pastel blue with occasional fluffy white clouds. The air was soft and balmy with very little humidity. Today it was impossible to believe the nation's capitol was built on a swamp.

It was late in the afternoon and the rush hour traffic was just beginning. Cars were still moving at a good pace up and down the broad expanse of Independence Avenue. The Mall was crowded with visitors from everywhere. Flags of all nations were furling and unfurling in a gentle breeze. The white marble government buildings shone in the sunlight each displaying the American Flag.

Washington was at its best – a fitting capitol for the most powerful nation on earth – impressive to all privileged to see it. The domed Capitol, situated halfway up the Hill, dominated the scene The broad marble steps invited all to make the climb.

Beside the Capitol, to the right, a road climbed upward and gave access to important buildings above.

On this road there was little traffic. On the first road to the left, along which were the Library of Congress and the United States Supreme Court, there was no traffic.

The broad marble steps of the Supreme Court, frequently the setting for loud debates, were empty.

This massive Roman structure was fronted by ten, gigantic, fluted Corinthian columns. Engraved above, chiseled in capital letters, are the words:

EQUAL JUSTICE UNDER LAW.

Possibly it was the hour or the fact that it was Friday.

A small black sedan, having turned into the road from the right, cruised slowly past the Library of Congress continued past the Supreme Court and disappeared. Moments later it reappeared going in the opposite direction. It came to a stop just below the center of the great marble steps. The motor was running. The occupants remained inside.

The massive door of the Court opened and a lone figure appeared at the top of the steps. He was tall and dressed for spring in a sand-colored khaki suit. He stood for a moment, able from his perspective, to see the back of the Capitol and part of the Mall beyond.

Still looking outward he began the descent.

At that moment both the rear and front windows in the black sedan lowered and the barrels of two weapons appeared. The tall figure was about half way down when the guns began firing.

Sharp staccato sounds as the guns, trained in tandem, fired into the man's body, slowly, systematically, riddling it. The figure collapsed slowly, its forward motion stopped; blood spurting and oozing from the myriad of wounds, staining the shreds of his sand–colored suit.

The firing continued upward, the bullets chipping pieces of marble, until they were bouncing and ricocheting off the massive doors – a potent deterrent to the guards, guns drawn, now crouched inside.

The firing ceased. The guns were withdrawn. The windows closed, and slowly – very slowly – the black sedan proceeded toward the end of the street and turned right into what had now become the full flow of rush hour traffic. The sedan merged – blended - into the main stream just below the Capitol.

**** **** ****** ***

President Walter Whitredge, seated behind his desk in the Oval Office, picked up the Washington Post from the top of a disorderly pile of papers.

The assassination of an Associate Justice of the Supreme Court was impossible to believe, an incomprehensible attack on an almost sacred instrument for American Justice. One journalist had already suggested it was more significant than the assassination of a President.

Walter Whitredge frowned. Had the columnist just degraded the office of the Presidency? As a newly elected President who had run as an Independent, possibly there were those who would consider a non-party electee more expendable. The President focused on the article below the black banner headlines. There were few facts beyond the name – Associate Justice Eliot Shapiro of the US Supreme Court.

The District Chief of police surmised, based on the concentration and intensity of fire, that there were at least two guns and therefore two gunmen and possibly also a driver. It was confirmed that it was Shapiro's custom in good weather to exit the building by the broad marble steps. No organization had claimed responsibility, but terrorism could not be ruled out. No witnesses had come forward.

Walter Whitredge put the paper into the wastebasket and regarded the jumble of papers on his desk that required his attention.

He stood up, stretched, and went to the windows that looked out onto the White House lawn.

Another beautiful day. Washington was showing off and he wished he could go for a long walk, well aware he could not go alone - even here. He returned across the beautiful royal blue rug, skirting the Official Seal woven into the carpet, questioning the design that made it possible for anyone to walk on the United States Official Seal.

His experience as a fighter pilot in Viet Nam had intensified his patriotism, even though he had not approved of that war.

He regarded the desk, a desk that had a name – ***Resolute***. It had been made from the remains of the ***Resolute***, sunk by the American Navy during the Revolution - a sardonic gift from Queen Victoria.

Whitredge inspected the oval room. There was history here – the scene of momentous decisions, some of which had been made alone without benefit of any advice or against advice. However made, the ultimate responsibility for decisions was the President's. Whitredge called to mind 'give 'em Hell', Harry. It was Truman who had said, "The buck stops here."

Walter Whitredge smiled. Harry's principal decision had been a whopper.

Whitredge frowned as he contemplated a decision he was about to make.

After being given permission, a short dapper man, apparently in his late forties, entered and sat in a chair to the right of the

President's desk. Cliff Sharp preferred sitting, having long ago decided he appeared taller when seated. He believed his lack of height was due to the shortness of his legs. Even sitting, however, he was still much shorter than President Whitredge who, at six foot six, Sharp concluded, was abnormally tall.

"Good Morning, Cliff. What's on your mind on this lovely day?"

President Whitredge was still an enigma and Sharp was wary of enigmas. Walter Whitredge was the first political naïf Sharp had ever encountered, and Sharp prided himself on his ability to assess and handicap every politician on the Washington scene

Sharp considered Whitredge a political freak, but one he could maneuver. Outwardly the man was perfect, commanding, tall, well spoken and apparently sincere. He was handsome, had a noble profile and a wide grin reminiscent of Eisenhower. The fact that Whitredge had told Sharp – and everyone – he believed in the people, had moved Sharp right down to his shoes.

"The assassination of Shapiro is one of the most pressing items on your agenda, Mr. President as I'm sure you agree."

"I had heard of the man, of course, Cliff. I had no clear idea of his stand - on anything. I suppose he'll be missed. I have the uneasy feeling we will never discover the assassins or their motive in taking such a terrible risk"

He frowned and looked thoughtfully into space.

"Professional assassins are always difficult to discover, Mr. President."

"What makes you think they're professional?"

"The absence of spontaneity, the careful planning. They must have had at least one informant as to Shapiro's schedule for that day and time."

"An inside job, Sharp?"

Sharp shrugged.

"Anything can happen in Washington. We have created a lot of enemies, sir."

Whitredge nodded, adding:

"At home as well as abroad."

"It's not too early to consider Shapiro's replacement. It's an excellent opportunity sir."

"We haven't had the man's funeral yet. What's the rush?"

Sharp ignored the question.

"You'll have lots of help, of course."

"From whom – beside you?"

Sharp blinked.

"The Committee of Fourteen."

"Who is the Committee of Fourteen?"

It was just the kind of question Sharp relished as it made him feel needed - and wise. He was invariably patient and replied in detail.

"The Committee of Fourteen is headed by the President of the American Bar Association who selects thirteen respected professionals, federal judges, graduates of the most prestigious law schools such as Harvard, Stanford and Yale – all with impeccable legal credentials. It is that Committee who will ultimately recommend to the President the names of suitable candidates."

"Sounds like the Wolves appointed to guard the chickens."

Sharp blinked again.

"But you make the final choice, Mr. President – and that will make the appointee your man."

"I doubt that, Sharp."

The President looked sternly at Sharp.

"You are obsessed with power, Cliff which may affect your judgment."

"Power is what it's all about."

Sharp suddenly found it difficult to control himself in the face of such naiveté. He started again - much more slowly.

"Without power, the President is helpless to get his agenda across. As an Independent you don't have the backing of any political party. If you hadn't received the support of your friend, Senator Bradford Justice, I'm not sure you would have made it. It's a damn shame he decided not to run for a second term."

Sharp paused for a moment.

"Every President has wanted the opportunity to get his man on the Supreme Court. It is after all a political institution. Roosevelt tried to pack the court. You're fortunate there is an opening for you to fill. I'm sure you can find a lawyer who will represent your opinions and back your agenda. You can appoint a woman. Of course we already have two."

"I wonder" Whitredge looked thoughtful. "I need to decide what my agenda is."

"I'm sure there are many lawyers who believe in the law as the only route to justice."

"Possibly that is the problem, Cliff."

"What?" Sharp was not sure he had heard his President."

"I repeat, Cliff – the law."

"But what else is there beside the Law? The Law is what we have!" Sharp was in danger of losing it. He tried to collect himself. He immediately apologized.

"Forgive me, Mister President. I got carried away."

The President nodded.

"That's quite alright, Cliff. I wouldn't keep you on as my Chief of Staff if you were afraid - or unwilling – to speak your mind."

Sharp realized he should feel relieved, but he didn't. Something was amiss.

"I don't know your reaction to the assassination of an Associate Justice, Cliff, but for my part I have to admit, although appalled, I don't feel any personal loss.

"Apparently you don't either, and I have the feeling we're not alone. I don't really know much about the Justices - as people, their likes and dislikes, their feelings. I don't know their legal credentials or their opinions and nothing whatever about their character. They are too remote, too isolated from the rest of us."

"And that is as it should be. Their sole duty is to uphold the Constitution. They should live apart from the rest of us."

"Do I detect a trace of worship, Clifford Sharp? You who are the ultimate pragmatist and cynic. I'm shocked."

Whitredge smiled. He decided he had gone too far with the little man.

"I never would have made it without your advice, Cliff, and I am grateful, though I have wondered why you were willing to act as my campaign manager. I know you don't believe in the people – as I do. I also know, even with all your help and know-how, I would not have succeeded without the people. It was the people who did the voting, prompted by the fact that I am not a politician and their belief that my primary concern is for them."

Sharp looked away to hide his disapproval. The idea that anyone could believe in the people was absurd. He knew better. He also knew there was no such thing as political loyalty. He had been the campaign manager for Whitredge's predecessor, and the son of a bitch had dropped him.

Sharp regarded this big handsome man with the Eisenhower grin and frowned. He had backed this coinable face and grin because he sensed Walter Whitredge was a possible winner, that with the right guidance – his guidance – Whitredge might even become an effective President and certainly Whitredge was undoubtedly the last opportunity Sharp would ever have to be the power behind the throne. Whitredge's apparent naiveté had proven public appeal. His frequently stated belief that the people, properly appealed to, could do anything was foolish, but Cliff Sharp had to admit that approach had certainly been effective – so far.

Walter Whitredge had been elected by the biggest landslide since Roosevelt, and Whitredge had constantly relied on Sharp for advice. It was turning out better than he had anticipated. Of course, Sharp had to recognize that Whitredge's popularity had been helped by his predecessor's misbehavior. The political climate had been right for the acceptance of an independent – non-party - candidate.

Walter Whitredge was smiling at the contrast between them. Cliff Sharp was quite small - not more than five feet six - and slight. People were already referring to Cliff as his mascot, but not to Sharp's face. It did not pay to make fun of a man so close to the President. Throughout the campaign Cliff liked to make the people constantly aware that his candidate had been captain of an undefeated University of Michigan football team and a fighter ace in Viet Nam.

"You do have a candidate, Cliff?."

"Not specifically, sir."

"Well?"

"Since the deceased was a Jew, I – we – you – should seriously consider appointing a Jew."

"As I understand it, one of our most distinguished Justices now serving is a Jew. Anyway, the only thing Jewish about Eliot

Shapiro is his last name. He married an Episcopalian of distinguished American lineage and joined the Episcopal Church." Whitredge smiled. "If his appointment was because he was a Jew, it was ridiculous."

"Possibly, but there will be a cry among Jewish groups that he was assassinated because he was a Jew and will demand that his replacement be a Jew."

"Nobody knows the identity or the motives of the assassins, but that idea never crossed my mind. I suppose, in our increasingly polyglot nation, there will probably always be hate groups, but American Jewry doesn't have to worry. My father's generation risked their lives to get rid of Hitler and his barbaric treatment of the Jews. This country has welcomed Jews, contributed billions to establish and support the Jewish State of Israel. Jewish political power in this country is substantial."

He paused. and regarded Sharp sternly.

"My Appointee's religion – if any – will be the last thing on my mind."

Cliff Sharp blinked again.

Whitredge decided this was not the time to tell Sharp he had already considered Shapiro's replacement. He knew his decision would be against Sharp's 'religion'. Up to now, he had thought Sharp didn't believe in anything – certainly not in the law.

The President returned his attention to the pile of reports on his desk and Sharp realized he had been dismissed. He squelched, with difficulty, the questions he suddenly – urgently - wanted to ask and left, closing the door quietly behind him.

Whitredge had noticed the blinks. It was the first time he had seen any uncertainty on Sharp's face. The man was astute. Maybe, for the first time, he was not quite so sure of his President.

He smiled. It was naïve, Whitredge savored the word, of Sharp to believe that anyone did not have a mind of his own – certainly not this President.

CHAPTER 2

Former US Senator, Bradford Justice, had already discovered a special vantage point on their newly acquired, colonial period farm from which to admire a panoramic view of lakes and mountains.

He stood there and filled his lungs with New Hampshire air. He never did that in Washington D.C. – not safely - and certainly not with the same satisfaction.

For the first time in years in the North Country, the calendar and the actual arrival of spring coincided. Frequently there were too many false starts, too many unfulfilled promises. In the past he had noted the appearance of the robins, one of the earliest harbingers, bouncing on the first patches of grass searching for worms one day, huddling grumpily at a surprise blizzard the next, but not this year – at least not so far.

He would have known it was spring with his eyes closed - the smell of leaves, still moist in the patches of snow. He could see the tiny buds in the hardwoods and on the long heretofore naked limbs of the tall maples that lined the driveway. They were a reassurance of continued and abundant life.

Brad longed one day to live year round in this country of wooded mountains and island dotted lakes with water still pure enough to drink. The timely introduction of zoning had not really slowed continued development but had made important conditions.

He couldn't blame people for wanting to live here, and realized he could not keep it to himself. That picture, always in his mind's eye, helped to sustain him during his three years as a prisoner of war in Viet Nam - the senseless beatings, brainwashing and long periods of isolation. They never gave up. Fortunately, neither had he.

Brad refused to believe it had all been for nothing. He had had a lot of time to think - to consider - what - if anything he had learned from it

Among other things was the necessity of coming face to face with himself. There had been no escape from that. That had been the most important lesson. Self-deceit had been practically impossible. Now, whenever he heard people talk about the necessity of finding themselves, to know who they really were, made him smile. It could be a painful discovery. He and his Dad had shared a lot of laughter about people finding themselves.

Bradford's most constant dream was finally a reality. He loved this small resort town in which he had spent almost every summer of his life. Though he had ample reason to know Wentworth Harbor was less than perfect, it was now his home and he accepted it with gratitude. It was not perfect, but then neither was he.

After detours as a fighter pilot, POW in Viet Nam and one term as United States Senator, he resolved not to allow any more detours.

Best of all he had Marilyn with whom to share this new life. He was still only forty-five, and in spite of his imprisonment, reasonably healthy.

He and his father had always been close. George Appleton Justice was Professor Emeritus of Bowdoin College. Brad had been close to his mother too. Meg Caulkins had been the calming advisor who provided the love and meaning to both their lives. Her fatal accident a year ago had been a tragic blow. Brad had never seen his father, this irrepressible, outspoken, essentially joyful man, so miserable. He and Marilyn had sent him off, grumbling, to Europe, and when he had returned, Brad had to tell him that the Petition for which they had both fought so hard had been defeated. The people had refused the opportunity to eliminate, by majority vote, a pornography site recommended by Town Counsel as a necessary protection from and in compliance with Free Speech in the First Amendment.

The Prof had shut himself up in the lakeside house he and Meg had winterized just before his retirement. He answered his phone, but was obviously annoyed at the interruption - and quite capable of letting his annoyance be known.

Brad got in his all-wheel drive Outback and drove to his father's camp (they still called the now quite spacious, modernized place a camp) on Lake Kabeyun. Kabeyun was Indian for the west wind which presaged good weather. For more than fifty years George and Meg had had the benefit of the favorable wind.

George opened the door for his son.

"I saw that sonofabitch, Roger Welman, downtown this morning. The smug bastard always waves to me with a shit-eating grin on his face. That's bad enough, but then when he's got me cornered in front of the Post Office, where everyone can hear him, says, 'Well, George, it's been more than a year and I don't see any dire consequences from the defeat of your son's amendment. Anyway, George, I did admire your efforts, but I'm awfully glad the towns people realized it would have been foolish - and expensive - to try to overturn the Supreme Court's ruling protecting pornography under the First Amendment."

"And then, the capper, Brad: No hard feelings, George?

"The sonofabitch cackled causing his Adams apple to bounce up and down. He looks like a plucked chicken.

"The bastard actually stuck out his hand! That man will never know how close he had come to death. I am still shaking I am so Goddamned mad!"

His father's expression was too much, and Brad grinned.

"What's so damn funny, for Christ sake? Your poor old man was insulted in front of the bloody Post Office in broad daylight and you're grinning like a fucking hyena!"

This was his father's first sign of life in a long time - and he was being funny, which he damned well knew.

"Well - I suppose - if you insist - I guess it is funny - It's all in the delivery." He grinned.

They stood there in the kitchen and laughed at each other.

CHAPTER 3

Two days later, Bradford Justice and President Walter Whitredge were alone in the Oval Office. It was still early. Brad had spent the night in Georgetown with one of his former Senate colleagues. He had not told his host he had requested an appointment with the President - only that he had arranged to pick up some personal items he had left behind in his former Senate office.

The President was reading. There was a pile of papers on his cluttered desk. He was not one who believed a clean desk was necessarily indicative of an orderly mind. For the next several moments, Whitredge was the picture of total concentration.

Brad was sure the papers were summaries, brief digests of current issues. That was the way he had tried to keep up with what was going on when he had been a Senator. The shortcoming was the inevitable slant the authors injected according to their particular interests or those they believed the reader might have. It was a weakness, but there was no way around it. The President couldn't observe everything first hand nor did he have the time to understand everything in detail. The truth suffered in the process and had been one of Brad's many frustrations with his job as Senator.

Looking across at this man with whom he had spent so many summers in Wentworth Harbor, he found it difficult to find the boy who had been up for any prank, with whom he had discovered some of life's secrets and illicit pleasures.

His boyhood pal was now the most powerful man on earth! Brad wondered what changes that would make and how long it would take Walter Whitredge to realize his awesome power?

Walter Whitredge could no longer be addressed as Whit. No more camaraderie, slaps on the back, bachelor drinking bouts, arm wrestling or other competitive feats of strength. They were both big men, though Whitredge had the advantage of height, by two inches. The old Whit had always claimed that his longer legs allowed him to hold more liquor.

President Whitredge put down what he had been reading, stretched and turned to Brad.

"How's the Prof?"

"He is definitely showing signs of life - finally. For a distinguished professor of English Literature, he has the vocabulary of Sinbad - at least in the company of men. He restrained himself in the classroom - after the arrival of coeds – most of the time. The college threatened to fire him several times. He, reluctantly, accepted tenure when it was finally offered."

"It was one of my regrets that I never heard him lecture, but Michigan's offer of a football scholarship was too tempting."

"You had plenty of lecturing. My father is always on."

"And well worth listening to. Well, my friend, what can I do for you, and I have chosen the word 'can' deliberately."

"I appreciate that, Mr. President."

Brad found it necessary to look away for a moment.

"May I assume we are truly alone - that we are not being recorded?"

"You may."

Whitredge looked grim.

"We have had considerable discussion about that. The Secret Service is never far away - even here at the White House - in addition to the Marines outside every damn door.

"I have had every recording instrument in this office disconnected by the FBI. I even had an audio man from the CIA in here sweeping the place. I finally agreed to wear a wire whenever I travel. Of course I objected to that too. I do not consider myself so goddamn precious - and I demand some privacy."

Whitredge had not raised his voice, but he had made his anger felt.

Brad knew his boyhood friend, though by no means a plaster saint, was a caring decent person who would try not to let power corrupt him. Brad wondered what even Whitredge, with the best of intentions, could do that would make things better for his country. The odds against his making important changes were overwhelming. It was that sense of extreme frustration that had convinced Brad not to run again for the Senate. He would never even consider running for President.

"I'm very sorry you aren't in the Senate to help me, Brad. I'll need all the support I can get. I thank you for your help in my campaign."

He paused and regarded his friend in silence.

"You didn't really think I had a chance, did you."

Whitredge smiled.

Justice was embarrassed, but it was true. He believed in Whitredge personally, but Walter had never held political office nor did he have the organized support of any political party. His win was a miracle.

"Had I felt you had a real chance, I wouldn't have resigned. The Prof thought you would win. He said the nation was sick and tired of leaders who had lost the fire in their bellies whose only concern was to be reelected. He also said the people were fed up with corruption as usual, influence peddling and particularly an amoral President who did nothing but lie and fuck."

"And he did say fuck."

"Oh yes, but he was talking to me at the time."

They both grinned.

"All right, Brad, out with it. You didn't leave paradise to come to Sodom and Gomorrah just for the hell of it."

"It's about the Supreme Court."

"Really?"

"I have a big problem with our Palais de Justice - the marble temple our lawyers have built for themselves. My father calls it the Law House."

"Bit strong, Brad - but I like it."

"I thought you might. I hoped you might."

Brad did not try to conceal his mounting excitement.

"I wasn't able to accomplish anything as a junior Senator. My fellow Senators' principal concern was getting reelected and the reputations of too many are incredibly poor. Voting for what would be best for the country was rare. It was one frustration after another, but, and I couldn't be more serious about this, I am hoping, now that my boyhood friend is President, that I just might be able to influence you on your appointment of a Justice to the Supreme Court."

Bradford paused and continued to regard Whitredge intently, which was unnecessary as he had Whitredge's undivided attention.

"Am I totally out of line? Tell me if I am."

"Friendship is always important, Brad. Of course you're not out of line. Your opinion is welcome - and timely."

"I believe you have the most important opportunity ever given to an American President."

Whitredge nodded.

"Before we go into that, Brad, and I certainly agree, do you have someone in mind?"

"No, but I can tell you what I want this Justice to be like, what his convictions should be, a person of character, of course."

"A good start, Brad."

The President smiled.

"I want the man or woman, the sex doesn't matter, to believe the Supreme Court's primary obligation is to make rulings based on truth and when the truth is in conflict with the law, to rule for the truth."

"I'm no legal scholar, Brad, but I've had – in business – considerable experience, invariably unpleasant, win or lose, with lawyers and our legal system. For all the lawyers I have known there is only one rule – to win. They apply laws only to that end – not to be fair or just. Their only obligation is to their client – their excuse for sometimes outrageous behavior. Their ethics are legal ethics which have almost no bearing on the moral code we've grown up with. The concept that what is legal must be accepted even if it is clearly unjust is preposterous."

"My god, we're on the same wavelength. I could be listening to myself!"

For the first time Brad was smiling.

"And we're not alone, Brad. Millions of Americans feel as we do. The entire system is in deep trouble and especially some of its practitioners. Have you ever counted the number of anti lawyer jokes? The number is amazing – and yet when someone is in trouble, they turn to a lawyer, and if they don't really have a case, they hire a lawyer who has a reputation for being aggressive and tricky. And there are always plenty of them available. Lawyers have been breeding like rabbits and are in every aspect of society. It's an invasion."

"You sound like the Prof. You should hear *him* on the subject of our legal system. So we feel the same anxiety, Mr. President. What are you going to do?"

"I thought you'd never ask."

He smiled.

"I am going to appoint a ***non-lawyer*** to the United States Supreme Court."

"No!"

"Yes!"

He paused, confronting Brad earnestly with an almost fierce intensity.

"I am going to appoint you, Brad – Mr. Justice Justice!"

Brad's jaw dropped.

"If you are willing – and available?"

Brad's face flushed, unable to respond.

"Obviously I have shocked you, although I wasn't prepared for such a reaction. I can't think of any other approach, Brad. I apologize".

Brad was short of breath, anticipating an asthma attack - a lung problem acquired as a POW. He tried to regain his composure. He hadn't been hospitalized for years and had been confident he had pretty well conquered it.

"Are you ok, Brad?"

"Yes. I'm ok, thank–you. I really am fine – and relieved."

He inhaled deeply and forced out his breath through pierced lips as prescribed. He was now breathing easily.

"Your idea to appoint a non-lawyer is certainly commendable. I think there should be laymen judges throughout the legal system, but the idea is Quixotic and will never happen. The system belongs to the lawyers and they have the power to prevent any such appointment.

"I am both astonished and grateful for the honor, but I must refuse."

The President exhaled slowly, and nodded.

"I am not as disappointed as you may think, Brad. If you had simply accepted immediately, I might have doubts. Your initial refusal convinces me you are the right man. Take your time. Think it out. I have not accepted your refusal, and I can wait, my friend."

CHAPTER 4

Brad happened to be looking out a window facing the long driveway, when he spotted his father approaching the house on foot. The Prof enjoyed walking, but this was some walk - all the way from Lake Kabeyun. It was at least six miles, much of it uphill!

Brad watched his father moving at a steady pace, downhill at last, his broad shoulders and deep chest betraying no sign of strain, although his age was finally catching up. His wind and lowered physical endurance had made him decide to give up tennis and skiing so he had turned to golf, a game to which he had found poor adaptability. He now insisted golf was for masochists. When asked if were a golfer his answer was

"No, but I refuse to quit."

When asked for his handicap, he would say either "None of your business, or - Me."

His father's complexion was ruddy and he still had a full head of hair although it was no longer blond. It had turned white years ago. Compliments on his hair, when extravagant, annoyed him because of the implication that it was his primary asset. He would frequently inform people that when he had courted Meg, he was in the military and his hair was very short – not a wave in sight.

Brad had noticed the signs of age in his dad - the crows feet around the eyes, the loosening of the flesh below his jaw, the brown spots on the backs of his still powerful hands, also some occasional awkwardness that evidenced stiffness in the joints, but the man was basically healthy, and Brad was grateful for that. The loss of his mother had made him particularly sensitive to his father's mortality.

By the time he met his father at the back door, Brad was grinning.

"Hello, George."

"Whoa there. What's this George bit? You'll know a lot of Georges in your lifetime, but there is only one man you can properly call Father. I remember when you called me father just as if I were a goddamn priest. How are you, my son?"

"Fine. You didn't walk the entire way from the camp?"

"I cannot tell a lie. I had a lift most of the way - to the bottom of Glidden Road, but it was all uphill from there. What's this news you are all excited about - that you refused to tell me over the phone?"

"Who gave you the lift?"

"Some woman who thinks I have beautiful hair."

"One of your casserole ladies?"

"Not yet, but I wouldn't be surprised. I tell you, son, being a widower in this town is amazing. There are widows out there just waiting to pounce even on an old coot like me."

"You're fishing, and I am not about to bite."

"OK. What's your news?"

Brad had been anticipating this moment, trying to come up with a way to approach the President's decision gradually - to let the suspense build, but now that the question was here ----.

"President Whitredge told me he has decided to appoint me to the Supreme Court."

Professor George Justice found it necessary to sit. Brad couldn't remember ever having seen his father so obviously astonished. Brad wasn't sure whether to be pleased or annoyed.

"What's the matter? Don't you believe I would be up to the job?"

"I don't know. I'll have to think about that, son. I mean what is your concept of the Supreme Court? What would you bring to that court that isn't already there?"

"Justice as the primary obligation of the Court."

"You've got to be kidding. I - I'm speechless!"

"A first, Dad. I'm impressed."

"I don't know which of you is the more naïve. I never would have considered Walter naïve, though he does sound a little sappy with his oft-stated belief in the people. Bull shit!"

"I remember my Government Professor's proviso, Dad. In order to believe in democracy one has to believe in the wisdom of the masses to make a wise decision, and Churchill's statement that all governments are evil, that democracy is simply the lesser of all evils."

"Wise sonofabitch." George stood up.

"That Temple, that Law House sanctifies the law. Read the inscription on the temple. Engraved in marble are the words EQUAL JUSTICE UNDER LAW. That, my son, says it all. The law comes first. Justice comes second – if considered at all."

"Well, well, do I hear some approval?"

"Although the fact that you are not a member of that brotherhood may be your greatest asset, it is also what will hang you. Our various Bar Associations and the lawyer members in our legislature will never *ever* permit a non-lawyer on their Supreme Court."

"There's no such modifier in the Preamble which names Justice the first and most important condition to be established, Dad."

The Professor smiled. "You've been reading."

"I have been reading our Constitution. I've read it and reread it. There's nothing in there which convinces me the Framers intended to restrict membership on the Supreme Court to lawyers, and by the way, that court is not their court. It is our court,"

"Let me pretend I'm a lawyer for the moment, Brad. I realize that's practically impossible, but if you're going to go into this, you have to understand them and their point of view. You've heard the expression the Devil's advocate. I like that because it implies that the Devil needs an advocate - and can always find one in our legal system."

They both smiled at that.

"Okay, Counselor, fire away."

"If it's true, Brad, that lawyers don't bother with the concept of justice, and I agree that it certainly is not their first consideration, I think the reason is that most lawyers have been trained to believe that justice, or the concept of what is fair or unfair, is too personal, too dependent on differing opinions. What I think is fair will not necessarily agree with your opinion. Fairness is not an absolute. It is always relative."

"I know and I understand that, Dad though I do subscribe to the belief held by many, that justice is an a priori absolute, has always been there and always will be. I justify that by starting with the discovery of the truth. Without truth, it is virtually impossible to decide what is just. Truth is difficult to find, especially when one side is doing its best to conceal it or have it ruled inadmissible, but again there ***is*** truth and that is what our legal system must regard as its primary obligation, the only basis on which to make just decisions. The law is handy but it is not an absolute and must never be accepted as a substitute for justice."

"Brad, I'm impressed. It's interesting not only because of your eloquence and clearly thought out point of view. It's true that millions of Americans don't respect our most important institution and its operatives, but most of us don't know why, what is wrong, and most important of all, what to do about it."

The Prof began pacing.

"I think you've made a great start, Brad. Do you know what to do now? Do you have the solution?"

"No and that's why I have refused. It's a wonderfully compelling idea, but impossible."

"You refused!"

George Justice found it necessary to sit down again. It took several hesitant starts to compose a reply.

"Well of course, the odds are probably insurmountable. Really no sense in devoting yourself to a lost cause. You have done more than enough in support of our country. You have a home you love, have enough income to enjoy a wonderful retirement with a woman who has stood by you and loves you. Your decision makes sense."

George paused and took a deep breath.

"I guess I was naively running off at the mouth – as usual. My enthusiasm overcame any sensible judgment. It is, as you said, Brad, a wonderfully compelling idea – having justice paramount in our judicial system. Every American citizen would be in favor of that though unfortunately too many of us actually believe that's what we have and believe in the so-called certainty in the law. We know that isn't true in too many instances." He nodded. "You made a wise and sensible decision." He paused and then added:

"By the way, did you read the quote in Boston Magazine? One of our most respected trial lawyers said that the OJ Simpson trial was our legal system's finest hour.

"I wonder what he meant by that. Probably would deny it anyway."

Brad looked thoughtful.

"Our President has not accepted my refusal. He insists I give it a lot of thought. He also said he could wait."

CHAPTER 5

It was noon and Marilyn was not at home as promised.

Now that he was retired and at home almost every day, Marilyn usually made him lunch. He was looking forward to a grilled bacon lettuce and tomato sandwich - maybe two, if she would let him. His waistline was beginning to thicken and she had cut down on eggs and his liberal use of butter and salt. They had agreed to limit their alcohol to no more than one two ounce drink per day - usually scotch and no more than three drinks before dinner at a party, no wine, and no alcohol after dinner. They both liked to drink and her intake had increased along with his.

Marilyn was generally a good sport and she did want to please, but some of her friends, wives of retirees, told her they loved their husbands, but not for lunch. Marilyn had reminded Brad that maybe he was retired, but he seemed to be making sure that she hadn't. The remark was so out of character it had shaken him.

Part of Brad's pleasure at being waited on was the comfortable feeling of domesticity. She was apparently oblivious to the effect certain moves had on him during house cleaning – bending over, the consequent movement of her full breasts, her lovely ass up ended. Sometimes he could stand it no longer and he would attack her. He reflected that though she may have been oblivious, she was always ready for a little slap and tickle. Brad gave sex many names including a romp and a roll in the hay. He had also adopted some of the locals' terms such as a nooner and matinee. He particularly enjoyed unscheduled sex for which he had had little time when he was working. Neither wanted to settle for perfunctory or scheduled sex.

Brad and Marilyn had been married for more than twenty years and for him their sex was never a disappointment. If possible, it continued to be even better. Marilyn appeared initially passive, but she always gave at least as good as she received. He loved the way she looked and the fact that she always dressed exceptionally well with a style of her own. He tried to do the same, convinced they made a handsome couple.

Marilyn loved the Prof, but told Brad he was more adult than his father who frequently moved too fast and was much too outspoken, but George could always make her laugh, and ever the gallant, he gave her lots of attention and appreciation. Marilyn had adored her mother-in-law, and missed Meg terribly. She worried about the Prof and had decided he should remarry. The man was lonely, and he was a man who needed a woman.

When Marilyn arrived - no more than fifteen minutes late - Brad wanted to give her hell, but one look at her in her brief skirted tennis dress he considered attacking her instead.

"Where have you been? I'm hungry."

"You poor thing. I'll put the bacon on right this minute. Would you like a bloody? I've had enough exercise to deserve one."

"Thought you'd never ask."

"You make them, dear, while I get lunch."

The phone rang and Brad answered it.

"Is this Bradford Justice?"

"Yes."

Brad did not recognize the voice.

"We know the President has decided to appoint you to the Supreme Court. We are ordering you to refuse. You are unacceptable. You will not pass the Senate Judiciary Committee, but in the meantime you will be a distraction we will not countenance. Your prompt compliance is mandatory."

The connection was broken.

Brad slowly placed the phone back on its cradle and stared out through the kitchen slider. The view was obscured by a persistent mist. If only he could have kept the man talking and could have asked him questions!

"Come and get it. Lunch is ready. You haven't finished making the bloodies."

One look at Brad's face was enough.

"Who was that? What's wrong?"

"I don't know who it was, and I don't know what to do about it."

"Tell me, Brad."

He looked into her eyes and knew he had to tell her. They consulted each other about everything, and Marilyn's understanding and immediate grasp of any problem was always helpful. Besides - that telephone call could concern her almost as much as him.

"Somebody had to be listening in on Whitredge's conversation with me. That call ordered me to refuse my appointment to the Supreme Court."

"My God!"

Apparently the listener did not record my refusal. I had asked Whitredge if our conversation was secure. He had assured me, with some agitation, that it was. Moreover, we had agreed to keep silent about his intention to appoint me until after we had had a strategy session. I'm sure he has not yet discussed this with anyone. The only person I've told, beside you, is my father, and I know he would not have confided in anyone."

"I can't believe our President is being surveilled. The idea is appalling!"

Both remained silent in contemplation of the consequences of that. Marilyn was the first to speak.

"You have got to confirm your refusal! I have almost lost you once. I'm still bitter at your sacrifice for your country in a senseless war that resulted in the murder of thousands of civilians and permitted our soldiers access to government supplied drugs.

"You left the Senate because of the corruption and lack of drive for anything but reelection. You have done enough for you country, Brad. Please, for all our sakes, refuse the appointment!"

"I hear you, dear, believe me, but the possibility of a place on the Supreme Court is compelling. The opportunity to try to refocus our judicial system on the search for truth and justice as its first consideration is exciting – far more meaningful than anything I could ever have imagined.

"Haven't you ever fantasized yourself in a position from which you could really do wonderful things for your country? The Prof would accept that challenge in a moment."

"Then let him have it. He no longer has a wife to worry about, but you have a wife - and two children! Thank God they're both in boarding school. If Meg were alive, I know she would support me in this."

"My dear, I don't want to put you in harm's way. You know that, and I am giving this a lot of thought, believe me."

"You can't take that disembodied voice casually, Brad. Whoever he is or represents, he has the ability to surveil the

President of the United States! I'm afraid. Don't tell me you aren't afraid."

"Well, at this point I am astonished. I certainly am concerned, but I am not afraid."

The argument went on for hours, and Bradford Justice was not winning any points. There were two things he had to do. He needed to consult his father and he had to warn Walter Whitredge!

CHAPTER 6

George Justice's reaction to the phone call and Marilyn's fear were pretty much as Brad had expected - with some interesting addenda.

"In the business of Intelligence, son, the paramount consideration is to take nothing at face value. You should understand that, having been a US Senator and a member of the Senate Intelligence Committee. Everybody has an angle though it's sometimes very difficult if not impossible to discover. The entire intelligence business is based on mistrust – which, by the way, is a helluva way to spend your life."

The Prof had taken the subject very seriously and his three plus years in the CIA had left an indelible impression. He had studied all that was available to him, believed he thoroughly understood the intelligence mission and was convinced the men in charge did not. He had often said they had both feet firmly planted in mid air.

George Justice could conduct a course in Intelligence, the tradecraft, the recruitment of agents, the identification of the best targets, motivation. One of the greatest mistakes, he believed, was the misuse of secrecy and the bureaucratizing of Intelligence. The two were absolutely incompatible. Another was the inadequacy of training not just in tradecraft but in the definition of what was intelligence and what was quasi-military interference with other nations. Plausible deniability was not only a farce but extremely dangerous as it had given Presidents a false sense of security. It was also a misguided use of power that almost always backfired. There was now even a term for it called blowback.

"OK, Professor, what is the worst case scenario?"

"This is pure speculation, understand."

Brad smiled.

"Since our President ran as an Independent, no matter how large his majority, he does not have the protection of either Party machine, and the dirty tricks departments are still alive and well.

"It seems likely that both Parties would want to know - in advance - the intentions of this man, and will use all possible means to find out - independently of each other, of course. And that would mean two surveillance teams. At the same time, since the news of your appointment has leaked - somehow - it may also be of particular interest to the American Bar Association who, it seems likely, will be against having a non-lawyer on the Supreme Court - the understatement of the century."

He grinned.

"It could be they, or someone they have hired, to get to you."

His grin vanished.

"So now there is a possibility of three interested listeners?"

Brad looked at the ceiling, but there was no help there.

"Yes, and there is the possibility of several more eve droppers."

George Justice frowned.

"We are still in the dark as to the identities of the assassins of Shapiro and what their motive was. Could they be one of the many militia organizations who, this time, instead of blowing up government buildings, have decided to attack important members of our judicial system? Maybe they don't want anyone to replace Shapiro just on general principle. I would certainly hate to believe that such an organization could be another customer for such information or be in the employ of some terrorist group who is determined to destroy our government."

"I hope you can't think of any more listeners."

"Unfortunately, I can. For example, if you were head of the FBI, wouldn't you like to know, in advance, the intentions of this as yet unknown President?"

"You're not going to leave out the CIA, I hope."

"Certainly not. It's an unholy mess, son, and anybody willing to get in the middle is a goddamn fool. Of course there may be an advantage in having too many enemies, son."

"Neither of us believes that, Dad."

"No. Neither of us does. Your wife is right, and I know Meg would have taken exactly the same position. The question you have to answer is whether or not you are a damn fool."

"You know, Dad, after my POW experience and the Senate fiasco, I swore that never again would I be willing to be a pawn in anything to do with the government. I think you must have felt the same way as a result of your war and the stint with the CIA. I've often wondered about your decision to become a professor."

George smiled and nodded.

"So now you know. It turned out to have been a good move."

He stood up and began pacing.

"I really believe in the importance of a layman on the Supreme Court, and at my age, and now that your mother is gone, I would be quite willing to accept that appointment - not because I'm ready to die, but because I am ready to get back into the fray. The problem is that Walter Whitredge offered to appoint you not me, and probably for very good reasons. My age is against me and the fact that I have never held political or appointive office, make my chances far less than yours.

"Anyway, Brad, I certainly will not blame you for your decision to reject the President's offer. You have already served your country so you have nothing with which to reproach yourself. I love you and I am, and always will be, very proud of you. Your mother adored you, but I am not willing to go that far."

His look belied that statement.

"Well," Brad shrugged and let out his breath, "The first thing I've got to do is warn Whitredge. He has got to know the President is being wired!"

"From now on, Brad, you must be sensitive to surveillance, be on the lookout for automobiles that are following you, keep your phone answering service on at all times. If you don't have the suction cup you can place on the phone so you can monitor all conversations, buy one at a Radio Shack. You may need a program called PGP, which as far as I know, permits secure E-Mail correspondence. I have it, though I've never used it. The FBI tried to get its programmer, a man named Zimmerman, to give them access, but he refused and they have either given up or have found a way to access it. It's complicated but both you and Whitredge are longtime computer buffs. You do have the President's E-mail address?"

Brad nodded.

"You're certainly keeping your hand in. Dad. Most of your contemporaries refuse to own a computer never mind understand its uses."

"That and my writing keep me out of the Pool Hall."

"Are you in the middle of a book?"

"I'm always in the middle of a book."

When he offered nothing further, Brad knew better than to pursue the matter.

"I think I'll look up Jock Walker. He's a former agency audio man and has recently retired to Wentworth Harbor. If you can get Whitredge up here for a family visit, maybe I can get the two together. I'll give you a call after I've talked with Jock."

The two men parted company and Brad realized he still had a lot of thinking to do. Clearly the Prof knew exactly what *he* would do, but as he had said, he was no longer a married man, and at almost seventy-nine he was too old. The Prof knew that - and hated it.

Brad drove home slowly, not wanting to confront Marilyn.

He was not the only non-lawyer the President could appoint. On the other hand, if he knew there was danger, he couldn't let some other character take his place – could he?

Brad was thinking about his father, the risks he had taken in WW II as a fighter pilot and one of America's aces, his evasion of the Germans after being shot down, the miraculous journey through Germany and into France where he had joined the Maquis only to discover that some were Communists and could be treacherous to an American who was not. He had participated in sabotage and lived with danger for another year. It was no wonder George Justice had in effect dropped out, returned to college and become a quarrelsome member of the faculty.

Brad knew his father's gesture was as much because he really would like to serve as an Associate Justice as to protect his son, but now that his father had pointed out the danger, Brad could not in conscience run for cover no matter how sensible.

When he drove down his driveway, Marilyn's car was not there. He turned the car around and headed to town. He decided he could use a drink.

CHAPTER 7

Brad drove up the long tree lined driveway. The tall old sugar maples provided shade in the summer. Unfortunately they were constantly shedding limbs. Planting sugar maples was one of the first priorities of the original settlers. He stopped and looked to his left just long enough to determine there was no car parked at the foot of his neighbor's driveway. A discontinued road continued past the house and sloped down into the valley. A car could park there and be invisible to both him and his neighbor. It was the only other house for more than a mile. He turned right and proceeded to the next intersection.

Between the ominous phone call, Marilyn's fear and the last conversation with his father, Brad was on edge.

He turned right at the three-way intersection in the direction of town and slowed down to a crawl, looking into his rear view mirror.

Within a minute a black sedan turned in from the direction of his house. Brad gradually increased his speed, all the while turning his head from side to side as if looking for something in the bordering fields. He lost sight of the car and didn't pick it up again until he was well along the valley road, and only seconds later, watched it turn off into a driveway behind him.

The driver was wearing a fedora hat. Brad couldn't see his face.

Brad parked at the local inn, the Wentworth Harbor Inn, and headed for the bar.

Breakfast at the Wentworth Cafe was probably the best source of information about town affairs - political and otherwise, but it was too late in the day for breakfast and the Cafe didn't serve liquor.

Brad waited for several moments while he looked around for a familiar face but was disappointed. In years past he had known almost everyone by face if not by name. The summer population of Wentworth Harbor had grown so much there had been occasions when he had been able to walk the length of the downtown area without seeing anyone he knew - and these newcomers looked different. Their attitude was different.

He found an empty place at the far end of the bar and ordered a Beefeater on the rocks with olives, making sure the barman had heard the s. Brad took a grateful swallow.

"I guess you needed that."

Brad turned to face a woman on the stool next to his. She was blonde - cleverly artificial, very attractive face - expertly applied makeup. She appeared to be in her middle twenties - maybe early thirties. Her hands were well shaped and fingernails manicured. She was wearing a white, short-sleeved blouse with a rich colored silk scarf around her neck. Her lipstick was ruby red and recently applied. Her lips were full and sensual. Surely this woman wasn't on the make. She didn't need to sit at a bar to find an eligible male. She must be waiting for someone.

"It's that obvious, eh? You've heard of Murphy's Law?"

"Everything that can go wrong will go wrong."

She smiled. Her teeth were perfect and white. She was immaculate. Brad ordered another martini.

When was the last time he had been alone in a bar beside a beautiful companion? She was a standout. Brad refused to make comparisons, probably in the hope that Marilyn would do the same for him. This woman had such smooth skin. How lucky she was. He hoped she realized and enjoyed her youth, for to Brad, she was young.

He didn't think women reached their full beauty and sexual potential until they were in their late thirties and forties. Then they were a promise fulfilled. That's what he had told Marilyn when she had, reluctantly, turned forty.

Brad was feeling the security of anonymity, forgetting for the moment that as their former Senator he was still something of a celebrity. He had received more local publicity from his decision not to run for a second term than from anything he had tried to do as Senator.

"Where are you from?"

The question was asked in a purely social tone, a natural curiosity. He always asked that of newcomers. Most of the time they were glad to answer.

"You have already concluded that I am not a local."

"Amen."

It was said with feeling.

"Do I detect the product of a boarding school - though you are a bit more stylish than those I have known."

"Only a couple of years. I was kicked out. The place was a nunnery. I live in Boston. I have my own fashion consulting business." She smiled into his eyes. "I'm just here for a couple of days. It's pleasant to be in a place where I'm not known; besides my business is full of fairies."

"I believe the current term for homosexuals is gay. Too bad really. Gay used to convey something effervescent and joyous. You're waiting for someone?"

"No." She smiled.

Brad remained silent.

"You're supposed to make an appropriate remark."

"I'm out of practice."

It was the understatement of the century.

"I'm too old to be of interest to you."

He hadn't been "in the market" for years, but he couldn't help flirting. He liked women, and every woman who knew him was well aware of that. It was one of the few regrets of the marriage state that the greatest game of all was over. He had played it well. He had wonderful memories. The ladies had been kind to him, and always full of wonderful surprises. It was far better than Parcheesi. The thought made him smile. Even the name Parcheesi dated him. He doubted she had ever heard of Parcheesi.

"Have you ever heard of Parcheesi?"

"Certainly. I'm not that young."

She faced him.

"You're having difficulty believing a woman my age could find an older man interesting?"

She really had a lovely smile.

"On the contrary, my dear."

Brad grinned and added.

"I am without doubt a most interesting man - but I am neither rich nor powerful. The men I know who are married to gorgeous younger women are both - and usually ugly."

"You're not ugly. In fact you're very striking - distinguished - and you have bedroom eyes."

Brad knew it was time to leave. He ordered another Beefeater on the rocks.

"That brings back a memory or two" Brad smiled.

"Dwelling on the past is definitely a sign of aging." She said.

Brad regarded her carefully. She held his gaze, her eyes full of promise.

"As is my refusal to believe in the sincerity of such a truly beautiful - and desirable - woman."

He paused.

"I want to know who hired you."

"I beg your pardon! Nobody hired me. I am not for hire. What an outrageous accusation!"

Her outrage was wonderfully convincing.

"It's wonderful what a few martinis and a beautiful, ego stroking woman can do. Now, I have no doubt there is someone here I could call on to take you into custody for soliciting. I have no wish to do that. What I want from you is the name of your employer."

Brad regarded her steadily.

"How did you know? What did I do wrong?"

"In addition to the come on, it's your cigarette lighter on the bar. I assume it's a recorder. You haven't smoked, nor is there anything in your appearance that would indicate that you are a smoker - no yellowing finger tips or telltale signs in your complexion."

Brad's hand beat hers to retrieve the lighter which he put in his pocket.

"You're very effective and my ego has been damaged."

He paused.

"Don't worry. I'm not going to ask what a nice girl is doing in a place like this - though I am willing to believe you have been acting out of some misconception as to my character. I want to know who has persuaded you that I am a suitable target, though I realize the role of vamp is frequently irresistible."

Brad waited.

"There's no crime in possessing a recorder."

"In a lawyer's hands the law can mean whatever he wants that to mean. I'm not even asking your name - just the name of your employer."

"You wouldn't believe it, if I gave it to you."

"Try me."

At that moment a man with a camera came up to Brad, asked if he was Bradford Justice, and took a picture. The flash blinded Brad. When he refocused, his lady friend was gone.

Brad got to his feet. The photographer was trembling, clearly expecting an attack.

Brad regarded him with contempt. The fellow looked seedy and had a paunch. Brad restrained himself and placed some cash on the bar.

"This is your lucky day, scum."

Brad left.

He went through the process of unlocking his car, opened the door - and waited. He was rewarded with the sight of another man getting into a black sedan. The man was wearing a fedora. He had a bland face reminiscent of a graduate of Oral Roberts College, either that or a young Mormon missionary.

Brad got into his car and tried the lighter. It wasn't a lighter. Not much professionalism here. In his father's day that "lighter" would have worked or he wouldn't have carried it. Brad sat for a moment.

She was certainly a beauty. He shook his head angrily.

CHAPTER 8

Jock Walker, at 68, a former member of the Agency, had retired to Wentworth Harbor some years ago. He had been a young man when George Justice was in the CIA.

Jock had learned his trade as an audio surveillance operator while in the Los Angeles Police Department. The Prof had been particularly impressed with the "wee Scot" because he was at that time one of the Agency's few professionals. It was an innovative policy in the Agency which the Prof had approved.

There were several times when George Justice had needed an audio specialist. The little bandy legged guy had always done a first rate job. Over the years, Justice believed Walker had probably bugged almost every Russian Embassy in the world and had also wired agents on both sides. George not only admired him professionally, he enjoyed his company. They had gotten together in Wentworth Harbor on several occasions.

George, after consultation with Brad, had set up a lunch meeting with Jock.

Fifteen minutes before Jock was due, at the suggestion of George, he and Brad stationed themselves some distance apart within sight of each other and the restaurant entrance.

George Justice had previously pointed out the reasons for this.

"In the old days, when I set up a time and place for an agent meeting, I would arrive early and would therefore be able to observe the approach of the person I was scheduled to meet and determine whether he was being followed, and if so, by whom. If he was someone I could trust, I might tell him where I was going to station myself so he could observe me and give me a signal if he suspected a tail. We know you are already being surveilled."

The Prof had given Brad a description of Walker and Walker a description of Brad.

"But how will I know if there is someone surveilling?"

"You probably won't, but you have already had a couple of glimpses of at least one of your surveillors."

"At least one? Christ!"

"I'm just trying to get you into a professional frame of mind."

"I don't think I like the professional frame of mind."

"I didn't either. If you see anything that disturbs you, give me the signal."

They parted company.

Within moments of the appointed time, Brad saw the wee Scot. His father's description was perfect. Walker was limping a bit, but he moved quickly and with confidence. It was the briefest glance, but Brad was certain Walker had picked him out. There wasn't the faintest sign of recognition that anyone not attuned to the situation could have noticed.

Brad looked at his Dad as he was in the process of following Walker into the restaurant. No one was following the Prof.

When Brad arrived at the restaurant on the second floor, the two men were seated. Brad joined them, and after a brief introduction, listened to their conversation.

"It's been a long time, laddie. Can I assume, sin' it's your invitation, that you're paying so I'll know what tae order?"

"Aye."

"Including, but not limited to a Glen Fiddich?'

"For that twinkle in your eye, it's as many Glenfiddichs as you like, Mon."

"Oh, now I'm worried. Please to remember that I am retired, and I like it that way, George."

"We can discuss that later at another place."

The Prof ordered three Glenfiddichs.

Several scotches and a hearty lunch later, the Prof paid the check and suggested they go for a walk.

About a hundred yards from the restaurant, following a path along the river that flowed from Lake Adam into Kabeyun, the Prof began to discuss his mission.

Jock was not interested. He said that since his retirement he had been offered employment on a contract basis not only from the Agency but also from the FBI, Industry, and possibly the Mafia.

At that point, the Prof told Walker why - all the details - everything. Brad was astonished - and worried. What had happened to his security conscious father?

Walker stopped abruptly and looked up at both men.

"I did my work for twenty years - sometimes at great risk - and this is the first time anyone has ever told me why - as if I were not to be trusted - or because I would not approve of their reason. I did the jobs because I believed I could. Even when I had my doubts, I kept working. I needed the money and my retirement was my only security."

He paused. The brogue had disappeared.

"Are you telling me that our President is being surveilled?"

"We're not certain, Jock, but we need to know - for everybody's sake."

Brad was no longer worried about Jock Walker.

"You will help us?"

"Aye. I will - and you knew I would. I should have ordered another Glen Fiddich!"

The three men then had a strategy discussion. They had to get President Whitredge to come to Brad's house and Jock had to have swept the house first. Brad had difficulty believing his house might have been wired.

CHAPTER 9

Having been informed by the Secret Service that it was against policy to commit the President's arrival to a certain date and time - except on State occasions - Brad was given a three day window within which to expect the President.

In the meantime, Jock Walker had swept Brad's house and found a telephone tap in the study. Jock said it was a very common type not one in use by the Agency. He had added, however, that it did not necessarily mean that it wasn't an Agency gadget as sometimes they deliberately used a common type, which started Brad muttering angrily about the Intelligence business.

"You people are so devious you remind me of the Kiki Bird a bird that flies in ever decreasing circles until it disappears up its own anus."

"Which would make a perfect symbol for the Agency."

Jock Walker, ever the dour Scot, had not laughed.

Both Jock and his father were on stand-by, but on the day of President Whitredge's arrival, the Prof was at Brad's house.

Brad had previously installed, at Marilyn's insistence, a security system. Brad's insistence that there was no need, that this was Wentworth Harbor, for God's sake, had not won the day. Since visitors arrived at the back of the house the occupants were blindsided because the focus was towards the panoramic view from the south side, Brad had suggested installing a trigger in the driveway that would trip a warning bell in the house and turn on the porch lights. It had thereafter been offered by the Security Company with some considerable success.

Brad heard the bell, moved to look out the rear window in time to see three black limousines moving down the long tree lined driveway. They came to a halt and men immediately emerged, guns drawn, from both the front and rear vehicles. They were in suits, but were not wearing hats because hat brims would obstruct visibility.

After some few minutes, while several of the men went around the front of the house and two went off to their right and disappeared behind the attached barn, President Whitredge appeared. Brad was impressed as always. Walter Whitredge looked sufficiently powerful to protect himself. He looked up at the window and waved.

Brad went down the covered steps to greet Whitredge. The moment he appeared a man arrived from nowhere, his pistol pointed at Brad's chest, and demanded his name. He was about to search Brad until Whitredge's voice commanded him to stop.

The two shook hands and started up the steps with the SS man immediately behind, begging the President to wait until he had had an opportunity to secure the place inside.

Whitredge stood still and Brad remained beside him. Brad was about to warn the SS man that his father was inside, when he heard an awful ruckus and immediately knew the two had found each other.

"You put away that fucking gun or I'll make you eat it!"

"Do as the man says, Henry! He just might do it. He is the senior Justice."

Brad and Walter Whitredge looked at each other and laughed. The tension left.

"I'm sorry, gentlemen, but these men are just doing their duty. Let Henry inspect the house, and then he will leave." Henry disappeared and returned ten minutes later.

"Everything seems to be in order, Mr. President." His voice was crisp and military to the core."

"Thank-you, Henry. I want you to leave us and go outside with the others."

Henry was startled and did not move. His orders were not to let the President out of sight.

Whitredge regarded him and waited.

"I do not expect to have to repeat myself."

"No, sir!" Henry left.

"You see what it's like to be President. I am aware that American Presidents have not had the best mortality rate in office, but I find this security business as upsetting as you, Prof. You know, I wouldn't be surprised if you could disarm Henry, but if you didn't succeed, he would shoot you."

"I have no doubt of it. He is much too programmed to suit me. He could start hostilities all by himself."

Then Jock Walker arrived, and he was mad as Hell.

"What kind of a greeting is this for your guests, Mr. President? I thought only the Mafia had goons like that."

The Scottish burr had returned.

"Aye." President Whitredge said. "My apologies."

"With the like a' them in your service, you can rest easy because no assassin would waste a bullet on you with such uglies to shoot at."

"Aye, Jock."

Brad directed them into what had originally been the parlor and except for parties was not much used. Marilyn kept the door closed. She said it was the one room she could always keep clean for visitors.

They all seated themselves, except for Jock.

"Before we have any discussions, Jock has a small job to do. When he returns, we can talk about old times."

Whitredge looked askance at Brad, and Brad put his finger up to his mouth. Whitredge remained silent.

When Jock returned, he gave Brad a nod and Brad resumed.

"Mr. President, I have asked you here because our conversation in the Oval Office was overheard."

"I beg your pardon."

"I received an anonymous phone call during which I was warned not to accept your appointment of me to the Supreme Court."

"When did you receive that call?"

"The evening of that same day."

"My God! I had just had my office swept by the FBI and every listening device disconnected. I told you that - and I can assure you I have not discussed the matter of your appointment with anyone."

"So now, with your permission, I would like Jock Walker, former Agency audio surveillance operator - par excellence - to sweep you. He has done this house and found a telephone tap so I believe this room at least is now secure."

Whitredge stood up.

"I am wearing one wire which I have their word was disconnected for this visit."

He looked down at the little man with the big temper, and smiled. He certainly was tiny.

"Be my guest, Jock. I do hope you don't find any but the one I am aware of."

Jock inspected the President carefully, first with a metal detector and then with his fingers. He found three in addition to the one the President had authorized. He looked up questioningly at Whitredge, made a motion as if to cut his throat.

Whitredge looked for confirmation at Brad and the Prof and they both nodded.

Jock placed all four in his pocket, and then stepped back.

"There's more, Mr. President. I found this little device on the other side of this wall."

He placed his hand on the wall the other side of which was the kitchen."

He held the device in his hand.

"This item, sir, is used for listening through walls. Clearly this had to have been placed there by whichever man inspected the inside of the house – before your entrance." Jock paused.

Whitredge's silence was ominous.

"If you decide to pursue the matter of Brad's appointment, sir, I will offer my services - without payment - except for a wee drop of Glen Fiddich now and again - and I can recommend a former associate of mine to look after you, sir. What is happening here is disgraceful, and I am no happy wi' the present judicial system mesel'.

"Any President who wants to put Bradford Justice on the Supreme Court is a man I can support."

Jock paused again.

"I have never come across a situation like this - not in twenty years. Ye've not one listener. Ye have at least four, probably not all with the same motive, but clearly you have powerful enemies.

"Well, I'll be off now. Keep me posted as to what you want of me. This, I must tell you, is the most important assignment I have ever had. Maybe that's because it's the first I have had fully explained. By the way, I believe I'll give these gadgets to you, Mr. President. I can and will testify as to where and when I found them, if you decide you want me to. I don't really need to examine them.

"Their presence is damning enough. Your bodyguard may decide to search me. I doubt they will have the brass to search their President."

He left three angry men.

CHAPTER 10

It was President Whitredge who spoke first.

"To say I am appalled at the discovery that all my conversations have been monitored, doesn't begin to express my concerns not only for myself but for the Presidency. Were it not for the credibility of Jock Walker himself and his recommendation by you, Professor, I would now find him suspect.

"I have known both of you all my life, and thank God for that. I need help and I need advice as to what my next move should be. Of one thing you can be certain," his words were measured, "I am not afraid. I will not be deterred from doing whatever I feel it necessary to do. I am President of this nation. I am indignant, and I am mad as Hell!"

George Justice stood up and began to pace.

"As your elder, and as one with some experience of life both inside and outside government, I would like to try to put this in some kind of perspective. I can only guess and I may be wrong, but" he smiled, "that is unlikely."

Some of the tension lessened. It was George Justice's favorite role.

"To begin with, this eavesdropping has been carried on from the beginning of your presidency and probably by both political parties, if only because you are an unknown quantity. That they may have had help from both the CIA and the FBI is possible. It is also possible that each of those agencies is doing this on their own for their own survival. J. Edgar was not above such tactics, which guaranteed his survival beyond the terms of many Presidents. It is probably impossible for any man with that much power not to abuse it in his own interests."

He faced the President.

"In your case, as a President with no wish to act in secret, I'm not really sure you should give a Goddamn what these Agencies and political Parties know. It is also entirely possible that a member of the Secret Service, in this case, Henry Saunders, has simply been programmed, is in fact following orders he believes are for your protection. I admit I don't care for such types. I prefer people who can and do think for themselves - people who cannot be programmed."

"I am obviously also a target for one of those eavesdroppers. Is the man who phoned me working for a group of lawyers?'

"Not necessarily, Brad. The number of militia groups has been growing. There is increasing unrest and disapproval of our government by foreign powers. Some, by now, may have friends in high places and may be funded by the enemies our foreign policies have created. Possibly it was one such group who assassinated Eliot Shapiro. I certainly don't know and possibly we will never know. It is vital that we realize we are vulnerable both from within and from without."

"Why would any American group upset with our Justice system want to prevent the appointment of someone who believes in justice for all?"

"Because, Brad, such groups thrive on chaos. Their primary motive is to destroy."

"Then it's possible that Shapiro was assassinated because he was a Jew as Sharp suggested to me. A lot of those militia organizations hate Jews and Blacks."

"That is also possible, Whit – Mister President. They don't really give a damn one way or the other. They frequently use such known prejudices to attract a larger membership and increase chaos. Did you ever hear the suggestion that Schikelgruber, Hitler's proper name, was a Jew? You're probably both too young. It was also circulated that Roosevelt was a Jew. Everything is fuel for the destroyers."

George Justice stopped pacing and regarded them both sternly.

"Since neither our politicians, our lawyers, our government and our judicial system are properly respected, the climate is ripe for revolt. Your determination, Whit – Mr. President - to place a non-lawyer on the United States Supreme Court, even if unsuccessful, is not only timely, but will be considered by many a vital step in the refocus of justice in our courts, and by example, in our Government. I really believe that you, Walter Whitredge, and Bradford Justice would make one helluva pair. Maybe you could win simply because you should win."

Walter Whitredge left the room and opened the back door. He went down a few steps so he would be visible.

"I want Henry Saunders to come inside - now."

Whitredge turned around and reentered the house. Saunders followed the President into the living room. Brad and the Prof had remained standing.

"You want to see me, Mr. President?"

Whitredge faced him.

"Give me your gun."

For one second Henry Saunders hesitated and then handed the President his pistol."

"Have you any other weapons, Saunders?"

"No, sir - except in the cars."

President Whitredge moved in front of Saunders and faced him. Saunders was standing at attention.

"Do you regard yourself as a loyal American citizen?"

"Yes, sir!"

"Do you regard spying on your President as serving your country?"

"Spying? I would never spy on my President. I would die to protect you, sir."

"Then why did you install this listening device on the kitchen wall? Don't deny it. I have your gun, Saunders."

Whitredge never raised his voice, but his anger was so apparent, Brad seriously wondered whether Whitredge was going to shoot the son of a bitch.

"Who ordered you to eavesdrop on your President?"

"I wasn't eavesdropping, sir! I don't know what's on those tapes. I turn them in to my Chief who turns them in to the FBI."

"But you knew this was done without my knowledge. I intend to have the truth, Saunders. Well?"

For the first time Henry Saunders seemed to slump. His head was bowed and he was looking down at the floor.

"I was told it was to protect you against any lies about any commitments or statements you might make - unwisely -- or --."

His voice trailed off.

"Do you realize you are in a conspiracy to betray your President? I have the power - and the right - to press charges against you as a traitor. Don't think for one moment you can blame your action on your superiors. Obedience to a traitorous order is no excuse – not in my administration. If you cannot think for yourself, I will certainly do without you."

Brad Justice was beginning to feel sorry for Saunders.

"A privileged conversation that took place in the Oval Office was overheard one result of which was a warning to the man with whom I had had that conversation and to whom I had promised silence - security."

All military stiffness disappeared. Henry Saunders looked miserable.

"What about these?"

Whitredge held out his hand with the four listening devices in it.

Saunders looked blank, and then shook his head vigorously.

"The only one I know about is the one I was told you had agreed to - and the only one I installed."

And then the light finally dawned.

"You don't mean to tell me those were discovered on your person by that peppery little Scot?"

"He didn't like you either." This was offered by Brad.

"Now, Henry Saunders, do you understand what I mean by a conspiracy?"

"I do. I sure as Hell do - sir!"

"Is there any reason I shouldn't pull this trigger?"

Saunders was not the only man in that room that was tense and silent. Walter Whitredge calmly checked the safety and offered the pistol to Saunders.

"Do you think you could handle the job as Chief of Security?"

Saunders was so astonished he couldn't find the words. Whitredge watched as Saunders' face went through a rapid transition from surprise to enormous relief.

"Well, Mr. Saunders?"

"Yes sir, Mr. President!"

Saunders straightened up, shoulders back, at rigid attention.

"Relax, Saunders. I do not want an automaton. I want a man who can and will think."

Saunders made a valiant attempt to relax.

“I think I understand, sir, and if I may speak freely, Mr. President?”

The President nodded.

“I had made up my mind that no matter what kind of a man the President turned out to be, my duty was to protect him with my life because he wasn’t just a man he was the symbol of our democracy.”

He paused almost overcome with emotion.

“You are not just a symbol any more. You can count on me, Mr. President.”

Brad turned to hide a grin. Oh, to be that young. He did not trust himself to look at his father. President Whitredge held back a smile too, wanting to believe he had found another man he could trust, surprised at his own intensity. There was so much to be done.

CHAPTER 11

It had been an awful night, and the morning was worse, but there was no good time to tell Marilyn of his decision to accept President Whitredge's appointment.

She had waited three years for him while he had been a prisoner of war in Vietnam. The thoughts of her and the promise of their reunion had been vital to his sanity. He had been able to conjure up her every gesture, her smile and her features. He loved her more than he had thought it possible to love anyone. He understood her fear, though he tried to minimize it.

The legal fraternity as one body, as a matter of policy, would be against the appointment of a layman to the Supreme Court, but he believed there were lawyers who fully understood the need for a far broader code of ethics and the institution of other important changes. Some of the law schools were introducing ethics courses into their curriculum, but without noticeable effect.

Brad had been reading copiously on the subject of the Supreme Court, including an enormous amount of material available on the Internet. He had read biographies of present and former Justices.

He had no intention of being purely negative. What he wanted was a positive approach, though the more he read the greater he realized the need for the perspective from non-lawyers. He also noted marked differences in attitudes between the old guard and the new.

He tried to make Marilyn understand what an important opportunity had been offered and why he could not refuse - indeed why he had to accept.

He spoke to her at breakfast.

"We, the American people, Marilyn, finally, have a President who really cares about the people - all the people. He wants to use the power of the Presidency to make this nation regain its promise. I think many Americans have forgotten the promise of America or, if they haven't forgotten, they feel alienated, and of course there are those who don't care as long as they have money to spend.

"Well, my dear, Walter Whitredge cares and he is no shrinking violet. I am convinced he is a strong leader, but he needs all the help he can get, and I want to help. I can't think of a more dramatic opportunity to turn things around, to give the people a voice in our legal system instead of the present legal monopoly not only in the courts but in our legislature."

"I thought you had had enough of being a pawn for your government, Brad. You felt frustrated in the Senate. God knows you felt helpless in Vietnam, held captive in a war we should never have entered.

"Please, Brad; come to your senses! You'll never make it to the Supreme Court. The lawyers who own it won't let you in, and if a miracle puts you there, they will treat you as a pariah - a threat to their sovereignty."

"Won't you please try to understand? I have to do this, Marilyn. I don't really have any acceptable choice."

There was a prolonged silence. Marilyn was weeping silently. Brad tried to put his arms around her and comfort her – and himself, but she turned away.

"I am sorry, dear – very sorry."

Marilyn stopped weeping and went to the phone in the living room leaving him in the kitchen. He heard her talking but couldn't hear what she was saying. He waited in the kitchen until she returned.

"I've phoned Mother. She was terribly upset because she loves you too, but she said I was welcome, of course. I will leave you until you come to your senses. You have a choice – apparently you have made it – without me."

The sight of her standing there, within easy reach, made his heart ache. He made no further move to embrace her - to keep her with him. He simply nodded.

It was best. Marilyn would be safer with her mother and hors de combat.

Brad helped her pack, took her suitcases down to her car and put them in the trunk, trying not to look too forlorn. He thought the wounded bull look just might do the trick, but it was better this way - well, maybe not better, but --.

They kissed good-by and he felt her tears on his cheek. He watched her drive up the length of the driveway and turn right. He watched the car until it disappeared. His face was no longer stern. He stumbled because he couldn't see. He managed the climb to the back door awkwardly.

He stopped, for the moment unable to enter what had so hopefully been the house of their dreams. At that precise moment Bradford Justice hated the world.

Wentworth Harbor had always been a safe haven against the deteriorating outside world. Not only was it a beautiful place, filled with wonderful memories, but people who needed to be awakened to the truth, to fully realize how important their legal system was and what had happened to it. He had to do something about it. He could not bear to join the apathetic, fearful, timid majority.

He had been through too bloody much. He couldn't quit now - not now there was an opportunity for him to do something. He knew it would probably be considered quixotic of the President to want to bring justice into our judicial system. The fact that it would be considered a stupid tilt at a windmill was in itself proof that it needed to be done. He began to pull himself together.

He did not want to be alone so he drove to town. He decided to have a cup of coffee and a doughnut at the Wentworth Cafe by the bridge in the center of town.

It was a modest place. The Prof described the decor as early Halloween. The fare was simple and Brad liked it and so did the locals. The moment he entered he was greeted.

"Mornin', Senator. Hello, Brad. Where ya been? Bet you're some glad to be outta Washington."

Every face was smiling and Brad found he could smile too. People in one of the booths made room for him.

Like his father, Brad was known as a talker and a politician who spoke his mind. Most of the locals were sorry he had not rerun for the Senate. They said of his predecessor that they had voted for him as the only way to get him out of town.

Brad wanted to tell them of the President's offer, but he had agreed with the President to make that announcement - officially, and in two parts.

The strategy had been the Prof's idea. Brad had to admit that the older he became the wiser his father became. He grinned. Profane as George Justice sometimes was, he had acquired one helluva lot of wisdom, and he was fun.

"Well, Rufus, what's new? I've been out of touch."

Rufus was a large man, powerful in his youth, who spoke with an honestly come by local speech not in any way tempered by his college degree in engineering at the University. He spoke low and generally quietly and people usually listened.

Rufus was a joiner. He was a member of organizations Brad had never heard of. He never missed a meetin', and never failed to offer his wisdom. Rufus liked to talk.

"New? God, I dunno where to begin. Well, I guess you've noticed the black stretch limmos comin' and goin' through town. When I say stretch, I mean to say stretch - half a block long and the windows so dark you can't even see who's drivin'."

"Can't say I have, Rufus. Who do they belong to - or don't you know?"

It was just the kind of challenge Rufus enjoyed.

"One of them belongs to a recent arrival name of Frascati, Salvatore Frascati, from Revere, Mass. They have a lot of Eyetalians down theyah, you know."

"Not too many of them heah, though we're becomin' cospoliton."

This was added by Lyle Brodrick, a local of many talents who had never worked for any one but himself. He could fix, build, wire, plumb anything. Prices were reasonable. He was honest and dependable - when you could get him. He had never really learned to read and his wife did his bookkeeping.

"You looked in your phone book lately? Startin' to look like the United Nations - Germans, Swedes, Dutch, even a few Orientals as summer folk."

Brad smiled at Pierre Cote's concept of a cosmopolitan community. The local phone book, with some notable exceptions, still read like a WASP nest.

The conversation went on and Brad was pleased just to listen. He enjoyed the accent. He had become familiar with it as a boy, could in fact imitate it perfectly - as could his dad. They often spoke to each other in the vernacular. His father always spoke to the locals in their language and none of them ever seemed to notice. He and the Prof shared a deep feeling for the locals and were saddened that their language was dying out. Too much radio and TV, and the yearly invasion of summer people many of whom were becoming year round residents.

"This fellah, Frascati, built himself one helluva waterfront home on the Big Lake, violated every known zoning regulation and requirement in both the State and the Town. House is too close to the water. The dock is so long it's a wharf and has a huge boathouse with a luxurious apartment above it. He even built a caretaker's cottage large enough to house a large family."

Rufus had Brad's undivided attention..

"How did he get away with that?"

"Nobody knows - for sure. He either ignored the need for a permit or he managed to get one. The man's spent a fortune - more than a million. Spent it locally, real estate broker, builder, insurance agency, architect. Established a big account in the local bank He bought everything he needed locally and paid cash on the barrel head."

"Have any of you seen this place?"

"Built a ten foot high concrete and stone wall with electrified barbed wire on the top all around it. The gates are closed and there's a sign warning folks to keep out. You can hear the guard dogs that seem to have the run of the place. Only way to see it is from the water, and even there you can't get up close. He has had buoys strung out in front to keep boats out - which is also against state law."

"What's it look like?"

"Eyetalian - lots a stone work and tiled roofs. Sure is huge - even bigger than the other million dollar places on either side. Neighbors can't be too pleased, and they are mighty big dogs - CEO's of some of the Fortune Five Hundred Corporations."

Brad found out later Frascati's wife had joined the Garden Club, was becoming active in the Parent Teachers Council, had joined the Newcomers Club and Frascati had become a member of Rotary - as the former president of a Laundry Supply company.

The Frascatis had enrolled their three daughters in the local schools. The youngest was only seven.

Rufus did not regard Frascati's arrival as a joke. Neither did Brad Justice.

CHAPTER 12

Salvatore Frascati stood on the balcony of the boathouse apartment. It afforded the best view of the lake and the mountains beyond. He was proud of this house for which he had paid cash.

Salvatore had started out poor - very poor - in Boston's North End where almost everybody was Italian. Wasn't too bad a place in which to be Italian, but he hated being poor. He wanted to become a big shot so he had put in his time. He did the dirty jobs no one wanted; that somebody said needed to be done. Today he was a big shot, not *the* big shot, but close. And now the man between him and the Capo di Capos, the Godfather of the Di Bianco family who ran everything in New England, was about to pay him a visit.

Giuseppe, Joe the Barber, Bonardi was coming here to this house. It was an honor and everything had been prepared.

Frascati heard the black limousine as it drove in through the gate. A warning bell had announced the arrival and Frascati went downstairs to greet Bonardi in person.

Bonardi was a short man and appeared even shorter in comparison with the two gorillas who accompanied him. Frascati took due note of the two brutes. They looked mean which was important.

"Hey, Giuseppe, you look great - a sight for these sore eyes. How come you look younger every time I see you? Welcome to my home. It's yours - whatever you want."

The bodyguards frisked Frascati. They found nothing. Frascati ignored them. The two men hugged.

"Hey, Sal, this what you wear in the country? You look like Gotti, a fucking fashion plate."

"In your honor, Joe."

Frascati was dressed like a golfer - slant front pockets, canary yellow stretch trousers, a white golf shirt over which was a red v-necked cashmere sweater. He was wearing beautifully shined tasseled loafers. He was taller than Bonardi and heavily built. Beside him Bonardi looked like a fireplug.

The two men went inside. The goons, in response to a signal from Bonardi, remained outside.

Sal gave his boss the tour and was gratified by Joe's grunts and nods of approval.

"I can see why you like this place, Sal. I like it too. I've been looking it over ever since you told me about it. It's too quiet for me, but the surroundings are as pretty as I've ever seen."

Bonardi sat in one of the deck chairs and looked out across the lake in silence for a moment, as if contemplating the beauty.

"Only one thing missing in Wentworth Harbor, far as I can see. Entertainment. You know how much money we make from entertainment? You know what I mean - nude broads, booze, bets - the works, and this is the very place. The wonder is that it's all legit. Too good to be true. I want you to set up a club here, Sal. We'll make a fucking fortune."

Salvatore Frascati was alarmed. He already had a fortune. He did not want a casino in Wentworth Harbor. This was where he wanted to live. He had brought his family his wife and three kids. He had even joined Rotary – a bunch a nobodies!

"A casino would never go here, Joe. The people wouldn't stand for it."

"Whaddya mean, Sal? The Welcome Mat is out. They've voted a porno zone in - not once but twice! That location won't do for my plans, and our shysters and the American Civil Liberties Union will fix all that. I tell ya , Sal this place is already a resort.. We bring in a club with dancing girls, booze, live sex shows and this place will begin to jump. Everybody will be rich – the real estate brokers, banks, lawyers, insurance companies, merchants, inn owners, restaurants – even the police. That Chief will be able to build an empire on the crimes we let him solve. The Selectmen will make money on the take along with the Permit Officer and members of the various Zoning Boards. We can't lose."

"Look, Joe, there's plenty of other places. The Season here is short. The winters are long and cold and we're sixty miles from the major ski areas."

"Fuck the skiers. They visit our place they'll give up skiing."

"I guess you haven't heard about our former Senator, Bradford Justice, and his father. Their Amendment almost made it, and they're still here. The Senator's a very persuasive man – a war hero. I believe they're regrouping. If we try to come in, they'll mobilize everyone. You'd be asking for a lot of trouble, Joe."

"Nothing we can't handle."

Bonardi regarded Frascati and frowned. Frascati did not like to see Bonardi frown.

"I'm surprised at you, Sal. This could be your baby. I was counting on you. What's the beef?"

Frascati was almost sick with anxiety. He fully understood the penalty for any interference with any plans. He shook his head.

"It's nice here, Giuseppi – not perfect – too much dope, too many unwed mothers, theft, aggressive behavior. I plan to have a talk with our police chief. I'll make him look like Dick Tracy. I'll clean up town management. I'll make Wentworth Harbor as good as they tell everybody it is."

He stood up.

"I plan to live here, Joe. I want to protect this place from casinos and porn shops. I've lived in those places. I know what they're like. Please, Joe, for old times sake, leave this town alone."

"Hey, what can I tell ya? I've run it past diBianco. He likes it. He likes you, Hey, don't look so sad, Sal. Maybe I can tell him you want to retire, Sal. Maybe he'll let you. I don't know."

"Maybe you'll keep me informed, Joe."

"Yeah, sure, Sal. After all you live here. This is your town.

CHAPTER 13

Salvatore Frascati found himself unable to look at the house of his dreams. All that money wasted.

To live in Wentworth Harbor had been his greatest wish, the compensation for a life promoting shit. He particularly hated drugs. Drugs were worse than a few assassinations. Hell, those guys had been scum, and after the first one, he hadn't really minded the others, but drugs turned people into animals, thieves, rapists, murderers. He hated the users and he hated the pushers even more.

Bonardi had asked him would he like to retire. Of course he wanted to retire. He'd only been in it for the money. Well, he had the money - more money than he could possibly use. He wanted out.

Bonardi had reminded him that he needed di Bianco's permission. Frascati swore. What could he tell di Bianco - that he no longer had the heart for the business, that he had hated many of the things he had been asked to do? Surely the man had to know that he, Salvatore Frascati, having taken the oath of omerta, would be silent to his grave!

Frascati had eliminated a couple of would be retirees. Di Bianco had said there was no better silencer than death.

Bonardi had told him the town was his, but he now knew Bonardi had been investigating on his own - and for some time. Joe knew more about Wentworth Harbor than he did. Son of a bitch wasn't after his permission. He had already laid it on and expected him to do the dirty work. And now, because of his big mouth, he was in trouble.

At that moment, Frascati wanted to call his broker and put the place on the market, which he knew the broker would be only too happy to do. Frascati shook his head. Hell, there was no place to hide. What was the point in cleaning up the town when Bonardi was planning to ruin it? He could refuse to help Bonardi, but he knew he hadn't the guts to try and stop him, and if he did find the guts, who in Wentworth Harbor would believe him, Salvatore Frascati, a man with Mafia written all over him?

From what he had heard about Bradford Justice, Justice would never accept a member of the Mafia as an ally. President Kennedy had, but Bradford Justice would not.

CHAPTER 14

On the 24th floor of Prestige Towers, one of Boston's newest office skyscrapers, were the offices of **TRICKEY, SLYE AND DIDDLE.**

T S AND D occupied the entire top floor immediately below the penthouse offices of the senior partners. Conservative opulence was established by oriental rugs over tightly woven, gray, wall-to-wall carpeting, hand carved molding bordering the top of walnut paneling throughout. Moroccan leather inlaid mahogany desks, sterling silver accessories (trays, pitchers and calendars), gilt framed oil paintings of sailing ships, oil paintings of former senior partners. The tallest portrayed Alvah Trickey wearing a worn New York Yacht Club cap. His hand was on the helm of a beautiful Hinckley sloop. The gold plaque beneath read:

Alvah Trickey at the Helm of
The Settlement

There were views of Boston Harbor from almost every window.

"Clients who come here," Bradford had said of his only visit to these exalted chambers, "could well believe that at least they have been fleeced in style."

Brad's visit had been to collect a cashier's check from William S. Diddle, scion of the prominent Boston Diddles, formerly manufacturers of textiles, who had supplied the Confederate with blankets and uniforms. They were firm believers in the axiom - business is business - a simple creed that had stood the Diddles in good stead lo these many years. It was a small but logical step for the family to go into the law.

The cashier's check was for a promised contribution to the Republican Party, the head of which had insisted on a certified or cashier's check which the then candidate for the Senate, had agreed to obtain. Brad had assumed his brief presence had gone unnoticed.

His assumption was incorrect.

Alvah Trickey had called a small meeting - senior partners only - to discuss 'a matter of interest to all'. They assembled in a small conference room in the penthouse. There was no view because there were no windows in the conference room. Once the door was closed the room was sound proof.

"If any of you gentlemen have recorders, please leave them on the table in the hallway. Several complied. There was no phone. Phones could be tapped. Apparently, for the lawyers who had left recorders on the table, recorders were standard equipment. Memory should never be counted on especially when dealing with chief executives of major corporations who rarely appeared without their counsel, presumably similarly equipped.

"Gentlemen, I have called us together to discuss President Whitredge's appointee to the United States Supreme Court. I refer to former Senator Bradford Justice."

"Where did you hear that? It isn't in the papers. It certainly isn't official. The President hasn't appointed anyone yet."

"Who is Bradford Justice?"

"Not only is the man not a lawyer, he believes in ***justice - above the law!"***

Alvah was gratified by the reaction. All his colleagues looked startled. Alvah was feeling smug that he was the only one of them who had known of the President's intention to appoint a non-lawyer to the US Supreme Court.

Alvah Trickey was already having trouble with the word Justice. He had an aversion even to the word. It tended to stick in his throat. The word had produced some nervous - sympathetic - giggles.

"I want your opinions and suggestions as to what we should do about the appointment of a non-lawyer to our highest court."

Alvah Trickey was a big man with enormous hands and thick fingers. He had large wrists and a fleshy nose shaped like a hatchet. He was ugly and could be very intimidating in court. He had a deep voice and an impressive vocabulary. Legal terms flowed like a torrent.

"Well, gentlemen?"

"I had an encounter with Justice a few years ago." Diddle began.

"Nothing catching, I hope, Diddle."

This from Martin Krook, the newest partner. Everyone but Trickey laughed.

"The fellow came here, as he said, to pick up a cashiers check - my generous contribution to the Republican Party. I had offered to put my personal check in the mail, but the fellow had the cheek to refuse my personal check."

"Now at least we know the man's not stupid."

Some more laughter.

"I resent that, Krook. The man immediately brought up the law, said that was what I had agreed to - in writing - above my signature. He suggested that, as a prominent attorney, my obligation to comply was clear. He also said to me that time was of the essence - another well known legal phrase - and asked the location of the nearest bank in which I had an account with sufficient funds to cover the amount."

Trickey paused.

"The man is annoyingly aggressive, and sure of himself, but he is not dumb and he understands legal argument."

Karl Grabb nodded as did the others who could never admit they did not always understand legal argument.

"It's an interesting idea. I never thought of having a non-lawyer on the Supreme Court."

"Of course you didn't! It's an obscene thought. We simply cannot permit it!"

Alvah Trickey left no doubt of his position on the matter.

"What in this world is justice, for god's sake?" Trickey continued. "It's simply an opinion. Everybody has his own idea of justice, of what is fair. We can't run a justice system that way."

Trickey didn't seem to notice the contradiction in terms, but his associate, Van Slyck, did.

"You can't have justice in a justice system?

"Of course you can, but it is adherence to the law that will bring that about."

"Certainly, Alvah, that's what we were all educated to believe - but I don't - and you don't either."

"That's legal blasphemy, Van Slyck. Bradford J--" Trickey could not use the word. "BJ is a damn heretic!"

"He can't be considered a heretic, Alvah, to something to which he never subscribed. If a lawyer does not agree with you, you may consider that lawyer a heretic, but Bradford Justice isn't a lawyer."

Van Slyck paused, hesitant to continue, but he couldn't resist saying what he felt.

"You simply deny its existence, Alvah."

He paused to collect his argument.

"It is truth that should be the first consideration. Far too often we have abandoned the search for truth and it is enriching us so we are not about to change anything. I think Bradford Justice is a breath of fresh air. I would like to see a non-lawyer on the Supreme Court."

The silence in that secure sound proof room was deafening. All of the other partners were shocked. Van Slyck was surprised that a group of super successful lawyers, used to years of argument and frequent legal nonsense, were so astonished. His was obviously the dissenting opinion, but these men should be used to dissenting opinions.

He searched their faces: Trickey, Diddle, Krook, Slye, Fogg, Grabb and Grimm. Grimm had said nothing, but his expression stated his disapproval, but then looking stern was his stock in trade.

Van Slyck realized his days with Trickey, Slye and Diddle were numbered. It had been a tactical error, but he felt a lot better. He'd been considering retirement for some time. He had just speeded up the process.

For years van Slyck had looked askance at the practice of law. He had surprised himself, however, when at a party, a stranger had asked him his opinion of the practice of law - this after the man had learned that Donald Van Slyck, a Harvard Law graduate, had been a trial attorney for more than forty years. He remembered his reply which had been immediate and heartfelt.

"It stinks!"

And then the man had asked - quietly, "What have you done about that?"

Van Slyck had learned from his hostess that the stranger was Bradford Justice, a name that had meant nothing to him then. Who was Bradford Justice? He couldn't be another Nader. Nader was a lawyer and used the law to get what he wanted. Bradford Justice looked like a gentleman. He was a big man. Van Slyck could still remember the intensity of the man's eyes. He appeared to be in his middle forties. His face was young though his hair was beginning to turn gray. At least he had all of his hair. Van Slyck remembered that because his own was scarce. The word bald stuck in his throat.

*** *** *** *** *** *** *** ***

Later that same day, Alvah Trickey had an unscheduled visitor.

Giuseppe, Joe the Barber, Bonardi ignored the secretary's request to announce him and barged into Trickey's office without knocking. Two huge goons remained standing just inside the reception area. Mary Barker tried to ignore them. Fortunately, Trickey was alone.

Alvah stood up. He was much taller than Bonardi.

"Siddown, Trickey. I got a couple guys outside a helluva lot taller than you."

Trickey sat down

"I would appreciate it if you would leave them in the car. You don't need them here."

"Don't tell me what I don't need. I'm here to tell you what I need, Trickey. I can't get over your name. A lawyer named Trickey. All lawyers should have that name."

Bonardi smiled and Trickey wished he hadn't. Bonardi's teeth were a brilliant white and looked as if they belonged to a much bigger man. Fortunately, he didn't smile often.

"OK, tell me."

Bonardi didn't like Trickey's accent either.

"Why don't you take the mush outta you mouth and talk like a man instead of a fuckin' fairy?"

Bonardi growled. "I need the name of a mouthpiece in a place called Wentworth Harbor in New Hampshire. If he can arrange things, I'll make him rich. I want a smart guy who is hungry - like you used to be before I made you rich."

Alvah Trickey barely hid his surprise. He opened his left hand top drawer and consulted a list of New Hampshire lawyers. He found eleven names and immediately picked out John Delaney. He wrote the name, address, phone and fax number on a scratch pad and handed it to Bonardi, but Bonardi did not take it.

"I also want the name of the largest law firm in Concord, New Hampshire and the man you think I should be talking to, you know, Mr. Fix Anything."

Trickey didn't have to look that man up - or his address, phone and fax number all of which he added to the scratch paper.

Bonardi took the paper, folded it and turned to leave.

Alvah Trickey did not know whether he was glad or sorry Bonardi had not told him anything. He was certainly not going to ask.

Bonardi ignored Mary Barker who looked too cool and distant. He left the office and the two goons filed in behind him.

CHAPTER 15

Alvah Trickey called another special meeting to which Donald Van Slyck was not invited. This time all present appeared to be of like mind.

The discussion was on the ways and means of assuring Bradford Justice's defeat.

Alvah Trickey asked, at the outset, that not one word of what transpired be brought to the attention of Van Slyck. They all nodded their agreement.

"As far as I can see, Alvah, there is not one chance in Hell that Justice will ever make the Supreme Court." Bill Diddle paused. "I don't mean that - not the way I just said that."

"We know what you meant, Diddle." Alvah Trickey cut in abruptly.

"Of course you do, I mean we all do. What I mean is that Bradford Justice will never obtain Senate approval because fifty-eight of the United States Senators are lawyers."

"But," Alvah said impatiently, "maybe as senators - and politicians - they will forget they are, or were, lawyers. If our own," he choked when he named Van Slyck, "Van Slyck says the idea is very interesting and Bradford Justice is a breath of fresh air, I don't believe all *those* lawyers can be trusted. I mean, now they are not only lawyers they are ***politicians* - and *nobody trusts politicians.*"**

"We're not considered too trustworthy ourselves, Alvah, though," Diddle added hastily, "that is an unfortunate combination."

"Never mind all that twaddle, Diddle."

Alvah was impatient to get on with the President's appointment.

George Grimm began to laugh which was completely out of character for the pale faced, hooded eyed, hunched backed man.

Grim was woefully unattractive, but could be very useful in court when detailing injuries that bordered on chronic and possibly permanent disfigurement.

Grimm was one of Alvah Trickey's favorites - as long as he didn't have to see too much of him.

Diddle's remarks produced some chuckles from everyone but Trickey. It was almost as if they were proud of their lousy reputation. After all, their legal skills had been producing millions every year.

It was enriching to be hated, and hopefully, feared. Grimm had the insurance companies so rattled they were constantly offering generous settlements the moment they found that the plaintiff was Grimm's client.

Diddle was determined to make his point so he continued.

"With just a little pressure from the ABA, I can't believe our Senator/Lawyers will confirm Bradford Justice's appointment. Really, gentlemen, there is nothing to worry about. Every lawyer knows on which side his bread is buttered.

"We certainly cannot afford to have some idiot on the Supreme Court spouting justice. I mean the idea is ludicrous. I'm old enough to remember Chief Justice Earl Warren telling lawyers who appeared in his court – *to forget the law*, to *consider first whether their case was fair*, for God's sake!

"That remark set our brothers spinning! Imagine any judge asking a lawyer whether he thought his case was fair! I tell you, my brothers, that would be the end of our profession as trial attorneys!"

All present looked appropriately solemn, and their frowns were deep in their contemplation of the consequences of justice.

"Diddle, I compliment you on your clear focus. You have just confirmed how serious the consequences would be, if the President's Appointee is confirmed by the Senate", he could no longer bear to use the Appointee's name, "but I cannot agree with your assurances as to the reliability of the Senators who are lawyers. We cannot leave his appointment to chance. The danger is simply too great."

He paused while he searched the serious faces of his partners.

"I have been contacted by someone, who shall remain nameless, who has offered help and has put before me the targets - and his analysis of the problem was right on the mark.

"The targets are, gentlemen: our President, Walter Whitredge, who has played too much football without a helmet, the Appointee, you know who, and the fifty-eight Senators. As the man pointed out so clearly, all the Appointee has, beside the President, is the public, and we all know how stupid the public is."

The latter remark elicited no smiles only a nodded agreement. Nobody in that room believed in the wisdom of the masses to make a wise decision. Anyway, the public, were not going to be needed - if the targets could be neutralized.

Slye, who had spent three years in the CIA, immediately associated the word target with neutralization and subversion, and wondered, with considerable alarm, if Mr. Anonymous was with the Agency or the FBI. Slye wasn't too sure he liked that possibility. He was well aware of the number of lawyers in both organizations. He frowned. This was indeed a very serious matter.

"Before we get too carried away, Alvah, with some very serious - uh - machinations, I think we should consider the consequences of such an approach. While I don't like the idea of a non-lawyer on the Supreme Court, he will after all, be only one man and so hemmed in by lawyers, he won't be able to do a thing. I have more confidence in our legal system perhaps than you do. Every man in this room has been practicing long enough to know that our legal system has been and is continuing to be abused, and most of us have not done anything to improve it. I do not believe that putting justice above the law is the answer and I would rather not have Mr. Justice running amok on the Supreme Court, but I believe the use of subversive tactics to keep him quiet will only make matters worse - for us - and for our country."

If Alvah's angry stare could kill, Martin Slye would have been dead. For Alvah Trickey the legal system was sacrosanct. He had soaked up his law training like a sponge and was able to rationalize – legalize – almost every one of the tactics he had employed over the years as justified by the so called principle of advocacy and had become wealthy because of it.

He ended the meeting almost immediately.

Martin Slye would not be invited to the next one.

Alvah Trickey was no stranger to the idea of ends justifying means. It was no secret that one of his clients was Joe, the Barber,

Bonardi. That client was never discussed although the fees had been shared. In legal terms the Partners were accessories before and after the fact. Alvah Trickey had never given any details of the various services he had performed as senior partner in Trickey, Slye and Diddle. Apparently they were relying on that old "I don't know." answer. They couldn't be convicted of perjury because, in fact, they didn't know.

CHAPTER 16

Before taking the first formal step in the appointment process, President Whitredge decided to deal with Cliff Sharp.

During the campaign and in the first months of his Presidency, Whitredge had relied heavily on Sharp's knowledge of politics and latterly the Washington scene. The little lawyer was as sharp as his name and had an encyclopedic memory, but Cliff Sharp was a lawyer whose ethics were always relative to any given situation. Whitredge knew, from the outset of their relationship, that Sharp was a pragmatist. When called on that, Sharp, after a telltale blink, had replied that he was simply a realist. Whitredge had used Sharp, but had no intention of depending on him.

President Whitredge and Bradford Justice were waiting in the Oval Office for the appearance of Cliff Sharp, and although the decision to inform Sharp of the decision had been made, Whitredge's feelings were mixed. Brad's reaction to the news that Cliff Sharp was a lawyer had not helped. Brad had said it was the ultimate inconsistency to choose a former lawyer as Chief of Staff and then appoint a non-lawyer to the Supreme Court. The President had replied that consistency was the hobgoblin of little minds. He hadn't laughed and neither had Brad.

Cliff Sharp, his knock acknowledged, entered the Oval Office and was immediately confronted by two very large men.

President Whitredge introduced Sharp to former Senator Bradford Justice.

"I assume you have heard of Senator Bradford Justice."

"Why yes, sir - former Senator from New Hampshire - Republican, if my memory serves me correctly."

Sharp offered his hand, and forewarned by Whitredge, Brad managed to seize it first and squeeze just a little harder than Sharp's determined attempt to impress. Sharp was immediately on guard.

"I wanted you to meet the Senator before I announce to the people that he is my appointee to the Supreme Court."

"I had no idea the Senator was a lawyer."

"The Senator is not a lawyer."

For the first time in their association Cliff was taken completely by surprise. His expression alone made it all worthwhile. For President Whitredge it was a moment.

The shock was so great Sharp forgot to control himself.

"You cannot be serious! After all you have been through to gain the Presidency, you are willing to throw it all away in an attempt to place someone who is not a lawyer on the Supreme Court. That will never happen. It can't happen! The lawyers of this country, though they do not always agree, will certainly unite against this, and make no mistake about it, they have the power to make his appointment impossible." His face was flushed and the words continued to pour out.

"You will be committing political suicide - and for what! The idea of a non-lawyer on the Supreme Court is unthinkable! I have nothing personal against you, Senator. You have impressive credentials. You have proven your patriotism in war and in peace, but you did give up your struggle in the Senate. You apparently didn't believe in yourself sufficiently to hang in there and run for a second term. Please, for the sake of a future in Office where you, Mister President, can make important differences, give up this quixotic idea."

Sharp was speaking for the opposition, as well as himself. Whitredge saw that Brad was about to reply. Whitredge interrupted him.

"Why is it so important to you, Sharp, that only lawyers can be Justices on the Supreme Court? You've already acknowledged there is no such requirement in the Constitution."

"A non-lawyer does not know the intricacies of the law, the vital nuances of legal procedure."

"Who's to say that a layman cannot know the law? Why can't a layman of intelligence and experience be equally astute in the interpretation of the Constitution? It is unlikely that anyone can point to any instances of Bradford's abuse of our Constitution. The Constitution belongs to all of the American people, not only to lawyers. I think you have forgotten that probably all of Brad's clerks will be lawyers ready to show off."

The President stood up and concentrated on Sharp.

"What is the primary obligation of our legal system other than the search for truth and justice? What is all this mumbo jumbo legalese about? Why is the law being kept a secret from the people? The only thing your legal fraternity lacks is a secret password. Can you tell me that the system is not constantly being abused - that it isn't in dire need of reform? Lawyers cannot seem to bring these necessary reforms about - even those who publicly admit they are needed. You, collectively, prevent change. It's time for men and women not brainwashed by the law to take a stand.

"I don't question either your knowledge of the law or your almost uncanny ability to handicap everybody with whom I will have to deal, Sharp. Believe it or not, I welcome your opposition and I would like to be able to continue to employ you, but –"

President Whitredge regarded Sharp carefully.

"I need to know whether you will be the *loyal* opposition. I require a yes or no, Cliff."

Sharp shook his head, turned his hands palm up, inhaled deeply, hesitated and let his breath out.

"Yes - reluctantly." And then he grinned and added. "And all this time I was thinking I was the power behind the Presidency. It is a low blow - Mister President. You know", Sharp addressed Bradford Justice, "with this President - and me - behind you, you just might make it. My God, what have I just said?"

What had begun as a confrontation was followed by a long strategy session and the discussion resulted in an increasing respect all around though after Sharp had left, Brad turned to Whitredge.

"I must offer a word of caution with regard to our lawyer. After all, you gave a clearly ambitious man no alternative. It was either join or be dismissed."

"I know. It may sound foolish, but I like the little guy. He is without doubt big in spirit."

"Yeah," Brad added. "Cliff Sharp is a legend in his own mind."

"But with him around I will always know what the opposition is thinking."

Brad left the Oval Office with the realization that his boyhood pal was not only a leader, he was a tactician.

CHAPTER 17

Whitredge was unquestionably someone to look up to. The press, that cynical body, liked that, though no one had said so in print. President Whitredge didn't have to wait for silence. Their anticipation improved their manners. There had already been several candidates from among the Federal Judges - three from the American Bar.

When President Whitredge appeared in the White House Pressroom, the place was packed. All any of them knew was that, finally, the President was going to announce his Appointee to the Supreme Court. Neither the President nor Bradford Justice need have worried there wouldn't be enough coverage. It had been agreed at the strategy session that this whole affair had to generate as much publicity as possible. Both men already realized their outside chance would come from convincing the people *they* should and *could* be an effective part of the process, that a Justice of the Supreme Court was *their* Justice because the Supreme Court was *their* court. The people could put him there by the pressure of *their voices and letters to their Senators*.

Brad would be promoted as an electable candidate

All stood upon President Whitredge's entrance. His appearance was, as always, impressive.

"It gives me great pleasure to appoint to the Supreme Court of the United States a long time friend. I am not prepared to tell you his name at this time, but I do want you to know ***that my appointee is not a lawyer."***

One moment of silence and the place went up. Everyone expressed astonishment, and less than a minute later, began yelling questions - so many questions with one drowning out the other, that it took several moments for everyone to quiet down so the President, who had waited patiently, calmly, could continue.

"The time is long overdue for the appointment of someone who is not a lawyer. Our Constitution made no such requirement for membership on the Supreme Court or candidates for the Presidency.

"I will be introducing my appointee personally in the very near future. Thank you for your interest in what I believe to be one of the most important appointments a President can make."

President Whitredge disappeared behind the curtain.

The interview was over, but the reporters milled around excitedly, shouting questions at one another until they finally discovered Press Secretary, Walter Hennessey, had also disappeared.

The next morning Brad Justice was busy at his computer, trying to prepare his acceptance speech. Its importance almost overwhelmed his ability to concentrate. Brad finally decided he should wing it. That thought almost paralyzed him. If they had the audience of the many millions anticipated, he had to at least make an outline or a list of the major topics.

When the phone rang, Bradford was glad of the interruption. It was Roger Welman, head of the Wentworth Harbor Planning Board. Bradford regarded the phone as if it were a communication from outer space. He and Roger Welman had nothing to say to each other since his Board had voted against their Amendment. They hadn't had any real clashes or ugly exchanges. That wasn't Bradford's style, though he had had to restrain himself, but was pleased his father had not.

Brad had expected defeat, discouraged by the herd like mentality that deprived most people of independent thought and action. If something was constitutional, right or wrong, it must not be questioned. The law was their king, besides any protest was prohibitively expensive and unlikely to succeed, and the final argument - the legal cost!

How many judges, in spite of personal conviction to the contrary, ruled on the basis of law that took precedence over what was just? Brad had encountered that attitude during his several appearances in the Legislature. Welman's presence on the other end of the line refreshed his memory.

"I'm calling to bring you up to date. We haven't seen you around town for quite awhile, and I think you may be out of touch."

Bradford was having difficulty focusing.

"Are you aware there is a lawyer in town who has visited our esteemed Permit Officer asking for a permit for a nightclub on the

Camp Mudgekiwis property. Apparently his company - New England Entertainment - has a Purchase and Sale Agreement for the Camp. The Club is for everything you can think of - nude dancing, liquor, live sex shows, films - the works, all the things permitted in the porno zone."

"Camp Mudgekiwis is not in the Porno Zone, Welman. So what's the problem?"

"Our Permit Officer issued a permit."

"That's not legal. Issue an injunction - and *fire* the permit officer. He should have been fired long ago."

"Well, uh, Town Counsel says that if we do issue an injunction, New England Entertainment will fight and the case will cost us a bundle."

"Still worried about costs, Welman?"

Cost was prominent in Welman's arguments against going to the Supreme Court to reverse that august body's endorsement of obscenity and pornography under freedom of speech in the First Amendment. The process was too expensive, and Welman was convinced, futile.

"Well, uh ---," Bradford could hear Welman attempting to swallow, "it's more than that."

"Of course. Town Counsel, Sam Smudge, is now telling you the outcome is dubious because New England Entertainment will cite discrimination - and probably win."

"Then you've heard."

"No, I haven't - *heard*! I had already made it clear that if a pornographer didn't like the designated zone, he could claim discrimination under the First Amendment - especially in our case since the citizens of Wentworth Harbor had already made sure of their welcome - twice!

"You did?"

"Yes, I did."

Bradford paused, trying to hold himself in check.

"Don't you think it's time to fire Smudge? There's got to be an attorney worth his salt somewhere - unfortunately not in Wentworth Harbor. None of them offered any help in the Amendment process.

"We have no choice except to fight, Roger. Maybe they won't pursue. Who in hell sold the property to New England Entertainment?"

"Banfield Realty. It's a new agency owned by Dick Banfield. Somebody with a lot of money has set him up. I don't know who. Banfield doesn't give a damn about Wentworth Harbor."

Brad let that remark pass.

"The Mafia don't wear signs and they always employ respectable looking front men. Who is their local attorney?"

"John Delaney."

"He hasn't been here very long, and he's so obvious I find it difficult to believe he has any clients. I hope you're not one of his clients, Roger. I'm sure that list would be revealing - if one judges a man by the company he keeps."

As far as Bradford could tell, no one in Wentworth Harbor had as yet any idea he was President Whitredge's appointee to the Supreme Court. They would know soon enough.

"What I need to know is what to do about all this, Brad."

"A little late, don't you think? I don't have the time to do anything. I have other things to attend to. Anyway what help can I be, if you and our esteemed Selectmen won't stand up and fight? Maybe it's not only the law our fearless leaders are afraid of this time, Welman."

"I resent that! I thought you were at least sincere. I didn't agree with your solution, Brad, but I never questioned your sincerity. I guess I was wrong." He hung up.

The phone rang again and this time it was the head Selectman, Lester Gardiner.

Les Gardiner had never been right on any matter of principle in all the years Bradford had known him. He had made his local political career by managing to be on the winning side - even when he had to do an about face at the last minute to get there. Bradford felt the man could have done much more, risen much higher in state politics. He had the brains and the looks. He spoke well, but lacked the stature or any real conviction.

"Hello, Mister Prophet. We are in a jam, Bradford, but I suppose you already know."

"Welman just told me."

"Where have you been? I haven't set eyes on you for a long time. I expected a call about now."

"I've been busy, What can I do for you?"

"I would like your suggestions as to how to proceed. I know you have a much wiser head than I do."

Les could pour it on when he wanted something.

"The Town has to issue an injunction and go to court - if necessary. You know that."

"Smudge says that's risky - that we could lose - and the process will be very expensive."

"Maybe you should just shoot them, or get hold of the owner of the camp and tell him to refuse to sell to New England Entertainment. What a name! Of course you would have to pay Banfield's Commission or ask him to give it up."

"I never thought of that. Aren't you going to offer any advice?"

"Fire Smudge. He's been giving this town bad advice for years, - and for once in your life, get on the side of the angels, forget the angles and see this thing through. Wentworth Harbor does not want that kind of a Club in which gambling will not be far behind that will change this town forever. You are one of the few locals still in power. Before this thing is over you will be tempted with offers, and if they fail, threats.

"Damn it, Les, the people of this town need you, so for once in your life, earn your keep and protect this town. Stand up to these bastards!"

After their conversation was over, Bradford Justice faced himself in the bathroom mirror, realizing fully the advice he had just given Les Gardiner applied to himself as well. His opposition, whoever they were, would not stop with one surveillor, a whore and a photographer.

For the first time he was almost glad Marilyn had left. He did not have to listen to her telling him to drop out - that it wasn't worth his life.

He regarded his face again and knew that it was worth whatever it might cost.

He wondered what kind of pressure the Mafia would bring to bear on President Walter Whitredge. Walter was the only one who could tell him to drop out. Maybe the opposition would know that. He and Walter would have to have another talk - soon.

CHAPTER 18

White House Press Secretary, Walter Hennessey, former Chief Correspondent for the Wall Street Journal, stepped to the front of the small podium, constructed for the occasion in front of but not blocking the view of Bradford Justice's home..

Bradford Justice's property was both pastoral and traditional. The Justice home, a 21/2 story central chimney, clapboard house, was built in 1820. From the audience perspective it was a significant reminder of their nation's colonial past. The house was painted white as was the large central chimney, the top brick border of which, had been painted black – said to be an indication of loyalty to the Crown. Brad couldn't verify that, but he liked the contrasting color.

The President had thought it a particularly fitting setting in which to make his announcement.

"Ladies and gentlemen, our President, Walter Whitredge."

Whitredge insisted he be introduced as "our President." Naive as it sounded to Cliff Sharp, it did truly reflect Walter Whitredge's concept of the Presidency.

Hennessey left the podium, leaving President Whitredge and Bradford Justice seated in full view of the audience and the TV cameras, which were everywhere.

The President stood up, a tall, commanding presence. His face was strong and his profile was coinable - as one day it probably would be.

The cameras were kind to him, which was fortunate, because many handsome people did not photograph well. When Whitredge smiled, it almost always became a grin and made him seem friendly and approachable.

Bradford, watching him closely, enjoyed and approved, believing that if any President could bring about important change, it was Walter Whitredge.

Brad tried to relax though he knew the next few minutes would be crucial - that any apparent nervousness, the slightest sign of doubt on the part of either, could destroy their chances for success. How, he wondered, could he manage to hide his nervousness, which, at that moment, was intense. He wanted to wipe his face, but knew that at least one camera was on him at all times. He likened the situation to someone trying to ignore an unbearable itch in a private place that could not possibly be scratched in public. The thought amused and calmed him.

The President waited until the crowd was silent, looked out over the people seated in portable chairs on the long lawn. He focused on the faces of those he knew and especially the US lawyer/Senators. He smiled at the locals some of whom had known him since he was a youngster.

"Good Morning, and it is indeed a beautiful morning. Mother Nature must be on our side."

He focused on the Senators, and smiled.

"Thank you one and all for being here. I hope Wentworth Harbor has found a way to accommodate you. It is now a residential resort so there aren't as many accommodations for visitors as there have been in the past. Many of the residents have registered their extra rooms at our Information Booth. I know the spirit is here if not enough spaces.

"This is indeed a special occasion - of vital importance to every citizen because, unfortunately, the concept of justice has come to be considered too vague and its search has been largely ignored in favor of many lawyers' acceptance of certainty in the law.

"I believe the rendering of justice is our system's most important obligation – in fact - its sole reason for being.

"The law has become an octopus reaching into every part of our lives. It is a system that has been abused by our lawyers and judges, dominated by them, frequently at the expense of truth without which the rendering of justice is impossible. Many of our legislators are lawyers as are almost all of our judges and several of our past presidents, including my predecessor.

"Our legal system, my fellow citizens, has come to be what our lawyers and judges say it is."

Whitredge paused, carefully, slowly, surveying all those present, and finally looking directly into the camera, said,

"The Law is not a substitute for truth, common sense and justice. I know, when you think about that, you will agree. The time is long overdue to take the first step to make our legal system fair -

for everyone. When I realized this monopoly, this stranglehold, had to be broken and a non-lawyer appointed to the United States Supreme Court, I immediately searched for someone I could support. The person I have chosen is Bradford Justice whose last name, though coincidental, was and is certainly appropriate."

He grinned and was rewarded by laughter.

"I have known Bradford Justice since I was ten years old, too afraid of the water to let anyone come near me to teach me to swim. Bradford won my confidence and succeeded where everyone else had failed. He and his father, Professor Emeritus of English at Bowdoin College, have been my mentors and confidants for thirty-five years. I have chosen Brad because I know he has the experience and wisdom to fill that job.

"Bradford Justice was a combat flyer who was shot down over Vietnam. He was their prisoner for three years. In spite of constant interrogations, beatings and long periods of solitary confinement, they could not break him or shake his belief in his country. He served as Senator from New Hampshire for a full term, but did not run again because of his disillusionment with Party politics, the abuse of privileges, and votes cast primarily with reelection in mind. Bradford Justice is married to a wonderful woman, and together they have raised two fine young people.

"By any standards Bradford Justice is a successful man with a strong ethical code who has served his country well. He too believes the search for truth is our legal system's most important aim. It is because of that and his willingness to continue to serve our country that you should have faith in his judgment and understanding of what our society should be.

"It gives me the greatest pleasure to announce, officially, my appointment of Bradford Justice to the United States Supreme Court, and ask for the support of every American citizen to put him there."

"Brad."

Whitredge extended his hand to bring him forward. Bradford stood beside him and smiled. The President took his seat on the podium.

The ensuing applause was enthusiastic. The President had done his job well.

Bradford Justice waited for the applause to subside and the audience to be quiet. Every pair of eyes focused on this man in whom the President had just demonstrated such obvious respect and faith.

Bradford searched the crowd for a familiar face. He focused on a few locals to whom he had issued invitations. They were all smiling up at him. For most of them he was one of theirs. He didn't trust himself to look at either Welman or Les Gardiner. He missed Marilyn, but at least she wasn't here betraying her great anxiety.

"Thank you, President Whitredge, for omitting my many flaws most of which you know so well."

President Whitredge shook his head slowly.

Brad looked searchingly, apparently calmly, over a sea of faces trying to encompass them all.

"Imagine, if you can, what it must have been like to have the President of the United States offer **you** an appointment to the Supreme Court of the United States. Over the years we had often discussed the urgent need for change in both our Justice system's primary focus and the behavior of many of its practitioners. It was a stunning surprise, but I knew immediately I wanted that appointment more than I ever wanted any other office."

Brad paused.

"So, of course, I refused."

There was an audible expression of surprise.

"Unfortunately, over the years I have come to the conclusion that people who seek power rarely should have it. Our President is a notable exception." Brad smiled.

"I reviewed my years of experience, both personal and vicarious, with our legal system, and the strength of my convictions returned, but I needed to assure myself that if the miracle occurred – if I could possibly receive the approval of the Senate Judiciary Committee, the majority of whom are lawyers and the Senate, fifty-eight percent of whom are lawyers, that I would not fail the President and those who would believe in me.

"I finally accepted because I believe in the need for change, and I believe in our President and share his faith in you."

There was enthusiastic applause.

Brad smiled, nodded and raised his hand for silence.

"There is a mounting despair of our legal system. More and more lawyers – and judges – have earned the contempt of many of us. I refer to those lawyers who continually abuse the system – for profit. Many of you are afraid of the courts with little or no belief in the judgments or the existence of even common sense. Aren't you, as I, appalled at the enormous costs?"

There were the sounds of many acknowledging groans.

"We know that all men are not created equal, certainly not, as intended, in the eyes of the law. As it is practiced now, the law is for those who can afford it."

Brad knew he had struck a chord by the emphatic nods.

"Lawyers speak about certainty in the law. There is no certainty in the law - nor should there be. The law, considered almost sacrosanct by some, is filled with contradictions, poorly written and frequently in legalese so abstruse that often lawyers don't understand it. The law and legal procedures should be available, for free, in every county courthouse, and the study of law should be a requirement in every high school curriculum.

"Since ignorance of the law is no excuse, there is no excuse for keeping the public in ignorance of it.

"It is difficult to believe that justice will ever be achieved, except coincidentally, in our adversarial system in which one lawyer is attempting to conceal the truth and too often getting away with it.

"The tragic result is the increasing lack of faith in our so-called justice system, the fear of our lawyers and judges. We are shocked by the decisions of haphazardly chosen jurors and their incredible decisions that frequently establish false precedents.

"Our justice system is failing and, ladies and gentlemen, it is without question our most important institution. Lawyers who share our concern, and there are many, agree that it is unlikely that important change will come from within. They have had that opportunity for more than a hundred years. Our present system is too profitable, too long established, and too invasive to expect change from within. We can make it better and we must make it better.

"The placement of a non-lawyer on the US Supreme Court is up to you. It is vital that you believe you can make a vital difference. President Walter Whitredge and I will be counting on your support.

"Thank-you."

The President and Bradford Justice shook hands amidst the flashing of cameras and great applause that became a standing ovation. It was apparent that, up to that minute, the lack of frequent applause during his speech was due to their wish not to interrupt and thereby miss anything.

Their smiles became wide grins.

At that triumphant moment neither really knew the power of the forces already at work to prevent victory.

CHAPTER 19

The newspapers had for the most part reacted favorably. The letters to the editors had been overwhelmingly enthusiastic about the idea of a non-lawyer on the Supreme Court. Whole sentences and phrases were quoted in all media.

President Whitredge and Brad Justice were gratified. Cliff Sharp insisted that all the hoopla was meaningless. It was the legal fraternity who controlled the issue. The absence of any reply from lawyers was significant.

There was nothing new in the resentment of lawyers. Lawyers had been reviled for hundreds of years. Shakespeare, Dickens and many other well-known writers, had expressed their disdain of lawyers. Dickens had devoted an entire novel to the subject. It had been a dreary, boring, heavy, dismal story of a case in Chancery Court that told the story, in painful detail, of the utter despoiliation of an originally wealthy estate which the lawyers had prolonged for generations and from which only the lawyers had benefited.

"When I tried to read *Bleak House* as a young man, I couldn't get through it. Dickens had been a court stenographer and clearly hated the system and every practitioner in it."

This had been volunteered by Sharp!

"I, my legal wizard, have printed out, from the Internet, thirty-five closely typed pages of anti lawyer jokes, and the list grows longer by the day. I have also become acquainted with an organization named HALT with sixty plus thousand dues paying members. I am sure there are many other similar organizations. At least one publisher thrives on books on how to avoid lawyers, and what about the militant organizations who deny the authority of the legal system. Surely, Cliff, all that anger must mean something."

"It proves that the people have no power, Brad."

"Did you hear the one about how to kill a lawyer?"

"Probably."

"Shoot him before his body hits the water.

"I also like the one that deals with an engineer who found himself in Hell. He did not like the conditions there so he brought in air conditioning and other comfort improvements. The Lord found out about this and told Satan that the engineer was not supposed to have been sent there and demanded that Satan send him up to Heaven where he belonged. When Satan refused, the Lord said he would sue. Satan laughed and replied,

"Where are you going to find a lawyer in Heaven?"

"Don't smile, Cliff."

But Cliff was already smiling.

Both Whitredge and Brad felt that lately the little guy had not been quite so ready to condemn, categorically, the idea of a non-lawyer on the Supreme Court – only its unlikelihood.

The conversation had taken place the day after the ceremony. Sharp had decided to stay over a day to look at real estate. He said he liked what he had seen on his first visit to Wentworth Harbor and wanted to get an idea of what property might be available.

Both Whitredge and Justice had been surprised.

They then learned that Sharp had been born on a farm, liked to hunt and fish, but said he hadn't had time for either for years.

Whereupon Justice and Whitredge had immediately slipped into the country vernacular they both knew so well.

"They say you kin take the boy out the country but you can't take the country out the boy, but you surely fooled me, Cliff." Brad smiled.

"Fooled yore Pres'dent, too. Time you come outta the closet."

"Gawd, I ain't been hidin' - jest carful. Don't want nobody to think I'm dumb jest 'cause I was born and raised on a farm."

Then, in unison, "Oh, we didn't think you was dumb."

Whitredge and Justice regarded each other in surprise. Brad waited for the President.

"Jest carful, Cliff."

"Now mor'n evah." Cliff could not suppress a smile.

It had been a moment.

Brad headed home. He had put it off as long as he could think of something else to do. He could not get used to coming home to an empty house. Marilyn was never far from his thoughts.

It was dark - really dark. The tree lined road helped keep out the sky. The branches, finally in leaf, seemed to be reaching out to each other. They created a welcome shade on the hot summer days, but tonight there were no stars.

He turned down his driveway, anticipating the sudden light triggered by the alarm system. It was always a welcome sight; hopefully a deterrent to any hostile visitors who would think the lights had been turned on by the occupants.

Brad had resisted. He hated the idea. His family had never locked their place. They had felt safe in their home. So had everyone else.

Both he and Marilyn loved this place because, in addition to their love of its colonial character, it was private. They were next to the last house on their road and invisible to it. There wasn't another house for half a mile. They were free to holler, dance around in the nude and make love on the grass - which they had done - a special, memorable christening. Brad had planned to write. It was the perfect place in which to write.

The outside lights did not come on, and he slowed down. There hadn't been a storm, some wind perhaps, but not strong enough to cause a line to be down. If there had been a problem, the road crew and the electric department would have been right on it. He knew everyone in both departments by name, and had often admired their skills.

He stopped the car, but didn't get out. At that moment he wished his dad were beside him. Age notwithstanding; he would have been a reliable partner. Brad recalled his advice. "For Christ sake, never be a hero. Be a survivor." Brad liked that advice.

Brad had no weapon to provide courage, and he cursed himself for that. He should have armed himself the moment after the warning phone call. His father would have. His father still had a snub-nosed Smith&Wesson.38 he had been issued by the CIA. He even had the shoulder holster.

Brad had no cell phone either - another oversight.

Brad switched off the car lights, got out of the car and immediately shut the car door, cursing the fact that the interior lights did not immediately turn off. He moved some distance away from the car into the dark, stood still - and listened.

He heard nothing but the night sounds. He could feel the darkness. He crouched to make himself as small a target as possible, devoutly wishing he wasn't so big..

Even after his eyes became accustomed to the dark, he couldn't really see. He could make out the house only because it was even blacker than the night. If there was someone inside who meant to kill him, he had been a far better target a few minutes ago.

He was fast working up some steam. Brad suddenly wanted an encounter - someone to lash out at - far better than this mounting fear. He tried to penetrate the darkness to determine whether there was a car. If there was a car, it would be easy to park it out of sight behind the barn.

Brad proceeded towards the covered stairway that led to the second floor, the first floor when viewed from the other side. The house had been built into the slope. On the driveway side the cellar was at ground level.

Brad had climbed the stairway and was on the second floor level before he realized what he was doing. He couldn't have said why he was deliberately putting himself in harm's way. When he tried to unlock the door, he was relieved that it was locked. He knew he had locked it after arming the alarm system. He fumbled for his key, fitted it into the lock, opened the door slowly expecting the shrill warning alarm, but there was only silence. The system was not supposed to be dependent on the electricity. It was supposed to switch automatically to a backup battery - an important feature for houses in the country during possible power failures.

Brad carefully closed the door behind him and stepped to one side to avoid whatever silhouette his body might have provided. Again he listened.

Old houses have noises of their own. Tell tale footsteps could cause creaks in the wide board pine floors. Even mice could make suspicious sounds. Old houses were perfect settings for ghostly memories of their past.

He could not remember where he had put a flashlight and he was reluctant to grope around the room for it. He found the light switch - and it worked! He let out his breath. He had no idea he had been holding it.

He was confronted by utterly wanton destruction!

Everything in his study had been destroyed! Couch pillows had been ripped open, the upholstery slashed, the TV tube smashed, books from the floor to ceiling bookcase had been ripped apart and thrown into the middle of the floor. Some leather bound limited editions of Dickens, Eliot, Shakespeare, Plutarch had been scarred their pages ripped out. The oriental rugs had been cut into jagged pieces!

He went into the kitchen and everything had been destroyed there too. Cabinet windows were broken, the doors wrenched off their hinges, canned goods smashed, their contents oozing all over the counters and floor. Bottles of liquor and tonic had been smashed. Every window had been broken - including the insulated glass slider.

In order to brake his fall on the slippery floors he had put his hands on the counter for support and they had been cut by broken glass, his blood mingling with the greasy contents.

Room after room that he and Marilyn had so carefully furnished with irreplaceable antiques, collected over the years or inherited from past generations, had been broken and striped with paint.

His body began to tremble, an involuntary response to his mounting fury. He had to fight a sudden giddiness, certain he was going to faint.

There was nothing left intact upstairs either except for their king-sized bed. The entire house had been systematically destroyed by vandals of the Devil!

Hot tears of rage and frustration streamed down his face. Nothing he had ever experienced had so devastated him. They, whoever they were, had hit him where he lived - in his home! His privacy had been invaded. The enormity of that overwhelmed him.

He stumbled into his computer room. Scissored diskettes were strewn on the floor, his monitor smashed and the innards of his CPU ripped out!

When he reached the bottom of the back stairs, on his way out of that awful place, he saw the blinking light of his answering machine. He was going to ignore it, but decided not to. He pushed the message button and waited.

"As you have probably observed by now, you have been paid a visit. I assume you are grateful for our consideration in leaving your nuptial bed in tact. We do want you to have a place in which to sleep. We decided you needed a reminder of your vulnerability, to make you realize the seriousness of our determination to prevent your appointment to the Supreme Court. We are not alone in this, but as you now know, you are. This is your last chance."

Brad pressed the save button. Later, he couldn't have said why, he had had the presence of mind to do so.

He left the house lights burning, switched on the outside lights and descended the covered outside stairway. He heard a car. It was already well up his driveway beyond the light from the house. The son of a bitch had been at the house waiting for his arrival!

CHAPTER 20

Minutes later Brad was knocking at his father's door. He restrained himself from bursting in. It had been a long established rule in the Justice household that every member's right to privacy was sacrosanct. When a door was closed, entrance was permitted, only after a knock and permission.

When George Justice answered the knock, he was annoyed and about to express himself. Brad's appearance stopped him.

"Come in, Brad. What's up? You look like hell."

"I've just come from there."

Brad followed his father into the den. George Justice was entertaining a woman - a damn attractive woman. His father introduced her. He was more awkward than Brad had ever seen him.

"This is Laura Peniman. I met her at the Whiteman's a couple of weeks ago. This little guy, Laura, is my son. I usually introduce him as my bodyguard."

The old man was recovering.

Laura stood up and they shook hands. Brad noted the firm handshake.

"I've heard a lot about you, Brad. Your father doesn't look as if he needs a bodyguard, though I suspect, you would make a good one."

Her smile was lovely and there was nothing awkward about her. She picked up her handbag and proceeded towards the door.

"It's obvious you two have something important to discuss. Anyway, it's time I was off. Thanks for a surprisingly good dinner, George. Nice to have met you, Brad. You have your father's strong profile."

The two men let her go.

George went to the wet bar and poured Brad a half a glass of Glen Fiddich, and watched with satisfaction as Brad drank it all.

"Well, son, whom do we kill?"

"I wish I knew. I just came from the house. It has been totally destroyed - every piece of equipment, furniture, rugs, kitchen cabinets, books - everything. The place looks as if it had been in an earthquake! Whoever did it - and there must have been more than one - were outside the house when I arrived and they didn't leave until just before I did. I heard their car as it drove out of the driveway. They left a message on my answering machine. I have brought the tape. The voice means nothing to me. Maybe it will to you. I'll play it for you."

Both men listened to it carefully.

"The voice means nothing to me, son. A bad trip, eh?"

"A very bad trip. I have to admit to you that I have never been so frightened in my life. The truth is I still am, and I don't know what to do."

"You can quit, son. I wouldn't blame you. It's bad enough to have an enemy and even worse not to know who."

"Amen. Mind if I have a refill? Sorry to take your good scotch. Haven't you got some regular stuff?"

"Don't you like it?"

"Of course I like it. It hits the spot." Brad poured himself another half glass. His hands shook and he spilled some. "Sorry about that."

"You damn well should be."

"The trouble is everything is happening at once. An outfit that calls itself New England Entertainment has a Purchase and Sale Agreement on Camp Mudgekiwis where they plan to establish a club in which everything permitted in our Porno Zone can be offered - and the Town is *debating* whether or not to fight them in court!"

"I've heard. I've also heard of Salvatore Frascati, a prominent new resident. You can't do it now because of your new celebrity status, but I can and will pay that gentleman a visit - for whatever good that will do. Is it possible the Mafia has been hired to harass you?"

"Anything is possible, but I find it very hard to believe any group of lawyers would do such a stupid and dangerous thing. They don't need to, and I can't believe they would think they needed to."

"Remember Nixon, son. He was a lawyer. He had no need to do what he and his henchmen did. On the other hand, I am inclined to agree with you. It would be just too goddamned stupid. The problem then is who else is so anxious to keep you off the Court? We still haven't found Associate Justice, Eliot Shapiro's assassins. That message might be from them. This goddamn country is going crazy - militia groups, mad bombers filled with hate for this government running amuck.

George Justice's matter of fact approach was beginning to settle Brad down and force him to face the future.

"The first thing for me to do is get some protection. I'm pretty sure a President's Appointee to the Supreme Court is entitled to protection, but regardless, our President will get it for me. I've got to call him immediately and establish that. The next thing I'm going to do is purchase a gun and get it registered. I may also buy a German shepherd guard dog. I'd appreciate it if you would put me up until I have a crew at the house to clean it up, repair the windows and install some new furniture."

"Of course, but you'll be cutting into my social life."

"Glad to see you have one. It's time, and Laura Peniman seems to me to be just what the doctor ordered."

"You think so?"

"I think so."

"I gather you've decided not to quit."

"I'm sensitive to the English language too. You could have chosen a less demeaning word, Professor."

George Justice ignored the comment.

"Has our President had a meeting with our latest G-Man? I think Freeman is his name."

"I don't know whether he has decided to confront him with the instruments of surveillance. Whitredge's appointment of Henry Saunders must have caused a raised eyebrow or two. You have a recommendation as to the kind of gun I should buy?"

"A semi-automatic 30-30, a sawed off twelve gauge shotgun and a regular .38 revolver. Of course, an AK-47 would be nice."

"You don't think I can hit anything. Since you trained me, it's your fault, if I can't."

"I'd rather you didn't miss."

"Me too, because if I killed anyone, I would have to hire a lawyer."

"Anything's better than going to the chair."

"I'll have to think about that."

CHAPTER 21

Within a few hours of Brad's phone call to President Whitredge, Henry Saunders appeared with a squad of Secret Service men. He stationed two at the entrance to the driveway, one to the front of the house, two by the back door and two on the south side of the house. Saunders had previously posted a roadblock at the intersection of Glidden Road and the Mountain Road.

"We will need a list of permitted visitors from you, sir. Two of my men will guard you personally. A bit of a nuisance and inconvenience, I know, but President Whitredge has informed me that if anything happens to you, my career is over."

Brad smiled. "I doubt that, Henry."

"I don't." He did not smile.

"I will be carrying a sidearm, Henry and I have a sawed off twelve gauge shot gun and an automatic 30\30 rifle. Make no mistake about it, this place was destroyed. I was threatened, and they are dangerous. I'm glad you're here."

"I will be personally guarding our President, but I have hand-picked every man I have assigned to you. Jim Grant is the head honcho. You will be able to contact each other 24 hours a day. I've passed along to them our President's message to me. I believe you will be in good hands."

"Thank-you, Henry."

Henry introduced Brad to Jim Grant. He was as big as Brad and at least ten years younger. He was blond with hazel eyes that were alert and very clear.

"I hope things are quiet for you, Jim, but as I told Saunders these people mean business. They may be the assassins who murdered Associate Justice Eliot Shapiro."

"President Whitredge told all of us who you are and why he has appointed you to the Supreme Court. We have been motivated to take good care of you, and speaking for myself, as a member of HALT, I think you're right on, sir!"

Grant smiled. Brad was sure it was a smile that must drive women crazy. Someone should teach Henry Saunders to smile.

Their presence was definitely a lift. Brad's morale had almost hit bottom. Once again he was impressed with Whitredge. The man functioned the way a leader should. He kept everyone in the picture. It was the only proper way to lead.

There was a very real risk for these men. They needed to know that - and the reason for it. He was glad Henry Saunders was looking after Whitredge who was probably at greater risk now that they knew his position. If he, Brad Justice, were to refuse the appointment, Whitredge would simply appoint another non-lawyer.

Brad understood what he believed to be the Bar Association's objections to the presence of a layman to the nation's highest court. It was just as well that none of their membership had been privy to the most recent discussion between President Whitredge, George Appleton Justice and Brad.

They would have realized that President Whitredge was not making merely a token or symbolic appointment. Whitredge had an agenda for his nominee.

Their most recent meeting had been filled with questions each to the other. Brad's disapproval of the way the so called justice system was run had been in part fueled by his own and others' negative experiences; also by the opinions of his father who, when all was said and done, though at times profane, was by no means solely a negative thinker.

George Justice had detailed some of the needed changes and had shown his deep concerns for what he too believed was his country's most important institution. He could be funny because he was a born entertainer, but humor was his way of expressing his frustration at people's apathetic acceptance of the status quo – especially among those who understood the problems.

Among the three there wasn't a shibboleth that was not questioned.

The Professor asked both the President and Brad,

"What do you think of the lawyer client confidentiality privilege? Is that good or should it be qualified? Suppose, for example, a male client admitted to his lawyer that he was guilty of raping a three-year-old girl. Should his attorney keep silent or should his obligation to society compel him to report it? If he fails to do that and tries to get a not guilty judgment, is he then not an accomplice? What is a priest's responsibility in such a situation?"

The three laymen had no trouble with that question. They agreed that any attempt to defeat truth was wrong.

"And what about the idea that no one can be tried twice for the same crime – even murder? I can't agree with such a blanket rule. If there is new convincing evidence of a freed person's guilt, he should be retried, as has been the case with convicted murderers. Those are just two of the many contradictions in our system that must be changed. If you can set a convicted murderer free then the reverse should also be possible.

"Why, in civil cases, when one is sued and forced to defend oneself, aren't all his legal and court fees automatically reimbursed to him when the judge or jury rule in his favor?

"And perhaps most important, why are lawyers who bring frivolous or malicious cases not fined, and upon repetition, disbarred for unprofessional conduct? There is no watchdog agency to police the system - only the American Bar Association."

"And what about contingency fees? The British do not permit them and neither should we."

The Prof answered his own question.

"The fault, Professor," Whitredge added, "begins in the law schools which send the wrong message. The idea that in the name of advocacy a lawyer can leave justice to God and represent his client, disregarding any responsibility to society. That is terrifying because it has become a belief - almost a religion. There is an ongoing move in California and other Bar Associations to bring ethics courses into law school curricula in realization of the fact that legal ethics are woefully inadequate. It is a good sign, but it has to change a long history of legal practice."

"I know a lawyer," Brad interjected, "when asked about his responsibility to society, replied that society is the enemy! I've wondered how many lawyers feel that way. If there is any excuse for such a wild statement, it may be that the poor devil thinks that Prosecutors are always truly representing society or that Prosecutors, since they have the awesome power of the state, can legitimately be considered the enemy. We talk about the need for justice in our legal system, but that is exactly what Americans, who have never been to court, probably still believe is the system's primary goal."

"I dunno, Brad, I believe the public has become pretty jaded about our so-called justice system. The hundreds of anti-lawyer jokes along with the militia organizations who refuse to acknowledge our legal system, prove that.

"What about Fred Rodell, Professor of Law at Yale? His book, **Woe unto you Lawyers!** published in 1939, the substance of which is still valid today? He insisted ***then*** that our legal system is the laughing stock among other nations. He also said the number of businesses who refuse to set up shop in the States is increasing. They feel the risk of inappropriate law suits that have resulted in huge, financially punishing settlements is much too high - not to mention the exorbitant insurance premiums now necessary to do business.

"His goal was a society *without lawyers!*

"And we have not yet considered another fundamental flaw."

Brad paused trying to phrase his question in a way that would be crystal clear with no possible confusion as to its significance. He had their undivided attention principally because between them perhaps they had thought they had already covered the most significant points.

"When is a lie not a lie?"

"I've always believed a lie is always a lie."

The President regarded all present assuming complete agreement."

"A lie, Mr. President, is a lie *only when stated under oath. That's our rule.* That is the Law."

Sharp's statement produced, instead of an immediate reply, a thoughtful silence.

"Another question, gentlemen. Does that possibly mean that participating attorneys can lie with impunity? What effect does that have on the discovery of truth?"

"I have to admit, Brad, I have not considered this point, and I am wondering how many people – even those well informed - have considered it.

"Well, Bradford Justice, what is the solution?"

"At risk of being considered too simplistic, naïve, place all participants in the court process under oath, as is the case with the witnesses who are always sworn in, and subject to the penalty of Perjury."

"I have to add, gentlemen, that all participants in a case are assumed to be under oath - as officers of the Court."

"Okay, Sharp, but I would like to actually see them sworn. I think it would be a very refreshing reminder to all concerned."

"I really don't think this will fly. I recommend silence on this one - at least until the Hearing."

"Possibly, Cliff, but it's the *legal* attitude. I know of a case in which a high up elected official at first refused to testify in front of a judicial committee – unless it was in a closed session and he would not be under oath. How about that for legal arrogance?"

There was no further comment.

President Whitredge thanked everyone for their input, declared it a most significant exchange providing further clarity and another compelling reason for the much needed changes in our Justice system.

CHAPTER 22

President Walter Whitredge summoned John Freeman, Director of the FBI, to the Oval Office. Freeman was definitely a suspect, and the enormity of that made Walter Whitredge very aware of his vulnerability and the loneliness of office. He was sure such a feeling had been shared by every President - even those with the backing of a major political party. It would take time to build loyalty in his Cabinet, all of whom had their own agenda. Opportunism was endemic. No President could really feel secure. Whitredge decided to take a leaf from Harry Truman - that there was little point in having power unless one used it.

John Freeman was short, pudgy and wore round, steel rimmed bifocals. He would have been a conspicuous anomaly in Hoover's reign. Hoover's insistence that his agents keep slim and fit had amounted to a fetish. Whitredge, after his first meeting, doubted that Freeman had ever been either, but he had a law degree plus certification as a CPA. A law degree, except during WW II, was the prerequisite for admission to the FBI. Whitredge wondered if that was because Hoover knew it took a lawyer to catch a lawyer, knowing how heavily the Mafia relied on lawyers.

Even seated Whitredge dwarfed Freeman.

"I have summoned you, Freeman because I expect you to tell me why you had authorized five audio bugs on my person. By the way, this meeting is being recorded."

Except for a brief twitch in his right eye there was no other discernable reaction from Freeman.

"I gave no such authorization, Mr. President though I was going to inform you that the Bureau has reason to feel, since your decision to appoint a non-lawyer to the Supreme Court, that there may well be some threats against your person. The authority for audio surveillance comes from the Secret Service who are charged with the responsibility for your personal safety. They report to the Attorney General." He paused. "I wondered about the dismissal of the Chief and your appointment of Henry Saunders."

"If you wondered about that, why didn't you inquire as to the reason?"

Freeman's right eye twitched again, but he did not reply.

"Are you unaware of the trashing of Bradford Justice's home - and the phone threats?"

"When?"

"Two days ago. In response to Justice's call for help, I ordered Saunders to send a guard team to Justice's home. Should I have called on you to protect him?"

"No, though we can provide protection - and will, if you so order. It is our mission to investigate the break-in, but only because Mr. Justice is your appointee to the Supreme Court which makes it a Federal matter, though that does not relieve the local police from their primary responsibility."

"Who, in your opinion, determines your investigations? From whom do you take orders?"

"The Attorney General."

"Since I have the power of appointment and dismissal of both, I assume I have the power to command both. You do understand that, Freeman?"

"Yes sir."

"Were I to ask for your resignation, what would you do?"

"I would tender my resignation immediately. Are you going to ask me to resign, Mr. President?"

"I haven't decided. What have you turned up with regard to the assassination of Justice Shapiro?"

"Nothing concrete, sir."

"What does that mean, Freeman?"

"It means we have nothing."

"Bradford Justice had the presence of mind to save the recording of the last message he received - after the destruction of his house. I have a copy that I will give you. Bradford Justice and his father, a former CIA Intelligence Officer, think it may indicate a connection with the assassination of Shapiro. The telephoners, whoever they are, do not want a non-lawyer on the Supreme Court. By the way, Freeman, how do you feel about that?"

"Your announcement came as a shock, sir. It is a novel idea, though I realize it is constitutionally possible."

"You have not answered my question."

"I haven't decided, sir. The idea is interesting, but I question the ability of a non-lawyer to cope with legal matters. On the other hand, it is entirely possible there has been too much coping with legal matters and not enough consideration of what is right and fair. It is hard for me, Mr. President, to ignore my legal training and experience. If it hadn't been for the introduction of the tax laws by our lawyer investigators, a lot of prominent members of the Mafia would still be free."

"But you may agree that if it were not for the legal technicalities employed by their defense attorneys, many of those Mafiosi are free who should not be free."

"A source of considerable frustration to the FBI, sir."

"We do not have to agree, Freeman, and I'm ready to listen, but what I do not hear I can't react to. Silence from you, or any other of the Agency chiefs, is not only not golden, it is grounds for prompt dismissal. Even the most tenuous relationship with any militia group and the Bar to keep a non-lawyer off the Supreme Court is wrong and must be investigated. Whitredge stood up,

"Here is the tape, analyze it and get to work. In the meantime, of course, I will let it be known, with pictures, the willful damage to Mr. Justice's home and the threats to make him refuse my appointment. Your investigation should include the legal fraternity. They should be quite willing to give you whatever assistance you will require. Should that not be forthcoming, I expect to be notified."

"Since you appear to prefer straight talk, Mr. President, I must tell you that it is almost impossible to prevent a determined assassin - especially when well funded. The FBI will employ all appropriate personnel and expertise to discover who is responsible for the threats and damage to Bradford Justice's property. I cannot believe any such behavior would be acceptable even to those lawyers who may not want a non-lawyer on the Supreme Court. Certainly your report of this matter should definitely put a damper on any possible future misbehavior from that source." Freeman stood up.

"Thanks for the tape, Mister President."

Freeman looked thoughtful.

"The practice of law has changed and not for the better. Maybe your idea has more merit than I had originally thought."

After Freeman had left, Whitredge realized he still was not sure of the man, but Freeman was now aware of the penalty for failure, and he had seemed shocked at the possibility of an organized lawyer connection.

Whitredge was also wondering what the FBI know about his past. FBI Directors made it one of their routine tasks to learn as much as possible about any political leader - or appointee. Such knowledge was their security blanket. It was unlikely any man who had had an active business or professional life had no secrets. Whitredge was wondering if his former wife was going to get him in trouble. She did like to talk and she was still smarting over their divorce - especially since he had initiated it before she knew he had any political ambitions. The Press loved to talk to her.

Whitredge also acknowledged his need for a woman, and the fact that even this increasingly loose society could suddenly become quite prim about their President's morals. Right now he was too damned busy to develop any serious female relationship. It was almost impossible to have any privacy.

CHAPTER 23

It was obvious the President's appointee to the United States Supreme Court could not properly have personal contact with a member of the Mafia, but George Justice decided he could and would.

It was important to determine, if possible, whether the Mafia had been employed to intimidate Brad. Intimidation was one of their most important tactics. Their reputation for ruthlessness, aided in large part by novelists and film makers who romanticized them, frequently made it unnecessary for them to do anything but appear, look threatening and their victims would comply. Such books and films were used as propaganda for which the Mafia must be very grateful. Americans ate this stuff up as did the publishers and film makers. George Justice felt the same way about so many of the spy writers who romanticized covert operators and the crimes they committed.

George Justice had had no experience with the Mafia during the three years he had served in the CIA. He would never have condoned their employment period, not even to assassinate Castro. The fact that a President of the United States had had sex with one of the Mafia chief's mistresses was both disgraceful and alarming. Power without responsibility is frightening.

George Justice phoned Salvatore Frascati. The phone call had been made from a pay phone in the next town. The voice was husky and barely audible.

"I want to meet with you. I have a matter that concerns you. I can be at your place in half an hour. I am driving a red car." He hung up. He had spoken with a pronounced local accent and had altered his voice.

Thirty minutes later George Justice was at the gate of the Frascati property.

The gate opened automatically and he drove in. He parked the car in front of the massive oak double door and waited. The stone courtyard was empty. The massive oak double door remained closed. The next move was apparently up to him.

George Justice opened his door and cursed himself for his obvious struggle to climb out. His large body was stiff and modern cars were not easy to negotiate. He had never been particularly agile and at seventy-three he was awkward. He also suffered from asthma and the effort had made him short of breath. He hated these signs of weakness, but once on his feet he still managed to look impressive.

One of the massive doors opened and Justice had a fleeting glimpse of a large, black haired man.

Frascati appeared in the doorway. He was not quite six feet and compact. The man was immaculate wearing a v-necked yellow cashmere sweater over a white sport shirt. His worsted trousers had a knife like press and his tasseled cordovan loafers were shined to perfection. His hair was black and short. He was clean-shaven, but his face was dark, evidence of a thick black beard. He appeared to be at ease and examined Justice with dispassionate, dark brown Italian eyes.

"Your name?"

"George Justice. You have heard of me?"

"I've heard."

"It's all true. I've heard of you, and I wonder how much of that is true."

"Every word. You wearing a wire or packing artillery?"

"No. Are you?"

"No."

"Come in. My house is yours. I'll give you the tour."

The place, Mediterranean in its decor, was huge, larger than any other waterfront home in Wentworth Harbor, where in more recent years; a number of quite large lakefront homes had been built. It was open from front to back on the first floor and the wall facing the lake was all sliders which gave onto a slate and stone terrace. Justice was impressed.

"It's a great day for a change. Let's sit out on the terrace."

Frascati led the way and motioned Justice to one of the several chaise lounges. George found a straight-backed chair, preferring to talk from an upright position. He did not want to get too comfortable.

Frascati chose another straight-backed chair, perhaps an acknowledgment that this was to be a business meeting.

"Can I offer you something to drink? Anything you like."

"No thanks. I guess you could live anywhere, Mr. Frascati. I wonder why you decided to live in Wentworth Harbor."

"I like it here - beautiful and quiet. Great place to raise kids. You been here a long time? I bet you've seen some changes."

"Nothing like the change your people want to make."

"I got nothing to do with that."

"Oh? They're your people."

"Who knows you're here?"

"Nobody. My car is known, of course."

"Why are you here? The name Bonardi mean anything to you?"

"No. Should it?"

Frascati shook his head angrily. He wouldn't put it past Bonardi to send someone to feel him out. However, upon further consideration, there was no way Bonardi could employ the man seated opposite.

"I just told you I have nothing to do with that. Look, Mr. Justice, I'm here to live in peace and raise my family. I don't want a club - or whatever - any more than you do. I would never have built this place if I had known there was such a plan for Wentworth Harbor, but there's nothing I can do to stop it. It's outta my hands. Capiche?"

"I find your attitude hard to believe. Maybe you've contracted a terminal illness and you want to try for heaven."

For one moment Frascati was incredulous. Who the Hell was this crazy bastard? And then he began to laugh.

"Me, Salvatore Frascati, trying for Heaven? Whatever else you are, you are a fucking comedian!"

"Hey! A known Mafia hoodlum who is against a sex club because he wants to live in peace and quiet? You're the fucking comedian!"

"I am fucking serious! I've lived in casino towns. They're full of crime and not only criminals but crazies addicted to gambling, booze and dope. Sexual perverts hang around watching sick sex acts live and on tape that drive them to try those things for themselves. Even the Mafia can't keep the streets safe in those places. What's going to happen here are things you never heard of, never mind lived with. You're talking to a man who knows what can happen. It will be worse than if somebody dropped a huge incendiary bomb. I wouldn't feel this way if I hadn't seen this place as it is now, but your leaders have no guts. Maybe some of them are too easily corrupted. The only excuse is that most of you have no idea what your people have welcomed."

"I can't resist pointing out to you, Frascati, the irony that this is your retirement haven after a life of crime. Seems strangely appropriate. Capiche? I'm not hearing any big laughs, Frascati."

"What are you, my priest? Are you waiting to hear my confession? I don't think you could fucking handle my confession!"

"I don't want to hear it. I can't offer you absolution, and I wouldn't even if I could!"

"You been mister perfect, I suppose. I don't believe that."

"You're right, and it's a cop-out for me to say compared to what. Now, if we're still talking?"

"You'll forgive me if I don't cross myself."

"You've got to find a way to get your people to forget about all this, Frascati."

"I would if I could - and still live. You spent some time in the CIA. You could learn from us about the need to know. This is a big organization and we make it a point not to inform anyone about anything without a serious need to know. I have already been cut out of this business because I made the mistake of letting someone know I was against it. My retirement was suggested, and only rarely is anyone ever permitted to retire. Those who do are generally eliminated. My neck is already way out.

"You and your son, the Senator, are the people to stop this thing. I can tell you this. If your town decides to fight, I think New England Entertainment will stop. You and your son have created a public awareness that the company will not want to fight right now, and this town's too small. I haven't been here very long, but I don't think your town has the guts to fight. You got a few spineless characters here - just like every other town - and guys with angles. However, if New England Entertainment decides to fight, New England Entertainment will be able to count on the lawyers of the American Civil Liberties Union to defend them. Between them and the First Amendment endorsing pornography and obscenity under

Freedom of Speech, New England Entertainment probably won't have to spend a dime."

"So, you're telling me Wentworth Harbor has no realistic choice but to fight. Right, Frascati?"

"I'm telling you nothing. I've never seen you. I don't know you."

Frascati stood up expecting George Justice to do the same.

"I have something else to discuss with you."

"Oh?"

"My son's home was broken into a couple of days ago. The place was trashed and he was warned not to accept the President's appointment to the Supreme Court. He would have come himself, but under the circumstances we decided it would be better for me to see you. We want to know whether the harassment was done by the Mafia, and if so why. We suspect the intruders were working for either a group of disgruntled lawyers or possibly some militia organization."

"After our little talk here, Mr. Justice, I know you will believe me when I say I have no knowledge of the break in or any threats. I will look into the matter, but it seems stupid that any of our people would be harassing an appointee to the Supreme Court. We don't like lawyers any more than you do. We use them a lot. We pay them one helluva lot. I have no respect for any of them. They're no better than we are, but," Frascati shrugged, "where would the Mafia be without our lawyers?"

Both men stood up. Frascati showed George Justice to the door.

"Stay too long and people might think we were friends."

CHAPTER 24

Bradford answered the telephone. He had moved back home before the work had been completed. He loved his father but not in such close quarters.

"Hello."

"Is this the Justice residence?"

Bradford looked around the room in disgust and answered "Partially."

"Hold for Dave Smith of the Dave Smith Show." Brad waited.

"Bradford Justice, former United States Senator?"

"Yes."

"I been trying to get you for days, Bradford."

"That so, Dave?"

There was a pause.

"Well - yes. Look, Bradford, you're hot news for the moment and I think we can make time for you."

"Time to do what, Dave?"

"Time for you on my show - for an interview."

"Do you know why the President has appointed me to the Supreme Court, Dave?"

"Well, no, not exactly."

The repeated use of his first name had thrown Smith off balance. He had never met the son of a bitch. He had only been trying to put him at ease, for Christ sake.

"Do you have any idea how big of an audience my show has?"

"Pretty large, Dave?"

"You bet your ass. Well, do you want to be on my show?"

"I hadn't given the idea any thought. You've phoned me, Dave. I assume that means you would like me to be on your show, Dave. How much are you offering?"

"You gotta be kiddin'! Bein' on my show will expose you and your cause to millions of people. We don't pay people like you. It's you who should pay me!"

Dave Smith's voice had climbed a whole octave.

"You mean your guests appear for nothing? You must have an unusually low budget, Dave."

Smith was on the verge of hanging up on this nut.

"Gracie Motherly has asked me to appear on her show. Her request is on my answering machine. I don't know what her offer will be. I understand she likes exclusives so it seems fair to assume she will pay for that. I'm sure your show has a wide audience, but I have already reached a far wider audience than yours. What our President is trying to do is important to every thinking American. His appointee, that's me, is news, not merely entertainment for those who peddle freaks and the generally trivial. If you want to upgrade your show and attract people of consequence, you will not only have to pay, but in my case, you will have to have read the material I would send you. If you don't read, there must be someone on your staff who can read it to you. Let me know your decision. Good-by -- -- Dave."

Brad hung up, certain he had gone much too far, but the opportunity had been irresistible. The Dave Smith Show was without doubt the smarmiest, most disgusting trash on the boob tube. Brad had tuned in twice, the second time because he couldn't believe the first.

The present reality however was his need for publicity which he could not possibly afford. The government did not hand out promotion money for political appointees. Bradford Justice wished he were rich. However, money hadn't put either Perot or Forbes into the Presidency. JFK's father's fortune had been an enormous help, but unlike Perot or Forbes, John Kennedy had had an enormous amount of almost magical charm.

Brad really hoped Dave Smith would pass him up, although he was aware Smith's popularity had attracted a raft of prominent people - including Walter Whitredge.

Twenty minutes later Dave Smith phoned back.

"How much do you want, Mr. Justice?"

"How long do you want the interview to be?"

Brad was stalling for time. He hadn't the vaguest idea how much to ask.

"I'll have you on solo - the whole hour."

"Do I have your word you will have read the material I will send you?"

"You have my word."

Whatever that might mean. Brad knew he had to quote a figure without hesitation.

"Twenty thousand - net, after first class accommodations, food and travel."

"You got a deal, Mr. Justice. I'll send you some alternative dates. My secretary will make your plane and hotel reservations."

The conversation was ended. Apparently it was worth twenty thousand dollars to Smith to tear him apart.

Ten minutes later the driveway buzzer announced the expected arrival of Arnold Marter. Brad frowned. He had definite misgivings about meeting with Marter. He had complained bitterly on the phone about his ongoing legal dispute, particularly the total absence of justice.

Marter's phone call wasn't the first from someone with grievances. Ever since the President's announcement of his appointment to the Supreme Court, Brad had received hundreds of letters and phone calls. He couldn't possibly hear or read a tenth of them. It was a continuing deluge and he had hired a staff to try and reply - a staff for which Whitredge, through Cliff Sharp's efforts, had made some funds available. The President and Brad agreed that some of those tales of woe would make good publicity. Also these complaints offered Brad opportunities to render judicial opinions. It was a challenge, but it had made it almost impossible to do anything else. Marter had revealed some mutual connections and Justice had agreed to meet with him.

The Prof's reaction to Brad's agreement to an interview with Marter was, as usual, dry and to the point.

"Too bad he doesn't spell his name with a y. Try not to spell it. Just pronounce it. Most people don't know the difference between Marter and martyr anyway."

Brad smiled at the memory. His father was acting like a schoolboy now that he appeared to be in love with Laura Peniman. He was writing poetry to her - mushy poetry. She loved it. The crafty old devil!

Certainly, Brad reflected, not to put too fine a point on it, he could use a martyr.

"Sorry you had to go through my security. I feel as if I'm under siege. Good of you to come. Let's go into the living room."

The furniture was new and of quality, but nothing like the feeling the oriental rugs and antiques had given the room. Brad became angry every time he entered it. The news of the desecration of the house had caused a terrible row. Marilyn had demanded all the gory details, made him recount every bit of damage. Her increasing dismay caused her to yell at him, berate him for exposing himself so recklessly, thoughtlessly, selfishly for an impossible cause. Brad had listened and tried to understand, but as important as their lifetime of collecting and the treasures received from their respective families were, they were only things after all - not worth the breakup of an heretofore good marriage. He was going to go and see her. She had stated her absolute refusal to set foot in their house. If, at that moment, after Marilyn had slammed down the phone, Brad could have confronted the bastards, he would have killed them. No law in this world could have stopped him.

Brad choked back his anger and faced Arnold Marter.

"As you know, I am concerned for those who have been denied justice. My request is that you be as precise as possible - you know - state the charges against you, the judge's ruling and your reasons for considering them unjust."

Arnold Marter emptied a full briefcase on the coffee table. It made an impressive pile of legal looking documents - 8x11 and 8x14.

Marter remained on his feet, pacing as he talked, using his arms and hands constantly.

"As you know I am a State Certified Land Surveyor. Although for most of my twenty-five year practice I have been independent, my business at the time of the complaint was a two-man partnership.

"The complaint was that my partner, who was doing the field work on a job some distance from our office, ran into a boundary problem which necessitated the expenditure of additional time. The complaint from both the landowner and a local surveyor was that my partner was not competent and was passing himself off as a surveyor though he was not registered with the Sate. The landowner complained about our fee and ordered him off the job. We have received no money for services already rendered.

"The Court removed my license to practice, and, of course, I instituted legal action.

"Finally, the plaintiffs agreed that I could have my license returned - provided that I dismiss my partner. My partner is black.

"I accepted the condition because I had no choice, but on the advice of my attorney, I have filed suit against the judge for a wrongful judgment. The case is ongoing. This has already lasted a long time and has cost me a great deal."

Marter stopped pacing and confronted Brad.

"I will continue my court actions if it costs me everything I own for which I have worked so hard for many years, and I will do it without complaint. I'll put that goddamned judge behind bars, if it's the last thing I do!"

Brad contemplated that angry face and had no doubt of the man's sincerity - and conviction. His face was that of a very ordinary man - not one that would be singled out in a crowd. Clearly Marter regarded himself a man of character who was in the right. If he had made a lot of money, it was not reflected in his clothes which though neat and pressed were of medium quality. Brad felt sympathy for an essentially honest, probably professionally capable, hard working man.

"Is your partner a registered surveyor?"

"No. He tried to pass the exam more than once. He's from South America and his English is not perfect. He is black and the surveyor who made the complaint does not want a black surveyor, and was upset we got a job he should have had."

Brad hesitated before asking the logical next question.

"Is it against the law in this state for an unlicensed surveyor to perform as one?"

"Yes, but I always checked his work. He did the work as well as anybody - better than some of the work I've seen."

"As a licensee are you responsible to see to it that all people in your employ who are performing as surveyors are duly licensed?"

After a pause. "Yes."

"Is the penalty for failure to do that the loss of license, a fine, or perhaps both?"

"I don't know - probably."

"Sit down, please, Arnold."

He did so reluctantly.

"I'm sure you believe, as I do, that an unjust decision is evidence of a failure in our Justice system."

"Amen."

There was a look of profound relief. Bradford Justice's questions had made him wonder where the man was heading.

"Well, Arnold, I see several flaws here. I haven't read that pile of papers, but from what you have told me I do not believe there has been a miscarriage of justice. I believe the Judge made a fair decision. When the Judge reinstated your license, justice was done. In fact, you should consider yourself fortunate that your license was not withheld longer and a fine issued. You broke the law, Arnold, and without any extenuating circumstances. The fact of your longevity entitles you to no sympathy. You had to have known better. The fact that your partner is black is irrelevant - and a shabby ploy."

Marter got to his feet. His face was crimson. His fists were clenched. Only Brad's size deterred him. Brad remained seated and ordered Marter to sit down.

"I am not finished, Arnold."

Brad took a deep breath.

"I am not trying to hurt your feelings. I believe you are convinced you are in the right here. I also believe you are essentially an honest man. It's obvious you feel injured - and I believe you will continue to feel injured - until you fire your lawyer and stop spending money on a suit you deserve to lose."

"You pompous son of a bitch. You're damn lucky you're bigger than I am!"

"And so are you, Arnold. Now, please, bear with me. I do want to help you, but you have to hear the truth. What has happened to you is an old story, Arnold. The moment you walked into that lawyer's office he knew what you wanted to hear and instead of giving you an honest professional opinion he was ready to engage in as much time and litigation as he could convince you to pay for. He convinced you he could show you how to get around the law, and when the first attempt failed, he filed suit against the Judge. It is your attorney who is the son of a bitch. In the last suit against the Judge he is guilty of filing a malicious suit, and the tragedy is there is no penalty for that. Oh, maybe a reprimand. There is no duly constituted government entity in the state or federal government to police the legal profession - only the various Bar Associations. It is like having the wolf guard the chickens."

Marter stood up and tried to stuff the legal documents back into the brief case, but he was so upset he couldn't and some of the papers fell on the floor. Brad helped pick them up and Marter took them angrily.

"I'll have you know my attorney is a partner in one of this state's most prominent law firms. It's obvious you know nothing about the law! You are unfit to be on the Supreme Court, and you can be sure I will use whatever influence I have to make certain you never get there!"

Marter tried to slam the door but Brad had hold of it. He closed it slowly after Marter.

Brad nodded. That was where he really belonged - judge on a Superior Court. Supreme Court Justices were reached too late. He would like to be in a position to nip malpractice in the bud.

CHAPTER 25

It was time for makeup before Brad's appearance on the Dave Smith show. As he sat in the chair while a professional makeup man was carefully examining his face, he felt an onset of nerves. He tried to assure himself the feeling was normal - was in fact essential to a good performance. He recalled performing in an amateur community production with a man who had proclaimed - loudly - the absence of nerves. He had been as calm as a corpse - until he appeared on stage. Then he began to sweat profusely causing his eye makeup to run. Worst of all he forgot his lines. Even though Brad had been able to cue him, there were constant, very awkward pauses, and it was a two-man play!

"Making you up is easy. You have wonderful bone structure and a strong face, and I don't have to pencil in hair. Poor David has lost too much hair and he absolutely refuses to get a hairpiece. They do such a marvelous job these days. No one would ever know."

He paused for a moment and pursed his lips.

"Shall I leave your amazingly few age lines? We refer to them as character lines. You don't want to look made up, I'm sure."

"No. I remember walking up to the podium to congratulate a Senator I had yet to meet. In front of the normal lights his pancake makeup was so thick, I felt embarrassed for him. He should have employed a professional."

"Indeed he should! Most of those politicians are too cheap to hire a professional and try to do it themselves."

"I don't object to the lines, and I'm aware there's a lot of mileage on this face. I just don't want to appear too worn or tired."

"Your tan helps, and I don't want to add any color. Dave looks sickly. I've told him to let me put some bronze makeup on, but he refuses. He won't listen to me. I don't know what I am going to do with that man."

"Tell me, Claude, what is Dave Smith really like?"

"Dave Smith is a truly wonderful man. I would sell myself to the Devil for him!"

Claude looked mortified.

"David Smith *is not gay*! I am, and I do love him, but he is *not gay*!"

"Neither his nor your sexual orientation are of my concern. What I am interested in is his character. His show does not indicate any purpose but to shock for money."

"There's nothing wrong with money. It's the people who have it - and what they do with it."

"What does Dave Smith do with it?"

"He saves it. He came from nothing and he knows that fame is fleeting."

"I certainly hope so. Notoriety hasn't done much for me, and the pay isn't too good either."

"Don't worry about your interview with David. I have a feeling you'll do all right. Tell it like it is. David likes that."

"I already have."

"He told me. That's why you're here. If I may say so, I think you'll make a very fair Justice." Claude paused. "Justice Justice. It has a nice ring to it. Good luck, Justice Justice."

"Write your Senator, Claude."

Smith and Justice had met briefly. Smith had looked Justice over and tried to hide his surprise. The man was big, apparently healthy and clear-eyed. He was wearing an expensive navy, single breasted blazer, a snow white, all cotton, button down shirt, yellow silk tie and summer weight charcoal gray, worsted, plain front trousers. His cordovan loafers gleamed. He was impressive and appeared to be entirely at ease - a well-educated man of the upper class. He and Bradford Justice did not and never would meet in the same social milieu. Dave was envious of the man's thick, graying hair.

"I would like you to wait in the wings while I introduce you, and then walk across the set past my desk and take a seat in the chair I have provided for you. How would you prefer to be introduced - as Senator or former Senator - or Mister?"

"Former Senator, and then Mister."

"How would you prefer to have me address you - as Dave or Mister Smith?"

"You call me Mr. Smith and no one will know who you're addressing. Dave will do."

"It's very considerate of you to ask, Dave, and while I'm aware that it's all first names these days, I am the President's nominee for the highest court in the land, and that is why I think Mister is appropriate. My friends call me Brad."

Dave Smith, who was known for his brass, was not about to presume friendship with Bradford Justice.

Brad, as instructed, remained in the wings. He felt the rush of adrenaline and this time acknowledged it gratefully. He enjoyed the feeling of being on. He had memorized nothing. He was free to wing it.

"My special guest this morning is former Senator Bradford Justice, President Whitredge's appointee to the United States Supreme Court. If the Senate Judiciary Committee ratifies his appointment, Mr. Justice will replace Associate Justice, Eliot Shapiro, who was assassinated on the steps of the Supreme Court.

"Mr. Justice and I have spoken only a few words. He is as new to me as to many of you. He was a combat flyer in Vietnam, was shot down and served more than three years as prisoner of the Viet Cong. Subsequently he served a term in the Senate. As you will shortly see, Mr. Justice is a handsome and imposing man.

"Please welcome -- Mr. Bradford Justice."

Brad stepped into the light, walked easily across the set, shook hands with Dave Smith who had remained standing, and seated himself at Smith's right. The applause seemed more than polite and when it subsided, Brad made the first remark.

"I think Dave Smith had me walk on to make certain I could."

Brad smiled and the applause seemed even warmer. He was puzzled by Smith's kind introduction - the lull before the storm?

"Tell me, Mr. Justice, why the Constitution doesn't require a law degree for admission to the Supreme Court - or was that simply an oversight?"

"I have a feeling that will be the position many lawyers will take from now on - whatever the outcome of my appointment - and may in fact attempt to introduce such a requirement.

"It should be remembered, Dave, that the framers of our Constitution were afraid of the law. We had just fought a war to rid ourselves of the English King - who was the law and could do no wrong. It was that fear of the law that inspired the right of protest against the law that is guaranteed in the First Amendment."

Brad paused and looked into the audience.

"As we all know, laws can be confusing, are frequently poorly written and in need of change. We are only human after all. That right to protest in the First Amendment is vital to all of us and must be preserved."

"Are you questioning the law?"

"Of course. Laws made by man are not sacred. Whenever a law is unjust and does not serve all the people, it must be challenged. At present laws are administered by lawyers too many of whom use and abuse them at enormous expense - our expense. Our judges are lawyers, their review panels are lawyers and the majority of our legislators are lawyers.

"That is simply too much power to be entrusted to people who frequently feel no responsibility to society who have been trained to believe their sole responsibility is to their clients. It is known as the principle of advocacy. It is a socially destructive rationale. It is difficult to believe that our present adversarial system in which one attorney is trying to conceal the truth will produce justice."

He paused and looked straight into the camera.

"That is not good enough for us. The courts belong to us and are *not the sole property of the lawyers."*

There was a prolonged silence as if the audience was waiting for more, and then a burst of deafening applause.

Dave Smith had not gotten where he was by ignoring audience reaction, but he felt compelled to ask the question he was certain would be on someone's mind.

"Since you don't think much of our legal system, why don't you leave?"

There was an audible gasp from the audience.

"I don't think you meant that, Dave, but I suppose it is a question of concern to some, so I will answer it."

Brad paused as if trying to organize his thoughts.

"I've risked my life for my country, and my father before me. One of my colonial ancestors was a Minute Man who died at Lexington; two were officers in the Battle of Bunker Hill. My roots are deep in our history. I want to make our legal system better.

"I want the laws to be clearer and much better written. There are several specific changes sorely needed.

"We need non-lawyers not only on the Supreme Court but throughout the system. It is presently this monopoly we can no longer afford."

"Thank you, Dave, and I thank this audience and those of you out there who have cared enough to listen. Now that we have become a truly polyglot nation we must have a judicial system everyone can respect and take pride in."

Brad stood up, shook hands with Dave Smith, acknowledged tremendous applause and left the set.

CHAPTER 26

After Brad's appearance on the Dave Smith Show, he received requests from other talk show hosts, and after consulting the Literary Market Place, signed with an agency that offered to book appearances all over the country. President Whitredge agreed that, if Brad were willing, it would be very helpful.

"We know, Brad," Whitredge said, "you are, in fact, running for that seat on the Supreme Court. The Senate Judiciary Committee, made up as it is of a higher percentage of lawyers than even the 57 percent majority in the Senate, will probably be against your ratification. We have to go to the people to convince them to write their Senators and Congressmen. It was the people who elected me, Brad, and it will be the people who will, in effect, elect you. Even though Smart has no faith in the people, he has offered some useful suggestions."

"Bless his little legal heart."

"He even had his secretary type them out. I think they're quite good."

The President smiled and handed him two sheets of closely typed paper.

"I'm sure you have already considered some of these."

Brad was reading Sharp's notes now that he was on the verge of keeping his first speaking engagement. The message was addressed to him.

"Brad, forgive the interference from an unbeliever in the people, but perhaps I am therefore able to look at this with considerably less passion and more, as you might call it, lawyer craft - with the addition of a y.

Appeal to the American pocketbook - the expense of grossly overpaid lawyers and the costly delays frequently caused at the insistence of lawyers with a weak case. Emphasize the collusion of the brotherhood who sometimes mutually agree to the script without the knowledge of the Parties. You know - first I'll do this and then you do that and we can really milk this case for all it's worth. And, I agree, there is no one to stop them or discipline them. There is no penalty for poor - even willfully poor - performance. Proving such cases is both expensive and success doubtful.

"Once the attorney is hired to represent a client, the client is out of the picture. His voice is gone though he might well do far better on his own.

"And there is something else you can tell the people. Since religion is divisive, religions are not a united force for justice. I remind you that in your and your father's battle for your amendment, the local churches did not unite and take a stand for its passage, nor did they offer to help finance an appeal by the Town to the Supreme Court. Why, when the majority of their parishioners did not want a porno district in their town? My wager is they never even discussed such an idea.

"The point to be stressed, when you are talking to the people, is that our justice system is the last stand for what is right - not just the legally possible. It is the only route to a just society for all the people.

"Yes, Brad, I would like to see you and Whitredge win. I know better than either of you the abuses of the system by lawyers - not all lawyers, goddamnit! We, this nation, do need to make justice for all the sole reason for the existence of our legal system.

"Up to now, you have been much too nice. Give them Hell, Brad!

Cliff "

Brad packed a garment bag, stopped to say good-by to his dad and began his journey to the people. He hated to leave because he was aware things were happening in Wentworth Harbor he would not be there to try and prevent. It was up to the Prof whose last words were:

"Full speed ahead, son. Save the world for democracy."

Brad got in his car, wondering if the old bastard had been smiling.

CHAPTER 27

When attorney, Warren Delaney, received a phone call from Alvah Trickey of Trickey, Slye and Diddle; he was impressed - and surprised. It was one of the well-known Boston law firms.

"You may expect a call or a visit from Joe Bonardi. Bonardi is head of New England Entertainment - a business that manages nightclubs, adult bookstores, and is an international distributor of pornographic tapes. I'm not sure what he wants to do in Wentworth Harbor. I have recommended you to represent his firm."

Delaney had been in practice for only ten years. He had set up practice in Wentworth Harbor five years ago, and was still feeling his way. He had a law degree from an undistinguished law school, but he had passed the New Hampshire Bar. A graduate of a community college, he had managed to acquire absolutely no culture. His language skills were limited. His legal vocabulary was minimal, but that did not stop him from using legal terms whenever possible, especially when he was with clients. He was heavy set, but appeared flabby. At the age of thirty-five he had acquired a paunch. The fact that he had no idea how to dress and was careless about his appearance had not seemed to make any difference to his few clients.

Delaney liked to appear shrewd and aggressive, and was always ready to go to court or threaten to go to court. Intimidation was his principal tool - that and the employment of legalese in front of ignorant clients. He was an embarrassment to the profession, but so far had managed to avoid an attack or anything more than a reprimand from the Bench. The miracle was that Delaney had managed to have any clients, which was proof of most people's total ignorance of the law and the legal profession.

"Well, Mr. Trickey, I appreciate the recommendation. I know your firm and its reputation. I will give Mr. Bonardi my full attention. Is there some fee involved or is he strictly my client?"

"Mr. Bonardi is all yours, Mr. Delaney." Alvah Trickey hung up.

There was to be no further communication between them. He never returned any of Delaney's phone calls, or replies to his correspondence.

Warren Delaney had been brought up tough in Boston's South End. His father, an alcoholic, drove a coal truck, and after coal was no longer the fuel of choice, delivered oil. A college education was Warren's way out. He was no good with his fists so he managed to lie low and always be pleasant to bullies. Delaney was not one of the boys, and he had no wish to become one. The man was not stupid. He was merely disadvantaged. Professor George Justice's analysis of Delaney was that, given a better background, he might have been a better man. The Prof also said such lawyers were the proof of the danger of public education.

A week later, Delaney received a call from Bonardi. Bonardi told Delaney to expect him at ten o'clock on the next Tuesday, and hung up.

Delaney reflected that Bonardi was a bully with dough. Delaney had known a lot of Italian Americans. Those kids had always traveled in bunches and acted tough. They almost never walked alone. Delaney was not a demonstrative man himself so he never appreciated the joyful side of the Italian character. Delaney was Irish but there was nothing expansive or joyful in his soul. He was an Irishman who did not drink.

On the appointed day at 10:00 Delaney was in his office, but he was not prepared for Bonardi and his two huge bodyguards.

The goons stationed themselves in the waiting room where his secretary was seated. Joan Simon was fascinated by the sight of two of the ugliest brutes she had ever seen. She had made no protest as Bonardi went past her to Delaney's office. She had little respect for her boss and most of his clients, but she had had no idea Delaney had sunk this low. She spent most of her time trying to keep Warren Delaney out of trouble. Joan was a certified paralegal. It was she who did most of the work. Instead of making her unhappy she was pleased at the opportunity to be in charge. She was convinced someone was backing Delaney - someone local. She had come to that conclusion because his income was insufficient to pay her the salary she demanded. Joan was probably the best-paid help in Wentworth Harbor.

She did not dislike Delaney. She simply had no respect for him either as a man or as an attorney. Delaney's wife was a drab little mouse of a woman and although Joan was a plain-faced woman, she had a spectacular body, and was surprised that Delaney had looked but had never made a pass.

It was tough being a divorced working woman in a small town, but the pay was good and Delaney had the wit to let her run the office and do all necessary research.

Bonardi's voice was raspy. Though Delaney wasn't much taller than he, Bonardi ordered him to "siddown".

"This will probably be the only time you'll see me. You will be my mouthpiece and do everything I tell you. I just wanted to see your face so I would be able to find you - if anything goes wrong. I will pay you more than you're worth - as long as you don't make any dumb mistakes.

"I want you to get a local real estate broker and have him get for me two pieces of property. One is the acre in the Porno Zone. The other is Camp Mudgekiwis an eighty five acre boys camp on the big lake in Wentworth Harbor."

"I can buy them direct since you know they are both for sale - unless there is an exclusive broker for either. I could probably get you a good price."

"You want to work for me, Delaney?"

"Yeah, sure, Mr. Bonardi."

"Then do as a I tell you. I haven't asked for your opinion and until I ask, don't give it. I want to use a local broker. I'll pay you a retainer of twenty-five thousand the first year."

"Am I a straw buyer?"

"Hell, no. New England Entertainment's the buyer - a legit business protected by the First Amendment. Strictly Kosher. You a Jew? You don't look Irish. We hire Jews. Jews are smart."

"I'm Irish and both parents were Irish."

"The Irish ain't that smart, but they're likable. You don't seem Irish to me. Now, when you have a Purchase and Sale Agreement on both properties, I want you to recommend the best local architect."

Delaney refrained from asking why.

"My next visit is to the local bank - the one that is locally owned. I will open an account there with a fifty thousand dollar deposit in return for their commitment to finance whatever I buy or build. I have a statement that will float their back teeth. You will talk, on behalf of New England Corp, to the largest insurance agency in town, telling them of New England's plan to build extensively and to be prepared to handle what will be the largest account they have. You will contact the best local builder and tell him I will want him to work exclusively for New England. I want you to contact the editor of the local weekly and tell him to expect a lot of advertising in return for some editorial support. Tell the Real Estate Broker to line up all acreage for sale and convince him he is and will be our boy for every acquisition we may decide to make." Bonardi paused.

"I want the names of all local business owners in a position of influence in this community."

Bonardi regarded Delaney balefully for a few moments.

"You don't really know much about this town, do you. Maybe Trickey picked a loser. Give me a rundown on the Selectmen. Who are they and what do you know about them? Rumors will do."

For the first time, Delaney showed some spark. That question was right down his alley. All his life, he had made it his business to know who was who, what made them tick and their ambitions if any. A lawyer could not know too much about those in power. One never knew when such knowledge would come in handy.

"We have three Selectmen - only one of whom is a local. They are in office by default - because no one with real ability is willing to run. Two of the men need the money - as little as that is. One of them is always on the verge of poverty. The other is simply lazy. He's retired and wants something to do and since his retirement pay is meager, he ran and won. He's a nice man, I guess, but wishy-washy. It's almost as if he wasn't there. The local could have amounted to something, but he is always looking for the angles. He constantly outsmarts himself. They are all vulnerable one way or the other. I've been looking for secrets. I'm sure there are some, but so far I haven't found any that are useful.

"Tell me, Mr. Bonardi, is what you plan to do illegal?"

"That's a pretty blunt question, Delaney."

He looked surprised.

"Strictly legal. The do gooders won't like it, but as usual, they will be useless, and also as usual, they will be too cheap to do anything that cost money - and it will cost one fuck of a lot of dough to go up against New England Entertainment. You afraid of what's illegal?"

"It's stupid to do what's illegal. I'm not squeamish. My job is to make whatever you want to do legal."

Bonardi nodded. Maybe this guy wasn't as dumb as he looked.

"Okay, you're hired. I'll be sending a messenger around with instructions and to take messages. You will not see me again - unless there's a reason. Capisce?"

Bonardi left and the goons followed close behind.

CHAPTER 28

Less than three weeks later, Roger Welman, Chairman of the Planning Board, called a meeting with Joe Smudge, Town Counsel, and Les Gardiner, Chief Selectman. The meeting was held at Welman's home on Elm Road in a recent subdivision. It had been extensively remodeled.

Welman, typical of almost every newcomer, believed he knew what was best for the Town, and had successfully run for the Planning Board.

The general attitude toward such people was frequently critical but resulted in little or no action - and no competition. As the Prof frequently said, it served the people right - they probably got what they deserved.

Zoning was a relatively new concept and quite a struggle for the old time Yankees to agree to. In the newcomers' hands, it became tougher and tougher for any real estate entrepreneur to do anything, yet it was a real estate broker, surprisingly enough, who had originally sold the idea to the people. He said the rich could afford to protect themselves for they had the money to buy up all around them, but Mr. Average couldn't, so zoning - intelligent zoning - was their only protection.

There had been times when Charlie Swett had wished he had not been so persuasive. The new do gooders were dedicated to the conviction that not one blade of grass should be cut and since he made his living by real estate; he chafed at that. He had gotten wind of the meeting and showed up uninvited. He was not turned away.

Swett, an impressive personality, was known to speak his mind and was highly thought of - even by some of the new super conservationists. He had been a year-round resident for thirty years and was fully accepted by most of the locals. He was almost as well liked as the Justice family with whom he had a very good rapport. He had never sought office, but almost every time he took up the cudgels, he had been successful.

Swett had chosen his causes carefully and selectively. He was not one of those whose lips were constantly flapping and kept writing to the local newspaper because he needed to see his name in print.

Roger Welman directed the men into the dining room where he had laid out yellow pads and pencils. He was a former middle executive in a Fortune Five Hundred corporation and accustomed to committees and meetings. He liked to think of himself as a take-charge executive.

As a self-employed operator of a small business Swett questioned Welman's real knowledge of business positioned as he had been in one segment of its burocracy. He liked Welman, even though he was taking zoning too far.

Welman asked his wife to get another yellow pad and pencil for Swett and took his place at the head of the table.

"I will be offering some refreshments a little later, but first I want our Town Counsel, Joe Smudge, to bring us up to date."

Joe looked like an accountant - or he could have passed for a schoolteacher. He wore tortoise shell glasses that made him look scholarly. His voice was thin - not made for trial work.

"As you know I have specialized in zoning law and I have been doing so for the last ten years. I became interested in zoning since its inception in New Hampshire. It is a subject that is becoming more and more complex."

"Thanks to you and some other lawyers. You fellows have sought too much power and have done your best to deprive people of their property rights."

"We are not here to discuss the theory of zoning, Charlie. We have been presented with a problem that is possibly the greatest crisis this town has ever faced. Please, let the town's expert on zoning continue."

"We have listened to him before - you and your board especially, Roger."

Smudge and Swett had had no personal contact, but Smudge was well aware of Swett's position. Swett, along with the Justices, wanted to change the law - because they believed the Supreme Court's ruling protecting obscenity was wrong. None of those three had any respect for the law. As far as Welman was concerned conversation with them was impossible.

"Well, if I am permitted to continue," Smudge looked to Welman for support. Welman nodded.

"What we are here to discuss, Smudge," Les Gardner interrupted, "is what you recommend we do in answer to New England Entertainment's threat of a law suit."

"What law suit, Les? This is the first time I've heard about any law suit."

"Well, we haven't broadcast it, Charlie, but New England Entertainment has a purchase and sale agreement on two parcels of land - one is the Town's Porno Zone and the other is Camp Mudgekiwis which has eighty acres and 1000 feet of shore front on the Big Lake. They want to build what amounts to a sexposition there because they consider the Porno Zone a poor location and insufficient land. When we threatened to deny them a zoning permit and to withdraw the building permit issued, in error, by our Permit Officer, they said they would sue us for discrimination. Joe Smudge here thinks we will lose and advises us to let them in."

Swett stood up, red faced.

"And I suppose you want to listen to him! We listened to him - and both of you - twice, and now look at the mess you're responsible for! If we had refused to sanction a porno zone in the first place, we wouldn't be in this bind. I don't know how you can face this town. When we voted the first time that was bad enough, but the second time, when Brad Justice gave us the chance to banish the Goddamn zone by vote, you did your damnedest to shoot him down. Where is Brad anyway?"

"He's touring the country trying to get himself on the Supreme Court. The idea is ridiculous!"

"After this last decision denying protection of our children from obscenity on the Internet, the idea of a non-lawyer on the Supreme Court seems better and better.

"You don't stand for a goddamn thing, Smudge. You certainly don't care about the community that is paying you for advice on how to protect itself from obscenity! The law alone is not enough. The law is not moral. It doesn't give one shit about the people it is supposed to serve. You're hopeless, Smudge. You - all of you - haven't faced the fact that what is permitted - what you have allowed in our porno zone - are defined as obscenities under

New Hampshire law, and obscenity is not protected under Freedom of Speech!

"Think about it! You've broken the law, goddamnit! Oh, you can weasel out of it, Smudge. You didn't do anything but offer legal advice, but, Les Gardner and you, Roger Welman, are guilty. If you capitulate to those bastards, I'll see to it you rot in Hell!"

Charlie Swett stormed out of Welman's home and slammed the door behind him.

The silence lasted for almost a minute. Finally Smudge spoke.

"The defeat of the Communications Decency Act proves that for this Town - any town - to take Brad Justice's Amendment to the Supreme Court is a waste of time." Smudge shrugged

"Charlie Swett is right, you know, Les."

Roger Welman shook his head angrily

"Strict adherence to a bad law is wrong. Trying to get around it by creating a zone was just subterfuge. We should have fought."

Welman shook his head.

The thought that we might have - obscenity - that is what so much of so called Pornography really is - is a catastrophe. We cannot let that happen, Les. You were born here. Surely you can stand up and take the right position on this."

Les nodded. His face was solemn. He turned to Smudge.

"You're fired, Smudge, and if you contest my authority, I guarantee that this town will blacken you name. Get out – now!"

After Smudge left, shaking his head in disgust, the two men regarded each other solemnly for a few moments.

"Well, now that has been done, where in Hell are we going to find an attorney who believes in anything but the law? There is obviously a cookie cutter similarity in the lawyers' lexicon that refuses to acknowledge the possibility that what has been ruled unconstitutional can be wrong. What we did here in Wentworth Harbor has been and continues to be done, on the advice of lawyers, all over the United States. Cities and towns everywhere have given up their rights to self-determination - by vote – to ban obscenity. Both Justices, father and son, have tried to tell me that, but I listened to the lawyers and was made to feel helpless, that it was better for our town to locate it in some undesirable place and thereby confine it "

Roger paused.

"I was wrong, but I don't know what to do. I know I want to fight these bastards, and I expect your help, Les."

"I never thought I would say it, Roger, but I hope Bradford Justice becomes a member of the Supreme Court, and his chief asset, I now realize, is that he is *not* a lawyer!"

CHAPTER 29

Brad Justice let himself into his hotel room. He had had dinner with his two security men and offered them the night off. Neither he nor they had detected any signs of surveillance. Although he and they were still suspicious, for the moment at least, the pressure seemed to be off. They had some discussions as to possible reasons for that.

"Your appearances have generated a lot of interest, sir. The people believe in you and what you stand for. The press is definitely going your way. I've been reading the editorials and most of the writers are very impressed - and frankly so am I. The crowds have given both of us considerable worry, but unless an assassin is ready to die in an attempt on your life, he can't possibly believe he could get away with the crime. I think he would be lynched on the spot.

"The people like you. You are convincing millions that this uncontrolled legal monopoly must be broken. I'm not suggesting that you're safe, but I'm convinced you are not the target you were."

"Thank you, Arthur. I do appreciate your vigilance. As to your feelings about the public attitude, the sole purpose of all these interviews is to convince them they can make a difference. Most of the time and for most of the people there's a feeling of alienation and helplessness in government matters especially when most of us are well fed and housed. We, and I must include myself, find it difficult to take any action."

Brad regarded the men for a moment in silence.

"I would really appreciate it if you would let me be on my own for tonight. As you know I am armed and I'm a light sleeper. I could do with some privacy, and I know you both could do with a night without responsibility maybe even a night on the town. How about it? See you at seven tomorrow morning?"

Bradford's hotel room was luxurious. His speaking engagement fees had allowed him to live handsomely on the road.

Alone in his room Brad wondered why he wanted to be alone, for in spite of the increasing crowds, he felt alone. When he had been a prisoner in Viet Nam, he had had Marilyn to look forward to, and he was then still a member of the Air Force serving his nation and had the feeling of company. He had felt alone in the Senate. Now touring the nation with a couple of Secret Service men, promoting a cause his wife considered anything but a dangerous waste of time was difficult to bear.

He hadn't spoken with his children about all of this. He had not as yet had the opportunity to become close to either. Marilyn had been father and mother and she had decided to keep them in boarding school.

Did he have anything left to give his country? The crowds were impressive, but did anyone really care enough to take some action?

His mood was dangerous. He had had plenty of time in which to experience mood swings so he knew this one was bad. If it hadn't been for Walter Whitredge, he might have quit as Marilyn had urged.

Whitredge was special. The man really believed in the people. There had not yet been enough of his political journey to remove that wonderful edge. The man was sure he could win this battle. Whitredge was a leader with a vision. Could the people be made to care enough to strengthen their most important institution? Bradford Justice had begun to doubt, but he knew he simply could not let that happen.

"Tell me not in mournful numbers life is but an empty dream!" He had quoted that line of Wordsworth many times. He refused to believe only the practical was possible. That was the philosophy of the defeated. Dreams could come true, if you continued to believe and work for them.

And then Brad thought of his father, the Prof, the brilliant talker, who could fascinate any but the faint of heart, who had been scarred by war and the consequences of American intelligence gone wrong. He had elected to seek peace on the campus - well - relative peace. Brad loved the Prof - George Appleton Justice - and never tired of listening to him, but the man had given up, thrown in the towel, had actually sought the atmosphere of a bunch of people he called socialists who had failed their students in the sixties! George Justice could have led, but he hadn't. Instead he had played the role of cynical social critic. The man had placed himself hors de combat.

That realization did not help. George Justice did not want his son to quit. His dropped baton was Brad's!

Brad switched on the TV.

He had had enough of thinking. He would let the boob tube take over.

Immediately the screen was filled with a naked woman - a damn fine, beautifully shaped, naked woman - possibly overripe - and the camera scanned her body - slowly focusing on her large breasts and nipples.

Brad sat mesmerized on the edge of the king-sized bed. He had not chosen the channel. It had simply come on. Every major hotel, for a fee, offered salacious tapes, but he had not requested a tape.

Her tongue appeared, licked her full lips and then extended and curled in an unbelievably long arc.

"My name is Violet and I can be yours for this evening for as long as you like. I saw you when you checked in and I want you. I like big men. I will wait for your call. My charge will be added to your room bill. I will wait one hour before I come to your room. Call soon or I will have to choose another."

There was more. He was sure there would be much more. He turned off the TV.

He had been set up!

CHAPTER 30

Violet would have performed. He had no doubt about that. Had the situation been different, had he not been the President's appointee to the US Supreme Court, would he have dialed Violet's number? He wasn't ready for that question.

He began searching the room for cameras. He couldn't find any, but he was certain they were there. What a scam for blackmail! Even in this age of promiscuity such photos would destroy anybody's credibility – especially the man who had tried so hard to keep pornography out of his community. He could feel the perspiration.

How had this worked? Who had been responsible? This was one of the major hotel - motel chains. They had to have knowledge of their offerings to their guests. The charge for services rendered were added to the room bill. What an outlet for pornography! Did they have their own library or hire a producer of pornography? Did the chain deal in blackmail? Surely not. Every major chain he had stayed in offered sex tapes, but it was clear this showing had been arranged especially for him. All he had done was turn on the TV. He would notify the FBI - via a request from President Whitredge.

The market for sex was so huge - and so compelling! The profit was enormous, as was the power that so much money created. Surely that result alone would make it dangerous to support. Brad tried to clear his head. He could still see that woman.

"Are we all so weak - so susceptible? There were tapes for all kinds of sex and for all sexes - with animals - children, sadistic sex, excretory sex, live rape, sometimes deliberately ending in death!

That information had been in the Attorney General's Report. There were clubs that showed live sex of all kinds. There was something for every kind of freak including sex with freaks and cripples. What he had just seen had been mild, quite ordinary, appealing to the heterosexual. There must be an important distinction between what most people would consider obscene and pornographic. The Supreme Court had failed to differentiate. Every porno zone, established on the advice of lawyers, permitted the gamut of smut!

The fundamental problem was that sex - in whatever form - was for sale. Sex had been for sale for centuries. It was only recently that the media had made it so graphically available to everyone. He could never believe the Supreme Court had the right to endorse obscenity and force communities all over the country to create zones for the unlimited purveyance of uncontrolled, salacious material both live and on tape or film. He was sure the FBI would obey Whitredge's order immediately. Whitredge had been making himself felt everywhere. They, whoever they were, were now attacking President Whitredge through his former wife who, lately, was being characterized in the press as the Silent Woman, caricaturized by a headless female figure, the classic presumption that the only silent woman was one without a head. The feminists had complained.

Brad phoned Marilyn who still had not tried to reach him. He always left his itinerary with his father. Marilyn answered and Brad immediately knew how much her voice meant.

"I miss you."

"Where are you, Brad?"

He told her and gave her the phone number.

"I'm going to be in Boston tomorrow for two days at the Ritz. Perhaps you would like to join me. It's been much too long, dear. I miss you."

"Well, I'm glad to hear that, Bradford."

Brad winced. The only times she called him Bradford was when she was upset with him. He waited.

"I'm busy. I can't possibly make it tomorrow - or the next day."

Her voice was crisp - definitely not her normally well modulated tone.

"How about the day after? I can manage to stay in Boston for another day - if you would come."

"There really isn't any point as long as you continue to persist in following the Holy Grail. Your appearances on TV are proof that you will not stop - for anything - or anyone. Have you heard what the press is doing to Whitredge? That wife of his is a bitch."

Brad was encouraged to detect the first real feeling.

"You think Whitredge's wife is a bitch?"

"Certainly. She has no business trying to hurt Whitredge's career. Whatever her grievances, real or imaginary, should remain between them and not be given to the public. She knows he can't really defend himself. Yes, she is a bitch!"

"Well, it's nice that we agree on something. I'm sure you're not talking me down - at least not in public, and I appreciate that. You don't have to live with me if you feel safer, but that shouldn't mean you will not spend any time with me. I need you. The sound of your voice, ***no matter how crisp***, makes my need for you even stronger. Do I detect a smile at the word crisp?"

There was a pause.

"Yes. You frequently make me laugh at your choice of words - but that does not alter my position." Marilyn paused. "In case you still do not fully understand my position, Brad, I am sick and tired of sacrifice. You have sacrificed too damn much for people who simply aren't worth it and don't give a damn. By the way, when is the big day?"

"Two weeks from today. Whitredge has already gotten two postponements. I suppose it's too much to ask for you to be there. I can get you a ringside seat."

"I don't think so."

"But if you're so sure of the outcome, I would think you would like to hear my swan song."

"Oh, Brad, I don't want to witness your defeat. You're trying so hard and so is the President, but it's useless. The lawyers are far too powerful. It will turn out to be business as usual. Give me a call - when it's all over."

She hung up.

Brad regarded the now dead phone

He would have stood by Marilyn no matter what. He shrugged. The word sacrifice had shaken him. He had never thought of himself as a martyr. The thought was appalling!

CHAPTER 31

Laura Peniman answered Brad's knock. He hadn't called first. His father had a right to have some female companionship. Knowing the old man as he did, Brad had no doubt the companionship was probably not strictly platonic - especially considering Laura Peniman, sexually appealing even at seventy plus. Brad felt a pang of jealousy. He smiled at her.

"Nice to see you again, Laura. Don't know what the hell you see in the old devil. The Prof's a lucky man. I hope he has cleaned up his language in your presence."

She laughed. Brad liked the sound of her laughter - full-bodied - definitely genuine.

"I'm prepared to make *any* sacrifice, though for such a well educated man, his vocabulary is sometimes lurid."

"I hate to put him in a bad mood, but I need to talk with him."

"I understand, Brad. I'll make myself scarce."

"That will really put him in a foul mood. I think you better stay. You know what I'm up to, I'm sure."

"I think what you and President Whitredge are trying to do is wonderful."

"Thanks."

He paused and looked at her intently. "Do you believe in the people?"

The Prof appeared.

"Don't put her on the spot. Nobody believes in the people."

"Walter Whitredge does. He really does."

"Remarkable. I agree with Sharp. It isn't people en masse that initiate anything. It's always an individual, starting with Christ and unfortunately, with some other notable exceptions, it has been all down hill from there."

"Then you don't applaud my tour and the speeches made by me and our President."

"Oh, I do. One can forget the masses, but there is always the hope that your efforts will produce some leaders who will carry the torch."

George Justice regarded his son.

"You look terrible. Come into the study and sit down. I'll pour you some Glen Fiddich."

Laura moved towards the standing coat rack - a homely affair that George had refused his wife's entreaties to get rid of.

"Where are you off to?'

"I don't mind, George. I know Brad wants to unload. Anyway it's late and time for me to go home."

"Don't go. Maybe you can help. I'm running out of stock phrases. I can't think of anything new that will help Brad. I can listen, and," he smiled. "I will. May I pour you one, my dear?"

Suddenly he was WC Fields.

"You mustn't drink water. Fish swim in it."

George Justice served drinks all round and then seated himself in 'his' leather chair in 'his' book-lined study and waited.

Brad proceeded to tell them the incident in the hotel room. He even went into some detail, which he prefaced with an apology to Laura.

The problem is, Laura," he had said, "without the detail, there is no impact. Even at that it's still only vicarious."

When he was finally through, he said, "If I had not been in the limelight, I would have called that woman. I guess I'm just as weak as any other male."

"Sounds normal and healthy to me, son."

Both men looked at Laura Peniman.

Laura smiled.

"I'm not a man so the exposure of Violet's delightful parts wouldn't have done anything for me. Even at my age, I don't think I ever felt I had such sexual power. I rather like the idea."

She laughed.

"Don't think you're going to get away with that, my love. You've known your sexual power since you were three! It is wonderful, but it's goddamned unfair!"

"Amen!" Brad nodded.

When the men laughed, Laura did not bother to look annoyed. Her laughter was wonderful.

"Don't worry about being human, Brad. That's what we women want you to be. After all we are the weaker sex. It would be cruel to take away the only power we have."

She did everything but bat her eyes coquettishly.

"You're not going to get away with that either, Laura Peniman!"

This time it was Brad who challenged her.

After that exchange, they were all very comfortably companionable, and for several moments sipped their Glen Fiddich quietly.

"That really is quite a scam, son. The more I think about it, the better it seems. With an operation like that one wouldn't have to do anything else. The money would roll in. I wonder we never thought of employing it in the CIA. What a way to make an enemy talk - about anything. It would certainly be an excellent recruiting tool."

"The reason, Dad, Gofkaufs never employed that one was because in your day television was not nearly as developed. The chains did not offer porno flicks."

"Oh, I know. I had a protected youth, son."

"Why don't you E-mail the idea to the Agency, Dad? Maybe they'll give you a medal."

"I don't know anybody in the Agency anymore. Anyway they'd probably have me investigated."

"I really don't think we should publicize that incident for lots of reasons." Brad paused.

"Wait a minute! Wait one goddamn minute! Why don't we use this against the members of the Senate Judiciary Committee? All we have to do is blackmail the majority and you're in. We'll get the FBI or the CIA to set the thing up. They could get the immediate cooperation of the Chains, of course. Those Senators are always traveling and staying in hotels or motels. It would be a cinch!"

"You're not serious!"

"No. I'm not serious, but they, whoever they are, did it to you."

"I'm shocked - profoundly shocked." Laura looked shocked.

"Is that really the way these things are done? I can't believe it. I don't want to believe it!"

"Believe it, Laura." Brad nodded. "It seems all right when you read it in a novel or see it on the screen, but when it's first hand, you're shocked. I'm glad you are, Laura. The tragedy is that most people are no longer shocked." Brad added. "I'm shocked!"

"I think it's time you people discover who is responsible. It is too late for guesswork. Certainly between you two, the CIA and the FBI you can find out."

"Hell, Laura, the FBI haven't yet discovered who assassinated an Associate Justice in broad daylight on the steps of the US Supreme Court!"

CHAPTER 32

Everywhere there was a news service, all the daily newspapers, radio and TV released the contents of an e-mail message, originally addressed to the New York Times.

It was a combination confession and manifesto. It was from a man who claimed to be one of the assassins of Associate Justice, Eliot Shapiro. The return address was bogus. It was a procedure available to anyone who could access the Internet. It read:

You may call me Jason. That is not my name. We are against a government that has become corrupt, run by greed and the lust for power. We reject a nation that has become a legalized, socialized tyranny.

Instead of bombing government buildings, putting false liens on property, creating guerilla forces or establishing religious cults, we have decided to attack the institutions that are the worst offenders and the men and women in the most sensitive positions therein.

Drastic? Possibly, but this tyranny calls for drastic measures since the people who care have lost their voice or have become silent - out of fear. Do not make the mistake of thinking we are alone. We are many including some in high places.

Are we afraid we will be caught and punished? No.

It is unlikely we will be found because our address has changed and will continue to change. The Internet is the greatest maze ever developed. You may never hear from us again - except through our deeds.

Brad and his father had met for the purpose of discussing Jason's message. The press was already calling him the Avenger, the Hangin' Judge of the Internet, the Hatchet Man.

"It's damn lucky he hasn't mentioned you, Brad."

"Amen!"

"What's that saying about strange bedfellows?"

"I don't want to assassinate anyone – though the thought is not entirely without merit."

Brad grinned.

"Haven't you ever felt sufficiently frustrated to wish you could physically stop anyone whom you felt refused to listen to reason – your reason – like the Queen in Alice in Wonderland, who was constantly shouting Off with their heads!"

"At least once a week, Brad, though such thoughts must never be acknowledged by a future Justice."

"I wouldn't be surprised at a similar feeling among our Justices when listening to pure blather coming out of the mouths of advocates. I wonder if it was Jason who trashed my house."

Brad shook his head in disgust.

"There's an awful lot of anger out there. There is reason to believe we are a violent society – bombings and assassinations. Destruction, wanton destruction of property, is awful and terrifying. I know the feeling. If Jason and his ilk hate what they term a socialized tyranny, why pick on people instead of changing the aspects of society which would improve it?"

"They want to destroy not change or cure. They would have no respect for you, Brad."

"The feeling is mutual! Well, I can't take the time to join the hunt for Jason. I have a pressing personal problem to attend to. Take care, Dad."

CHAPTER 33

Brad awakened early. He envied those who could sleep at least eight hours no matter when they got to bed. He'd been in harness too long. He sat up, placed his feet on the floor and proceeded to the bathroom, a journey no longer exactly smooth. He had acquired some aches and pains in POW camp, and he was not getting the necessary exercise. He resolved to take a long walk immediately after breakfast

His thoughts turned to Marilyn – her coolness. He was acutely aware of the absence of promise for their future. What if his efforts, by some miracle, succeeded? What if they failed? He had tried to make her understand his urgency and the possibilities for good from such an appointment.

He could not turn his back on all that. One could not go through life always avoiding conflict. He could not join the ranks of the socially numb – unaware of so much that required their attention. He could not help caring any more than he could help breathing. Life was so very short and there was so much to do that needed to be done. As a prisoner of the Communists he had had three years to think about life and some way to give it meaning. It had been a forced intermission, but he had to believe it had been worthwhile. He needed a wife who would understand and care and make him believe he was not alone.

It was time to visit Marilyn, but he needed that walk first.

It was summer now in the North Country. The woods were full of various shades of green and the maples, oaks and beech that lined the back roads provided a leafy bower and a cooling shade. His only neighbors had moved to the lake for the summer. Except for the mailman the road was his, and he was grateful.

He stopped to return the chatter of a chipmunk sitting on a stone wall that lined the road. He did it well, and for a moment the yellow and brown striped animal stopped, stared his confusion and then disappeared into the wall. He watched a gray squirrel as it traveled along a branch in the hardwoods. Suddenly, silent as the grave, a large horned owl glided across the road, his huge wingspan wide open, banked into the thick woods and disappeared without disturbing a leaf – a remarkable feat. That silent foreboding flight must bring terror to his nocturnal victims. The owl's flat face, hooked beak, unblinking eyes and sharp talons were merciless. The owl was nature's stealth bomber.

The birds had returned. It had been Marilyn who fed them, and in her absence Brad had taken over. He particularly enjoyed watching the feisty humming birds that rarely stood still and flew almost as fast as bullets. He called the tiny yellow finches his lemon drops. They had watched through the kitchen slider the bird's comings, goings and their sometimes antic behavior. He called that ever-changing scene their floorshow.

There was so much to be seen. If he were lucky, during his various walks, he would startle a deer and he and the deer would remain motionless facing each other. Brad knew the deer would not really recognize him unless he moved. Brad had been able to hold that scene for as much as ten seconds. His slightest movement would cause the deer to bound away. Only his white tail, which hunters called his flag, was briefly visible as it disappeared quickly into the woods.

Brad was not a hunter. He had agreed with his father that the only game worthy of the hunt was man. When deer were considered too numerous and a nuisance, the 'surplus' were periodically killed. It was called harvesting. Brad wondered when the population of people would be considered a nuisance and the 'surplus' harvested. All the wars hadn't really slowed down population growth. He shrugged.

He heard the woodpecker's rapid thocking sounds as they searched the bark of the trees for insects. As attentive as he was, he knew there was much he did not and could not see. He let nature distract him, occupy his full attention, and he was grateful. He loved the land and felt at peace when alone in it. This was a reality he understood. Here he could almost believe in God. Certainly this was a creation worthy of a God.

Brad had learned to walk softy when he was in the woods or, as now, on a deserted country lane. He enjoyed joining in the communications of the loquacious crows noting their increasing number, and admiring their crafty ways of avoiding hunters. He remembered, years back, when he felt the challenge of those black talkative birds of prey. He had been given a twelve gauge double-barreled shotgun, a weapon in which he had become an expert on the skeet range in the Air Force, but he had never been able to get a good shot at a crow no matter how crafty his tactics. He had tried leaning his gun against a tree near his house. The crows had bounced nonchalantly around it without apparent heed. When he had walked carefully toward it, looking the other way, the crows were still engrossed in conversation, but the moment he had reached for that gun they were away screeching warnings.

He had opened his upstairs window without a sound. He had stuck his head out the window. The crows were busy inspecting the lawn. He had reached for the shotgun and, ever so slowly and quietly, brought it to his shoulder – admittedly an awkward procedure, but just before he was in a position to fire, off they flew. It had been useless.

He developed a great admiration for crows and their ability to communicate with each other for their common good. Maybe some day people would catch on.

***** ***** ***** *****

Brad arrived, unannounced, at Marilyn's mother's house just after 1:00 PM. Lunch should be over, and if neither she nor her mother were home, he could leave a note – or wait.

He started to park in front of the white cape because there was a car he did not recognize in the driveway in front of the separate two-car garage. One of the two doors was open exposing an empty bay. For reasons he did not immediately articulate, he changed his mind and pulled in behind the car, effectively blocking it.

He got out of his Outback and went up across the lawn to the front door and knocked. He had to wait several moments and when Marilyn opened the door, she was out of breath.

"Hello, my dear. Hope I'm not the bad penny. If you won't come to the mountain???"

Brad remained just below the front step and smiled hopefully.

"No – I mean, of course."

She appeared distracted and stepped outside. Neither made any attempt to embrace.

A man Brad had never seen before appeared around the corner of the house. He must have left the house by the back door.

"Sorry, old man, but your car is blocking mine. I was just leaving. Really, old man, the front door would have been quicker for you."

"Do I detect a little pique - old man? I don't believe I know you."

Brad looked enquiringly at Marilyn.

"Aren't you going to introduce me?"

"Of course. Ah - this," nodding in the man's direction, "is Tom Blodget."

There was a pause.

"Aren't you going to tell him who I am?" He faced Blodget.

"I am Bradford Justice – her husband."

"Oh."

Marilyn was alarmed. She had never seen Brad like this. He seemed under control but ---?

"Tom is a friend of mother's." Her words came fast. "He dropped by to see her, but she's shopping."

Tom confirmed Marilyn's explanations with what seemed an unnecessarily enthusiastic nod.

Brad inspected Blodget carefully. The man was probably in his forties, well dressed, Ivy League type, clean-shaven, good features, altogether presentable. It was difficult to judge his height since he was standing on the lawn a little below the steps, so possibly he seemed shorter than he really was. He was unquestionably better looking, but he looked soft.

"Tell me about yourself, - Tom. What 's your line of work?"

Brad detected a brief flicker of annoyance and was sorely tempted to warn him to remain calm.

"As a matter of fact, I'm retired."

"Really, from what?"

"I recently sold the family business."

"For a handsome profit, I assume. What was your family business?"

"We manufactured industrial waxes. It is a niche business and so far we've been free of competition from the big companies."

"Sounds interesting. I trust all of your family is satisfied at losing such a unique business. How do your children feel about that or was money the only consideration?"

"Brad, Tom was just leaving, and your car is blocking his way."

"I'm just checking to discover whether a new friend of yours is not an enemy of mine." Brad continued regarding Tom closely.

"You can understand that – Tom, I'm sure."

Blodget tried to appear manly, but failed. He remained silent.

"Well, I don't want to stand in the way of your new friend."

"Really, old man, I must be off. I have an appointment."

"I would have thought, now you are retired from your family's great niche business, you would be done with appointments."

Brad remained silent for several moments, allowing the tension to increase.

"Well, if you must rush off, - old man. Catch."

Blodget bobbled the keys and they landed on the lawn. He picked them up hurriedly almost bobbling them again, climbed awkwardly into the Outback, backed it up, parked it in front of the house and returned wordlessly to his BMW convertible. He did not wave as he passed them still standing on the front step.

Brad turned Marilyn around and propelled her into the house.

CHAPTER 34

Once inside the house Marilyn moved as far away from Brad as possible, which wasn't far since the living room was not large. Her mother's house was one of the smallest in a middle class neighborhood. She was a widow living on modest means. He reflected that the BMW convertible probably made quite an impression on the neighbors.

The furnishings were imitation early American – no antique heirlooms here, nothing like the carefully chosen antiques he and Marilyn had acquired over the years. The vandalism of their home was a hard blow. Her refusal to see it first hand made it worse though he understood why she did not want to.

Marilyn remained standing, her posture rigid. She was angry. Was anger an indication of guilt? He had to take a deep breath. Marilyn had never looked more beautiful.

"Why did you hustle your mother's friend out the back door?"

Marilyn did not answer.

"Are you having an affair with your mother's friend?"

"I don't have to answer that!"

"Is your refusal to answer an admission of guilt?"

"Think whatever you like."

"You think I like to believe my wife, who refused to be with me when I needed her, is whiling away the hours having sex with another man? I can assure you I haven't been whiling away the lonely hours with understanding females."

"Of course not. You've been too busy saving the world. All our prize possessions have been destroyed and much of the house as well!" Marilyn's eyes were blazing. This was not the woman he thought he had known for more than twenty years.

She tried to regain control.

"You had to go to war in Vietnam because you were a professional - in spite of the fact that you knew that war was a terrible mistake. We talked about that. You admitted the US was wrong. I begged you not to go – but that had no effect on you. Your country, right or wrong, meant more to you than your marriage to me."

Tears were starting, but she wiped them away. When Brad started to speak, she cut him off.

"Let me finish!" She took a deep breath.

"And there I was – the little adoring housewife – left alone for three damn years not knowing when or if you were coming back or in what condition. I was expected to be the long-suffering faithful wife, raise the children by myself – and I tried. You can believe me or not. I don't give a damn!" She regarded Brad defiantly.

"Well, you did come back – thin as a rail and with asthma, but once again we were able to make plans for retirement to Wentworth Harbor. I allowed myself to believe we could finally live like a family, but not Bradford Justice. You decided to serve your country as a United States Senator so I joined you on the campaign trial and all that entailed. Once again I had to appear the adoring supportive wife. It wasn't what I wanted. I was sick and tired of serving my country – and finally so were you. Your disillusionment with government at first hand finally brought you to your senses. You – not I – decided not to run for another term, but to settle down to the good life in Wentworth Harbor. It had been a long route for me. I had almost given up, but I dared to be happy and look forward to a wonderful future with you and our children whom you hadn't taken the time to get to know."

She paused, her eyes continuing to focus on Brad.

"And then, your childhood pal, now President of this crazy nation, decides to put a non-lawyer on the Supreme Court. Once again, you answered your country's call, and put your marriage – and me – in second place. I'm sorry, Brad, but I am not up to another challenge – especially since you, as well as I, know your cause, no matter how noble, is doomed to failure."

The tears were unstoppable now.

"Our marriage is over, Brad. It has been over for a long time."s

Brad regarded Marilyn steadily, trying hard to keep himself in some kind of control. She had certainly made her case, and he felt terrible. His anger at her suspected affair with Blodget was gone. She had succeeded in making him feel guilty. He had not realized how much she had gone through when he had been in Viet Nam. He had not compared his suffering with hers. No doubt he had been thinking of his own situation – the beatings, the interminable interrogations, long periods of isolation, the insistence that the American way of life was bankrupt, greedy and immoral. He knew now his thoughts of her were not realistic. She was a vision of love for him and constancy in his dreadful situation, and that vision as much as anything else had helped to steady and sustain him. Now she had told him he had been selfish – wrong.

"I don't want to lose you, Marilyn. I do understand what you've just told me. It hurts like hell, but, I don't know." He floundered – at a loss,

"I never wanted to hurt you. I thought you would understand that this offer of Whitredge's, this opportunity to break this dangerous legal monopoly, was larger than either of us. I know it seems impossible – a quixotic attempt, but the President wanted to try and asked for my help. I couldn't refuse. I believe our nation is in real trouble, that faith in government and its justice system is at a new low. There was some truth in what the communists said about us. I wanted, more than anything, to prove them wrong!

"We have the ability to change – hopefully without bloodshed - and change we must. The reason I agreed to let you go to your mother's was because I wanted you out of harm's way, but make no mistake, I did it because I love you. I regarded our separation as my greatest sacrifice. I did not want you to leave me. I had no idea it might become permanent.

"I realize now we ask too much of our women – to stand by us no matter what – to be constant in your love forever. I guess that, along with my other quixotic ideas, is foolish. The thing is I had faith in you.

"I will never forgive myself for making your life so unhappy. I am so terribly sorry."

They had been standing facing each other no more than two arm lengths away. They were both crying now. For perhaps the first time in their marriage they had made contact.

Brad stood there, arms at his sides, unable to make a move, and suddenly, Marilyn was in his arms.

Brad was the first to find a voice.

“Ohh,” he said, “that feels so damn good. I do love you, my dear. Please, find it in your heart to love me too.”

CHAPTER 35

"You're not an easy going man, Brad."

Marilyn smiled and then looked thoughtful.

"You were you know. When we first met, you were like the Prof. He has very definite opinions about government, politics, society, and he may be somewhat profane at times, but he makes his opinions fun. He makes you laugh when you want to cry.

"I have to tell you, my dear, you have to learn how to loosen up – get your sense of humor back. I know you have been through an awful lot, but I want you, as I first knew you, full of a truly great wit. I think you need that for both your cause and yourself. You are after all your father's son – and I love you both."

"Listen, I'm running for the Supreme Court. I'm not in vaudeville. I can't be a clown in cap and bells. I can't run around filled with a lot of cheap chatter. I'm supposed to be as close to perfect as a man can be. We know I'm not. Oh, yes *I* know I'm not! I almost shacked up with a sex artist and had I not been *perfect* I would have. My God she was a sexy creature and thanks to your absence I've been on a sex free diet. I'm sure that Bludger or whatever his name is not half the man I am. No reply necessary.

"I do have a good sense of humor, but I don't have a repertoire of jokes most of which I wouldn't remember anyway."

"And that's what made you so entertaining. Your humor was spontaneous, topical, on the mark Who do you want the people to see – a personality that is so perfect no one will like you? Have you become a Johnny One Note?"

"Ok, next time I appear on TV or in a lecture hall I'll do a soft shoe, learn to play the saxophone, end with a brisk patter and then get down to the business of saving our justice system from finally committing suicide."

Brad started to grin.

"I really would like to loosen up. Frequently I bore myself. I ask myself who's kidding whom. I'm an imposter!"

Brad regarded Marilyn for a moment and then, throwing up his hands.

"I could sure use a laugh right about now. Say something funny. I'll try to laugh." He grinned. "As a matter of fact I just thought of something funny."

"Really?"

"It's kind of stupid for a sex starved husband whose wife can drive him into a sexual frenzy, to be standing here instead of attacking. I mean we have admitted, if not declared, our love. Isn't it time for a honeymoon? I'll make you giggle all the way through - if you can."

Brad picked her up, cradled her in his arms and laid her down gently on the bed in what he remembered was her room.

"I'd forgotten how big you are. I can't resist you – and I don't want to. Now slow down, dear. Give me a chance to make it up to you. Oh – I have missed you so – in spite of all I said. I don't want anyone but you and I don't give a damn even if you are an imposter."

When, after they were both delightfully spent, Marilyn said,

"You were so wonderful, so tender, with so much sensitivity to me, I think I should continue to keep you on a sex free diet. On the other hand, I guess I could never do that again."

"Do I detect a purr? I remember once making you purr."

"The purr is back."

"Can you face the house now? I want you back home. There is plenty of protection there, and my traveling is over. It's the court or bust, and believe me I'm prepared for either."

They heard the back door open.

"Oh, my god, it's mother. Let's get dressed!"

"Hey, aren't you forgetting something?"

"What's that?"

"We're married. Take your time."

The bedroom door was closed and they waited until they could hear her mother at the other side of their door.

"Is that you, Brad?"

"None other, dear."

"About time."

She moved off.

"That mother of yours really is a Yankee isn't she?"

`"Ayeh!

CHAPTER 36

It was word of mouth that brought the Senate Judiciary Committee members together at a place not frequented by any of them. The route was advisedly circuitous with prescribed intervals of time between each arrival.

It was virtually impossible to have a secret meeting in Washington D.C. especially for political leaders. The Washington underground – a loosely knit affair - was nevertheless more efficient than the FBI. Everyone spied on everyone officially and unofficially. It was the most exciting game in town. It was generally agreed that the Columnists were the best and as a consequence their columns were required reading by all intelligence and law enforcement agencies.

When all but one of the members of the Judiciary Committee had finally assembled and had seated themselves around a conference table, there was confusion as to which one of them would be conducting the meeting, each one regarding the man next to him quizzically. When nothing positive resulted from the attempt to identify a chairman, everyone began talking at once. – until - finally, the sound of a gavel brought everyone to attention.

The gavel belonged to the Senator from Massachusetts, Senator Joseph Callahan – an old hand with long experience in the Senate – and the Chairman of the Judiciary Committee.

Callahan was a politician's politician – a man who could turn on a broad smile and pick up a baby with the best of them. He enjoyed political life and planned to stay on in the Senate as long as possible, even though his voting record showed him in favor of limited terms. He felt safe because he was well aware there would never be a majority, and his vote made him look less greedy and far more sincere than his fellow senators.

"The purpose of this informal meeting is to find out how many of you have felt pressure from the press and your constituents with regard to the appointment of Bradford Justice to the Supreme Court. I have checked with the mailrooms in both the House and the Senate and they're running out of space with letters addressed not only to the members of this committee but also to every senator and representative as well. Frankly, I have never seen anything like this response on any previous issue.

"Of course I haven't opened any letters but my own so I don't know the percentage of favorable or unfavorable responses for others. I would like to hear from each of you."

Joseph Callahan regarded his fellow members with a serious expression. His dull red-blossomed nose seemed to join in. It always attracted attention even among his pals.

"I don't know the tenor of any of the other mail, Joe, but mine is almost one hundred percent in favor of the man's approval. In fact, I am convinced a vote against him may cause me to lose my seat."

"So can I deduce from that a vote in the affirmative, Senator Floyd?"

"Not necessarily, Joe. Depends how many of us agree. I mean, if the vote is unanimous against the appointment, that would make a difference."

"You want company either way, Norman – a shaky perch."

"I'd like to hear from you, Senator Morris. How do your constituents in Connecticut feel about a non-lawyer on the Supreme Court?"

"They love the idea, but their feelings are irrelevant. We can't possibly approve the appointment of a non-lawyer to the Supreme Court – especially this man who believes in justice first and the law second. I mean the idea is insane."

"Justice is insane?"

This was asked by the Senator from New Hampshire, Evan Moody, a gangling man with large bony wrists and a long face.

"You're one of the few non-lawyers on this committee. You simply don't understand. Sure we want to have justice, but justice under the law. That is what's engraved on the Supreme Court building."

"Not what it says in the Preamble to the Constitution, Senator. No such qualifier there – just plain justice. Now why do you suppose that is, Senator Morris?"

"Well, the Preamble was a statement of ideals which the Constitution refined - made practical. Justice is a matter of opinion that must be strained through the legal process. Justice is the result. I mean, who knows what justice is, Senator Moody?"

"I do. Have always known. Maybe in Connecticut it isn't so simple. Lot more people in Connecticut."

There was laughter in spite of the antagonism already made apparent by the expressions of disapproval among the majority. Most of his fellow Senators found Evan's crisp delivery amusing. He had a way of cutting issues to the bone. There was wisdom in the old Yankee, but he could be cantankerous and stubborn as a mule – a description that pleased him even though he was a Republican.

Senator from California, Donald Rafter, decided to offer his opinion.

"I don't know how many of you remember Earl Warren. He was our governor, so popular, he was voted in by both parties, and he continued to be popular – until Eisenhower appointed him to the Supreme Court, which Eisenhower later said was his greatest mistake. There was even a movement to impeach him. You know why – because he put justice before the law. He would actually ask counsel if he thought his cause was just! The man single-handedly was destroying our entire legal system. It was outrageous!" He paused. "And that, gentlemen is the answer to any argument for placing Bradford Justice on the Supreme Court."

"Impressive, Rafter, so your vote will be in the negative – even though it may cost your reelection."

"Well – I would prefer a compromise, Joe."

"Can't give half a vote, Rafter." Evan smiled.

"What troubles me, gentlemen, is a vote in the negative will be construed as a vote against justice. I don't want to be on record as against justice. I mean, goddamn it the man's name is Justice."

"A stroke of genius on the President's part, Rafter. Don't you agree, Hamilton? Will your Connecticut constituents stand for that?"

"I don't know. It's incredible really. I'm well aware our profession is not well thought of. Actually I no longer offer the fact that at one time I was a practicing attorney. Being an attorney is no longer a political asset. I objected to the jury findings in the OJ Simpson trial. I'm sure almost everyone but Dershowitz felt the same as I, yet as a lawyer, I had to agree the damn trial was legal.

"Judge Ito was simply no match for that legal team. I guess most of us have read legal novels in which all the representatives of the law including judges are on the take or are just mean and disreputable. The people eat them up, but none of those books try to explain the fundamental flaw in our system. We act as the readers expect us to act. I'm sure none of us will ever forget, during our previous President's term, the special prosecutor who spent fifty million dollars trying to get that President impeached for trying to cover up a consensual adulterous affair. He employed, I don't remember how many lawyers, who intimidated witnesses and because of the law he - and they - were untouchable.

"It had all seemed so simple in the beginning. Bradford Justice didn't have a prayer.

"We have the votes, you know. All we have to do is vote no."

"We can still do just that – and we must. We won't all lose our seats, and I believe we have no choice."

"Spoken like a man who is a true believer, like a true Texan, McClure. Ready to die with your boots on."

"Is the alternative really that bad?" Evan Moody asked the Senator from New Mexico. "You were a judge for some years, Jacques. When you reached a verdict, were you always sure it was a just verdict or did some law interfere with a decision you knew was the right one?"

"I always made sure the law was on my side, you can bet your tamales on that, Evan. If I didn't do that, opposing counsel could have my verdict over turned."

Joe Callahan regarded his fellow committee members in silence, particularly those who had so far refrained from offering any comments.

"Do any of you know - Justice?" He was beginning to have trouble with the word

"He spent a term with us in the Senate. I'm sure you will agree he was definitely not one of the boys. Oh, he was pleasant enough, polite and all, but it was obvious to me that he did not approve of most of his fellow Senators."

"That's true, Joe, but I got to know him at a purely social occasion. Believe me, he was a man who loved to party. Great sense of humor, an earthy wit, and fun. I remember that because it came as a surprise. My wife said he was a wonderful dancer even though he is a big man. It was obvious his wife adored him. I liked him and wanted to get to know him better. I think you'll agree, Joe, that Bradford Justice could be pretty persuasive and got things of interest to him through in spite of being a junior senator."

"Oh yes. I was the frequent brunt of his sarcastic wit. What bothered me was that the man believed in himself and his opinions."

"I can see how you might find that a bit hard to cope with, Joe"

Several chuckles at the Senator from New Hampshire. Evan Moody had the grace to smile.

"You must have gotten to know Justice, Evan. Give us your opinion."

"As a layman, I am definitely in the minority on this issue, but perhaps since I don't have the lawyer perspective, I can provide a different point of view."

Evan paused and cleared his throat. It was awfully dry in that room.

"It has seemed to me for some time now that it is the Law that so often obscures justice – that the law is the main problem with our so called justice system. In the search for a just and common sense judgment, the law is often the detour, the blockage, that prevents common sense decisions; that the search for truth is being ignored and sadly lost. Just finished a book by one frustrated judge who said that justice had been ignored in favor of contradictory and stupid laws. Getting tough on crime and criminals was the only way for her. I understood her frustration, but she missed the point. We will never have a just system until the enforcement of all laws is proportionate and appropriate to the circumstances of the transgression. For our legal system to be respected it must be just. It should not read as presently engraved on the Supreme Court: Equal Justice under Law. It should read: Justice For All."

There was complete silence as much because it was Evan Moody's longest speech as at its content. For some of the lawyers present, the statement was tantamount to heresy.

"No question as to your vote, Evan."

"Glad I got that across, Joe."

"Are you also saying that the change is so fundamental that it must start at the top, Evan?"

"Couldn't put it better myself, Joe. Couldn't be a better place for the truth."

That ended the meeting with several of the committee still not heard from though there was no doubt in Callahan's mind that they were desperate to keep things as they were. Their faces were grim."

CHAPTER 37

Alvah Trickey was not accustomed to waiting. He was accustomed to keeping others waiting. As with so many lawyers that was policy. The other policy was not to return calls, and when Trickey did accept a client's call, he would offer a reminder that all client attorney telephone conversations were charged at the hourly fee - that if there was an important development, the client would receive a call.

Keep the client off balance, let him know time was valuable, that his lawyer was in control and didn't need to keep the client informed about legal details he probably wouldn't understand.

Alvah had followed President Whitredge's and Bradford Justice's efforts to reach out to the American people and was now viewing the results with alarm. He was in touch with one of the members of the Senate Judiciary Committee, a former law school classmate, who felt as he did, and was now, after the informal, secret meeting conducted by Joe Callahan, badly shaken. He had asked for a meeting with Trickey.

The Senator's choice was the Ritz Bar in Boston. Trickey muttered to himself that it was probably because the man couldn't think without a drink in his hand. Trickey prided himself on being a moderate drinker. He was not a moderate eater to which his size was a witness. He loved to eat but as a connoisseur not as a glutton.

Alvah was about to order something, when his Senator finally appeared.

"Sorry I'm late, Alvah. I know how you hate to wait, but I had trouble getting a flight from Washington. Senators don't have the clout we used to have. You haven't ordered? I think you better have a drink this time, Alvah. I don't think we have a majority. Too many of our Committee think we might not get reelected, if we don't approve the President's nominee."

The Senator was also finding it difficult to say Bradford's last name.

"I can't believe it. What a bunch of cowards!"

"Whoever heard of a brave Senator, Alvah?"

A waiter arrived. The Senator ordered a double martini on the rocks, no garbage. The waiter looked enquiringly at Trickey who hesitated for a moment and said what the hell, make it two of the same.

"I am not a drinking man, you know."

"Oh, I know, Alvah."

What the Senator did know was that Alvah didn't drink because he couldn't hold his liquor.

"It's that bad?"

Service was swift at the Ritz especially during the lunch hour and the drinks arrived promptly. Neither man waited to begin.

"I'd almost forgotten how damn good a martini tastes. I remember how I detested my first one." Alvah looked surprised.

"I can feel it already." He took another grateful swallow.

"It's a disgrace, you know. Those lawyer-members stand to lose a lot more than their seats. Once that goddamn justice lover gets on that Court it will be the beginning of the end of the practice of law as we have known it. You have got to convince them of that. Surely the Bar Association has taken a stand. They must have made their position clear."

"Of course – but in a far subtler way than I would have thought. It's that damn word that has slowed them down. Why in the world did he have to pick a man named Justice?"

The waiter was alert and asked if they wanted another round. He received a nod of agreement from both.

Two martinis later Trickey began to whisper and the Senator had to bend toward Trickey in order to hear him. The Senator was not a large man and his head was much smaller than Trickey's and it now looked like an appendage rather than a separate entity.

"I have been giving this problem a lot of thought, and I now realize that what your Committee is looking for is a way to approve the President's nominee, but have the assurance that he will never serve. Do you follow me, my boy?"

The question was said in a normal voice, which startled the Senator causing him to raise his head and hit Trickey on his chin.

Trickey took it in stride, but suggested that his companion couldn't hold his liquor at the same time announcing proudly that he could hold his.

"What you're suggesting, Alvah, is impossible."

"Ah, but it is possible. Consider what has happened."

"What has happened?"

"You see? You don't even know what has happened."

"Tell me what has happened."

"See, you have to deal with the pissable."

"The pissable?"

"Right. Remember the assassination of Shapiro and the person who claimed responsibility. Called himself the Avenger or something."

"Well?"

"**He**'s going to 'sassinate Bradford – you know who – after your committee votes him in."

"How're you going to get him to do that?"

"Because,"

Trickey started whispering again,

"I know how to find an assassin who will do the job and we can blame the Avenger, and everybody'll live happily ever after."

Both men waved at the waiter for another round.

The Senator's head was once again resting on Alvah Trickey's chest just below his chin.

They were both sound asleep.

CHAPTER 38

Alvah Trickey's later rationalization of the Ritz incident was that lunchtime drinks always made him sleepy, the emphasis was on the word sleepy. He had not been drunk.

He had not heard from his Senator since that luncheon, and he wondered whether the man remembered their conversation and finally decided that the Senator had not because if he had, there would have been an urgent request for another meeting.

Alvah was certain of that. His man, as upset as he was at the thought of confirmation of Bradford Justice, would never be a party to the Trickey solution.

That was the trouble with politicians. They could never make the hard decisions especially when they knew a decision was unpopular and might make reelection unlikely.

On the other hand, his man in the Senate was not absolutely sure of the outcome. There were others on that committee who were not against the possibility of having a non-lawyer on the US Supreme Court. It seemed a toss up, and that was enough for Trickey.

His secretary announced the arrival of Mr. Bonardi, but the office door opened before Trickey could acknowledge the man's arrival. As usual Bonardi walked past the secretary, stationed his two goons in the waiting room and barged in.

"Siddown, Trickey. I don't see how a man as fat as you can stand anyway. Whaddya want? I'm a busy man."

Trickey regarded Bonardi distastefully. With all his money, he had no idea how to dress and seemed to pride himself on being uncouth.

"I want the name of a hit man."

"Yeah?" Bonardi looked surprised. "Really? You got some trouble only a killing can get you out of? I never thought you'd go for a killing."

Bonardi nodded as if he was pleased at the thought and sat down. He got to his feet immediately as soon as he realized he was shorter even when Trickey was seated.

"I can understand your surprise, and I approve, Bonardi. It's for a client."

"Some client."

Bonardi looked disappointed.

"You don't have your own source for a killer?"

"Of course not!"

"Of course not." He mimicked Trickey. "Cut all that thick gray hair and you'd look just like Mr. Clean. Even if your head was as bald as an egg, you wouldn't look clean to me, Trickey."

"Well, can you give me a name?"

"A name? A name! Fer Christ sake, you dumb son of a bitch. I suppose you'd like his address and phone number too!" Bonardi was disgusted. "They don't give their names and locations out to anyone. Even I don't have a direct line on a hatchet man."

"I didn't suppose you did."

Trickey tried to look as if he were in the know and then thought better of it.

"Why would you expect me to know about such things? I don't go around killing people."

"But you want to kill someone now."

"A client of mine wants to eliminate someone. What do such people charge for their services?"

"Depends on the victim. Anyway, I don't know. That's a matter between you and the killer."

Trickey wished Bonardi would choose another word, not that Trickey was squeamish. This was a good cause and no one else had the guts to do anything about it.

"You do know how to contact such a service?"

"Yeah, I know, but it'll cost ya."

"How much?"

"Ten grand."

"Just for a contact?'

"Take it or leave it, Trickey."

"Cash, I presume?"

"On the barrel head. In my hand."

He held out his hand.

Trickey opened his desk drawer, counted out ten 1000-dollar bills and handed them to Bonardi.

"I shoulda asked more, but, unlike you, Trickey, my word is good. Anyway, your expense has just begun, and I warn you, dealing with this killer will make you scareder than you have ever been in your life. I wouldn't deal with him, if my life depended on it. Ciao, Alvah."

CHAPTER 39

Alvah Trickey stopped in the hallway just beyond the reception desk and stood, as he often did, contemplating the oil painting that showed him standing at the helm of his yacht with his large hands on the helm. The NYYC cap on his head, deliberately worn at a jaunty angle, had given him what he considered the look of an old salt, a man who had sailed the seven seas, looked death in the eye and would continue to face the sea with confidence.

The Justice situation looked bad – very bad. There was no assurance of a majority, in spite of the fact that there were twelve lawyers on that eighteen-man committee. Trickey's jaw muscles rippled. His plan would give them their cake and eat it too. He frowned. He had picked that expression up from his mother and though he used it he hadn't really thought it made any sense. Of course you couldn't eat your cake and have it too. His mother had thought it profound. However, in this particular case, that is exactly what the lawyers on that Committee would be able to have. Had the appointee's name not been Justice, no self-respecting lawyer/politician would have voted him in.

Well, he squared his shoulders, somebody had to maintain the purity of the judicial system and clearly he was the one to do it. He was convinced his cause was sufficiently important to justify all means necessary to assure its success. After all, that has been the policy of his nation for many years and had included assassination, blackmail, bribery, fomenting of revolutions, sabotage – the commission of every crime possible, and the people had been buying it. Novelists had been romanticizing and trivializing all of it for years.

The legal system was about to be threatened and he was the one man with the courage and conviction to preserve it. After all, as most lawyers say in their defense, a nation without laws would be chaotic. Our courts are the last stand against social chaos.

He went into his office and told his secretary he was not to be disturbed. He opened his copy of the Boston Globe and turned to the Classifieds. He looked under the Services section – and there it was.

Man for all occasions
Rates on request
Reply to address below.

Alvah put the paper down on his desk. He was surprised, possibly a bit disappointed. Was this all there was to finding an assassin? My God, this world really was in a mess! Surely the Globe had no idea what this small ad was all about. He supposed there was neither the time nor the interest to investigate all the classified ads.

He examined several of the other ads, but at first they all seemed the same, and then he realized the indicated PO Box was not a Globe address. It was a box number at a specific Post Office. He frowned. Was he supposed to put his request for a killing in writing! Not this lawyer! He frowned. He must have been looking at the wrong ad. It was a stupid ad!

And then he remembered Bonardi's instructions. After you find the man of all occasions ad, look for another ad that gives the same address.

Trickey muttered something about nonsense, but he put the classified section on his desk and looked again. There were a lot of ads. One finally caught his attention.

Key to success
Frank Mason
General Delivery
80 Daniel St, Portsmouth NH

Trickey went over the list of ads again and again, but none seemed to fit. He looked puzzled and then frowned.

He was supposed to go to that Portsmouth Post Office and ask for mail for Frank Mason – if that was indeed the right ad. Would he have to prove he was Frank Mason? How could he do that? He couldn't. He hadn't found the right ad.

He looked again. This time he found another with the word key in the headline.

Key Computers fmason@aol.com

He had the right ad. Both previous ads were essential, and the man had chosen the largest server on the Internet for the maximum anonymity. Trickey was impressed both with the hit man

- and himself. No doubt the e-mail address would be changed after the next contact.

Alvah Trickey was beginning to enjoy himself. His training in the CIA was beginning to reassert itself. He had joined during the Viet Nam war in order to avoid being called up. He had discovered quite a few lawyers in the CIA. Apparently the Agency believed legal training was particularly useful in the Intelligence game. He had not remained any longer than was necessary. The pay was not nearly good enough and he had decided the CIA was no place for a grown man with brains and ambition. He had been too smart to have let himself be placed in danger. He had remained in Washington for his entire employment – strictly a Headquarters man.

As the senior partner of TS&D, Trickey knew he was in a particularly sensitive position. Above all he had to avoid the appearance of evil. His emphasis was on the word appearance. Law practice, particularly in a large firm, was bound to be fraught with problems of conflict of interest. It was practically unavoidable. The fact that Bonardi had been a longtime client was not as troublesome to him as it was to some of his associates, but his answer that everyone was entitled to legal representation seemed to satisfy most of the doubters. It was, after all, the law.

Trickey had his own computer and e-mail addresses. Yahoo was his home page and he used the Internet frequently. He remembered buying the Encyclopedia Britannica on a CD. He had thought it quite wonderful until he had hooked himself into the Internet after which he never used the Britannica.

He sent the following message to the e-mail address in the newspaper.

Request meeting

His message was unsigned and he sent it from an address that he would cancel later. The reply to sender read:

> Have lunch at Ritz Bar 23 July. Be alone and sit at a table. Remain from 12:30 to 1:15. Place golf visor cap on table next to your right hand. Order Rum Collins. You will be paged as Frank Mason. Accept message. Follow instructions. Don't try to use this address again. It will be invalid. This is a one-time shot. If you are not paged, it will be because I think you are unsafe. The ad will not be run again.
>
> Frank

Trickey shut down the computer. Obviously the man was trying to protect his identity, and he wanted to have a look at his employer. Were he Frank, Trickey preferred to refer to a name instead of the occupation, he would insist on knowing the identity of his employer. There was always the tempting possibility of blackmail.

At that thought, Trickey seriously considered quitting. He was well known around Boston. A lot of people could identify him on sight.

Decisions decisions, but Trickey was caught up in the game. He couldn't bring himself not to continue. Anyway, he'd find a way out – if necessary. He'd managed to extricate himself from predicaments before. There always seemed to be a law that protected him or at least that distracted the issue and discouraged further pursuit.

On the other hand it seemed logical that beyond Mason's identification of him, Mason would thereafter separate himself, hopefully realizing that any attempt at blackmail could lead to his own disaster. Assassins should stick to their trade. Trickey derived some small comfort from that thought – until it was rapidly superseded by the conviction that an assassin had to be a pathological killer - certifiably insane.

CHAPTER 40

Alvah Trickey was not a golfer. He was a sailor, and the request for a golf cap annoyed him.

When he arrived at the Ritz, he was seated immediately. He was pleased to be recognized until the same waiter asked if he would like the usual.

"No, a rum collins."

Trickey could not tell whether the waiter was relieved or disappointed. Why would a killer choose the Ritz Bar as a meeting place?

When the waiter returned with the rum collins, he handed Trickey a small sealed envelope.

"Wait. Who handed you this?"

Trickey scanned the lounge. He had no idea whom to look for. What did a killer look like?

"I couldn't rightly say, sir. The man was wearing a hat, glasses, and had a rather thick mustache."

Of course he did, thought Trickey.

"How did you know where to deliver it?"

"The golf cap, sir."

Trickey dismissed the waiter and opened the envelope. The message had been typed – probably, Trickey guessed, on a computer printer. Was that as traceable as a typewriter? Trickey was now aware the preservation of the man's identity was important to him as well. Should the assassin be picked up, he could be made to disclose the identities of his various employers. Trickey nodded slowly.

He read and reread the instructions.

Dial this number: 893 7945 at precisely 2:00 today. We will have a two-way conversation during which you will name the target and any conditions you want to make. I will tell you my fee. If you agree, I will instruct you on the means of payment. I suggest, for your security, you phone from a nearby booth where you will not be overheard. Don't have the number checked. If you do, you will be my next target. Destroy this message.

Frank

Trickey began to sweat. He wiped his neck with his breast pocket handkerchief. Trickey looked around him.

It was such a pleasant atmosphere – well-dressed people engrossed in each other, talking about mundane matters. There were a couple of young men talking business. The number of young women also talking business was a reminder of his age. He was almost sixty and planning to retire and spend the rest of his life sailing his yacht or possibly buying a considerably larger one in order to take longer voyages. He was still looking for a wife or a companion who wanted to do the same thing. His wife had divorced him several years ago because, she insisted, he was in love with the law and had no time for her. Also she did not like being confined to such a small boat. Alvah reflected that the Queen Mary would have been too small for her. Alvah had been delightfully surprised to discover the number of women eager to please - especially divorcees and widows. It had given him an inflated sense of his charms.

Frank had deliberately given him very little time, and although Trickey understood the reasons, he suddenly wanted more time – much more time. Did he really want to go through with this? He now considered how much he could look forward to. He believed he had found the woman who would sail the world with him. He looked at his watch. He had to make that call. There were telephone booths in the Ritz right near the Bar.

He paid the bill, was disgusted at the price of a rum Collins, and left.

The waiter looked after him and decided that England had no monopoly on eccentrics. By now the US held few surprises though he did wonder about the man who had given him the envelope. Wearing a hat indoors in the Ritz was definitely unusual.

Trickey found an empty booth, closed the door, and stood there unmoving for several moments. When he punched the numbers, his thick fingers moved slowly. When the operator told him he had dialed an incorrect number and to dial again, he let out his breath, shook his head and waited. Finally, he tried again and this time somebody answered.

"Frank here. You're five minutes late."

"I considered not phoning. I don't like threats."

"That wasn't a threat – only a fact. Who's the target?"

"His name is Bradford Justice, a former Senator from New Hampshire, and presently the President's appointee to the United States Supreme Court."

"You don't want him to be successful."

"No, I sure as Hell do not, and I think the lawyers on the Senate Judiciary Committee don't want him on that court either, but they may approve his nomination anyway."

"But you're not sure." There was a pause. "The best way to prevent that possibility is to eliminate him now."

"If he is not approved, he is no longer of interest. He can live as long as he likes. If he is eliminated now, people might believe lawyers did it. If he is approved, people might believe the assassins of Shapiro did it."

"You want my services only if he is approved? I don't like that."

"Why not?"

"If your man is approved and becomes an Associate Justice of the United States Supreme Court, he will be a far more difficult target."

"And you can't handle that."

Trickey was almost relieved.

"I didn't say that. I can eliminate anyone, but it will cost you a helluva lot more."

"How much?"

"One hundred thousand – cash."

"No. Fifty thousand now and the remainder after the completion of your assignment."

"What happens if he is not approved?"

"You keep the fifty thousand."

"Fifty grand for doing nothing. I like that – only I want a hundred and fifty grand if I have to kill him."

"You asked for a hundred."

"I am thinking of the odds."

"The assassins of Shapiro are still loose."

"True, but Supreme Court security is much tighter now."

"You don't sound too confident, Frank. Maybe you're not the man."

"I'm the man."

"I have to make one thing absolutely clear. If you kill the man - after his rejection – you will receive no further payment. Understood?"

"Yes, but I hope he is approved."

"And I hope he isn't."

"Payment will be in cash – Swiss francs at the present exchange rate."

"No. I don't want to be on record anywhere as the purchaser, for whatever reason, of such a large amount of foreign currency – particularly Swiss francs."

Trickey reflected that he could take the fifty thousand out of his escrow account.

"I can create an account in whatever bank you wish in whatever name you give me. You can give me a signature I can send to that bank"

"No. I don't want your address. Now listen carefully I want you to have the fifty thousand in twenties and fifties. You will put the resultant package in a public locker. I don't care where as long as it isn't in Boston. You will send the key separately, with no accompanying info, to Arnold Williams at PO Box 1028 Grammercy Park Post Office, NY, NY. 10016. You will send the location of the locker to Oscar Wineburg at Box 560 Chicago. You better write this down."

"How will I know you have received the money?"

"Its receipt will be noted in the Globe Classified next week or the week after that. It will be under Personals. It will read: Thanks – Frank

"How will you get in touch with me?"

"No problem."

"How will I get in touch with you?"

"You can't – just pay the balance, if Justice is successful. I'll instruct you as to the delivery of the hundred thousand."

There was no point in arguing the amount now.

Alvah Trickey wiped his neck again. He stuffed the handkerchief in his trouser pocket. He wrote the pertinent addresses down in his little black notebook, and then verified them.

This was it. He had let himself become terribly exposed and there was no way out. There had always been a way out of every agreement. He always left at least one opening for future litigation, but this fellow had left no openings. This man, Frank, was wasting his time. He should have been a lawyer.

Alvah Trickey left the booth mumbling. He bumped into a man who had been waiting and almost knocked him down. Trickey's 270 pounds was intimidating and the considerably slighter individual satisfied his anger with a look – almost.

An hour later in the security of his office, Alvah had some time in which to think – and he did a lot of thinking.

Frank – whoever he was – was not only smart as hell, he was well spoken – not one word of slang or obscenity. He sounded well educated and very professional – which was even more intimidating.

That delivery procedure had been cleverly worked out. Trickey was certain both addresses were not only temporary, but had two different forwarding addresses. Probably Frank was a long way from both locations and would immediately cancel the addresses.

Well, Alvah reflected, if he were an assassin, he would go to any length to protect his identity.

Alvah managed to move his bulk out of his chair. He had work to do. He had to withdraw fifty thousand dollars from his escrow account – that untouchable escrow account. It was the perfect fund. He had dipped into it before. It would be entered as an administrative expense.

CHAPTER 41

Time was running out. Brad was going over his presentation to the Senate Judiciary Committee. He composed it on his computer, left it for a day so he could sleep on it, rewrote it and presented it to the Prof.

As usual the Prof.'s comments were amusing, but Brad wasn't exactly in the mood for humor.

"I have read your speech with great interest - and some satisfaction, but it is too good for them – and far too gentle – so gentle the people won't get it. Since you haven't got one chance in hell, you should take this occasion to let 'em have it – both barrels!"

The Prof leaned back in 'his' lounger and took a swallow of his Glen Fiddich. Drinking for him was anytime he was in the mood.

It was too much for Brad. He laughed – a big laugh worthy of a big man. His father's frown made him laugh even harder.

"You old fake! This isn't a classroom at Bowdoin where you can give any advice you want without censure. I'm not in a position of power or privilege in front of the Senate Judiciary Committee. I will have to live with their answer for the rest of my life."

Brad had offended his father, but this wasn't to be a debate in front of still naïve students and their tenured professors. He was angry at the odds against his approval, but he would have to restrain it and not let the Senators and the world know how he felt about some of them. He had seen all of them in action and or lack thereof during his time in the Senate.

"I'm sorry if I've offended you, Dad, but I want that job. I really want to be an Associate Justice of the United States Supreme Court. I know I can make a difference. Mother often said to you, when you were being obstreperous, "You can catch more fly with honey than with vinegar." Brad paused. "I believe she's right."

Brad began pacing just missing floor lamps and end tables.

"I know that Committee will not want to hear any drastic changes, and they certainly will not want a non-lawyer telling them of plans that will frighten them even more. The concept of justice first is anathema."

"That disturbs me too, of course, Brad, and it should disturb every thinking American citizen – but it doesn't. Too many of us say that our system, with all its faults, is still the best in the world. It is a smug and stupid attitude. Our system is not working for all the people and is not always satisfactory for the wealthy either. Ask any litigant, winner or loser, what he thinks of the system. Most people have not suffered through a legal battle so they simply do not know or understand how terrible it is. This appearance of yours will be televised all over the US and probably the world. This is your best, and probably your only chance, to make your position crystal clear. You and Whitredge have created an image – a force for justice as the sole reason for the existence of our judicial system. Don't show the slightest sign of doubt about that. You don't have any doubts, Brad. Do you?"

"None!"

"Well, then, you must show that."

The Prof. stood up and refilled his glass and Brad's. He raised his, waited for Brad to do the same, and looked his son in the eye.

"Here's to victory!"

Brad swallowed his drink, hugged his dad, told him he was incorrigible and left.

Brad had much to attend to. He was sorry he hadn't had time to devote to the Town, but he had been thinking about the pending law suit against New England Entertainment – Joe Bonardi – and had finally come up with an idea.

Brad entered the Town Offices and told the receptionist he had an appointment with Les. Les met him at his office door.

"Well, I'm glad to see you, Brad. Thought you had forgotten us – now that you're running for the Supreme Court."

"I haven't much time, Les, so hear me out."

"I'm listening." He seated himself. Brad did the same.

"There's money in Bonardi's proposal – big bucks for a lot of people – including you, which you know very well."

Les started to protest. Brad ignored him and continued.

"It's hard to do the right thing – especially when there are financial reasons not to – and you, Les, have always been an angle man, though following the angles has not brought you much. Don't jump on this angle as being your main chance. Fronting for the right when your mind is elsewhere simply will not do. This is your chance to be the savior of your town, and I want you to hang in there no matter what terms you are offered. Now, having said that, I am going to offer a suggestion."

Les threw up his hands. "Believe it or not, I'm still listening."

"There are several towns in NH who have made the same mistakes that we did. I was going to say you did, but I'm responsible too because I should have engaged this issue the first time it came up. I simply didn't believe this town would ever have voted for the establishment of a porno zone so I did nothing to oppose it the first time around. I could not and still can not believe we would give up our right to determine the standards for our community."

Brad inhaled deeply and continued.

"Contact the selectmen of all the towns and cities who have created porno zones and convince them to join forces in what would amount to a class action, and agree to share all legal expenses. Such an action will save Wentworth Harbor some legal expense and at the same time make a far more persuasive case."

"You know you have just insulted me, Brad. I've known you a long time and I could point out your weaknesses. I know a lot about you as a younger man – and Walter Whitredge too."

"And it's below the belt time, is it, Les?"

Les shrugged.

"I don't have millions to use for such an investigation."

"Now, will you do what I have suggested?"

"Will you help?"

"If I ever get on that court which, by the way, has ruled both ways on the protection of pornography under freedom of speech in the First Amendment. The first decision was *not* to protect it. Probably 99% of the people don't know that.

"I will do my best to convince the Justices that freedom of speech – the First Amendment – should not be used to compel towns and cities all over this nation to create pornographic zones and in the process ignore their votes to the contrary. Of course I will only have one vote. In the meantime I probably should remain silent on any specific issue." Brad paused

"Incidentally, Les, I have no evidence of any untoward behavior by you – only rumors, and so far, even our judicial system does not officially credit rumors – or does it?"

"You know what, Bradford Justice?" Les grinned. "If you do get on that court, God help them. I believe you're really going to stir up the pot!"

Brad grinned and nodded.

"And you know what, Lester Gardiner? I'm going to love every minute of it!"

Les watched Brad as he left the office and smiled. The big bastard looked positively jaunty.

.CHAPTER 42

Even though Les Gardiner was going to take his advice and try for a class action suit to be presented to the Supreme Court, Brad was indignant at the necessity for such a costly legal procedure.

Hadn't the Justices read the **Final Report of the Attorney General's Commission on Pornography?** The results of that investigation clearly established the catastrophic consequences of their second ruling of, among other things, the protection of Organized Crime. The Supreme Court had previously ruled that such activity was not protected – so why, now the evidence was in, hadn't the Supreme Court changed the ruling within itself, thus saving all the time, money and frustration involved in a law suit? Didn't the Supreme Court bear the responsibility for its decisions? Was it unable to rectify its own mistakes? Maybe they were too isolated and protected from the outside world. Brad likened them to the weathermen who never looked out the window.

Was it just or fair to condone the degradation of women and children, to protect the obscene acts committed? Freedom without responsibility to society is tyranny.

Brad groaned at the thought of this bureaucratic legal tangle. If nothing else, we had to simplify, to clarify our laws, to cut this huge, legal red tape that was costing the people billions.

How in the world was he going to face 12 lawyers with their mixed up sense of ethics? How could he obtain their approval when he spoke an entirely different language and had a stricter set of ethics? Most people don't know that legal ethics and their ethics are frequently incompatible. Lawyers can - legally - march to a different moral drummer than the rest of us.

His musing was a rehearsal.

He returned to his computer and rewrote his presentation to the Senate Judiciary Committee. He felt as if he were writing his Last Will and Testament.

CHAPTER 43

Contrary to Frascati's assurances to George Bradford, New England Entertainment filed suit against the Town of Wentworth Harbor for Unlawful Discrimination under Freedom of Speech in the First Amendment.

The new Town Attorney, former Judge Harold Wilson, advised the Selectmen to settle, in the amount of $50,000 dollars to New England Entertainment, for damages and legal costs. Co-counsel for NE was a female attorney from the Civil Rights Committee.

It was discovered that one of Harold Wilson's more important clients had a vested interest in the success of New England's plan for Wentworth Harbor. Wilson was on retainer with Rufus White who had a substantial interest in the local bank as well as the real estate company Bonardi had selected to be New England Entertainment's Real Estate Company. White also had a large share of the local insurance agency, which was scheduled to be the Agency for NE Entertainment.

Bonardi did not know anything about either Wilson or Rufus White, and neither of them knew Bonardi. They were simply out to feather their own nests. Had they known this was a Mafia operation, neither Brad nor George Justice thought it would have made any difference. Self-interest – money – was king.

The Town's informant, real estate broker, Charles Swett, had made it his business to do some investigating on his own. As the Real Estate Broker with the best reputation for integrity in Town, and an avowed enemy of attorney, Warren Delaney, Swett began his investigation with Joan Simon, Delaney's paralegal. They had had a couple of drinks together and respected each other. She was sexually available, but Swett was not, though he was tempted by her sensational body. He had suggested several times that she find employment elsewhere, or better still, open her own office.

One bit of information led to another until Swett had solved most of the puzzle. When he brought his information to the attention of both Justices, they had a conference as to what to do about the situation. Charlie had already informed the Selectmen, but he wanted to make certain something would be done.

"There are times, Brad, when I wish I could act on impulse and raise Hell. You know, hire a few thugs, have them beat the Hell out of Rufus White thereby neutralizing him and then turn to Attorney Wilson and repeat the process.

"Unfortunately, Charlie, there are too many beneficiaries from Bonardi's plans for Wentworth Harbor and not enough citizens to take up the fight. I find that the most disheartening of all. I realize I shouldn't admit to such feelings, but I feel that way too, especially after the way I've been treated."

"Scratch anyone deeply enough and you'll uncover violence, gentlemen. Wars are the evidence of that. Unfortunately, in so-called peacetime there is still war, but hopefully the disputes can be settled in our courts. When that process fails, we have violence such as the assassination of people in power, as in the death of Associate Justice, Eliot Shapiro. Our justice system is in reality the court of last resort. When that system fails to be even handed and fair to all who come before it, our country suffers."

Brad and Charlie nodded.

"This situation in Town is not going to be settled fairly in our courts."

Brad's face flushed.

"Attorney Wilson will cover up his relationship with White. None of the key people will come forward and the town will lose its battle with NE Entertainment. Imagine being joined in their suit by the Civil Rights organization – and by a woman at that! It's a cinch she never read **the Attorney General's Report on Pornography** with eloquent and moving testimony of children and female victims."

"So, Mr. Justice Justice, what are we going to do?"

"We are going to fire Attorney Wilson for conflict of interest and search for an attorney who is not only able but cares about all this. There must be someone who can argue this all the way to the Supreme Court."

"How about you, Brad?"

"Thanks, Charlie, but only approved lawyers are eligible. Now how do you suppose they managed that?"

Brad inhaled deeply.

"We have to find a lawyer who is on the approved list of attorneys qualified to appear before that court."

"How is that list appointed?"

"The list of Supreme Court Attorneys is made up by some Committee appointed by the American Bar Association – or some other damn group of lawyers."

"Close enough, Charlie, and those chosen are expected to adhere to the rules of the Justice System. They are unlikely to work up some genuine enthusiasm for representing clients who are challenging a ruling of the United State Supreme Court which all judges are sworn to uphold."

"The people's Catch 22! It's a goddamn mess! So many legal cases are exactly that. Playing strictly by the rules, the whole mess is treated as a game. Known facts, due to legal rules, cannot be admitted into evidence, and after the whole charade, the court will find for New England Entertainment – and this without the necessity of a paid off judge – but a judge who believes his duty is to uphold the Constitution of the United States!"

"My God! You sure you want to be on the Supreme Court, Brad?'

"More than ever, Charlie."

"And right now, son, you can't even appear interested in this. The Judiciary Committee will be certain you are a threat, and they'll vote you down even if it means the loss of their seats in the Senate. They will never let a man in who bites the hand of the legal system that feeds them!"

Charlie Swett shook his head in despair.

"I'm just a business man who has been trying to make a decent living. I've never fought a war as you two have, but I have always believed in my country, and I am now embarrassed to admit, I believed that justice in our courts was possible because that was what you went to court for. Oh, I knew it could take a long time and be too expensive, but justice would triumph in the end. I had no idea it had come to this. In my business I have seen attempts at corruption, but I just ignored them and went my own way, but we can't ignore this. We have got to get a fair hearing!"

Charlie stopped.

"How much do assassins charge these days? I'm only kidding! Anyway he'd need a machine gun."

The meeting broke up. Charlie Swett left.

"We'd need a bazooka! I'm going to find a qualified attorney."

"Lots of luck, son."

Brad fired up his computer and linked down to attorneys qualified to practice before the Supreme Court. The list was long, some with E-Mail addresses. To them he wrote the following message:

"Wanted: a trial attorney – a litigator - who believes that justice is our system's most important product – not under law – but with, hopefully, the assistance of the law. 'The quality of justice is not strained - 'etc.

"The right of protest is guaranteed under the First Amendment. We need a lawyer who believes that and will represent that in the United States Supreme Court.

"His replies will be secure."

Brad used a friend's e-mail address – with his permission, of course.

CHAPTER 44

Brad seized the paper, seated himself on the other leather chair and proceeded to read. In response to his father's brief, cryptic phone call, Brad entered his father's house and was faced with the front page of the Manchester Union Leader, the headlines of which, were presented to him at eye level.

Attorney General of the US appoints a Special Prosecutor to Investigate President Walter Whitredge.

Whitredge's ex-wife testified, under oath, that President Whitredge was having an affair with another woman during their marriage to her and about which he had lied. President Whitredge replied that his marital difficulties were nobody's business.

"Ours is not the first marriage to go on the rocks. Neither of us were happy and I didn't want to add insult to injury to her by admitting an affair with another woman."

When asked if he cared to admit that the lover in question was still his lover, President Whitredge replied that he is not *admitting* anything.

"I am making a statement. Yes we are still seeing each other, though not as often as I would like as I am very busy."

Brad lowered the paper and regarded his father.

"My God! The timing is incredible. I'm due to appear next week."

"Maybe," George Justice frowned, "Just maybe, ***that was on their mind***. Our nation has gone berserk – and, of course, there is precedent for this latest attack. A disgruntled political party wants to get rid of a President, and at a loss to nail him for any high crime, they attack his sex life. That has already happened, God Damn it!"

"And in this case, Dad, our President has no party behind him.

"It reminds me, Dad, of a friend of mine's law suit against a competitor he was determined to put out of business. He knew his competitor was at a critical financial point and he wanted to find a way to tie him up financially. My friend's lawyer provided the solution which was to trump up some charges, bring suit, attach all assets and paralyze his competitor's business. Eventually, the competitor's lawyer got everything dismissed, but in the expensive, time-consuming, legal process the business was bankrupted. My friend was triumphant at scoring such a coup.

"I have since understood such tactics are quite common. It was one of the many incidents that convinced me our legal system was in serious need of reform. In that case, all legal and court costs should have automatically been paid to the defendant and the lawyer given a heavy fine." Brad shook his head.

"So? What's next?"

"A private talk with our President. You have got to see him – yesterday!"

Brad got his appointment with the President the next day.

The weather was still not too hot and they walked along the Reflecting Pool to the Lincoln Memorial. The President commanded his security guard to remain at the sidewalk while he and Brad walked up the steps and into the memorial building.

They were two large men who stood tall, and to a casual observer, looked confident and strong, able to face down any opposition.

"I had no idea, Brad, how vulnerable the Presidency has become. At this moment, I cannot believe any man or woman would want to become President. I have done nothing I am ashamed of. My mistake was marrying the wrong woman, but it was a personal matter hardly a high crime on which impeachment proceedings should be based. At this point I'm not sure whether I lied under oath, not that it makes any difference to me. A lie is a lie."

Whitredge looked thoughtful.

"For some, men especially, power seems to act as an aphrodisiac. Men with power are attractive to women. It's a magnet that pulls both ways. We haven't had very many presidents who were particularly attractive physically – neither handsome nor even particularly charming, but most of them had illicit sexual relationships. It's not behavior I condone. It's simply a fact of life. It is the person's performance in office that is paramount. Once in awhile, a man is elected to office whose personal behavior is above reproach, but that doesn't mean he can rule the nation effectively. I have already learned that effective power is achieved through the art of compromise.

"Sharp has taught me that. I don't like it, but I'm beginning to respect it, primarily because I want to get things done."

Whitredge paused and regarded his friend steadily for a moment.

"I don't like this job anymore. I can't believe any President in these times would. The only thing that keeps me here is the possibility of accomplishment."

He looked up to the huge figure of Lincoln.

"Lincoln knew who the enemy was, and it wasn't the south, it was us – all of us. The union of both into one nation was his goal, He set the stage that made it possible – and he was assassinated for it. One thing no President should expect from the people is gratitude." He paused. "I can't say this in public, of course. Yes. I lied to her, and you can now see why. Just between us that woman is hell on wheels!"

Brad laughed, and - finally, so did Walter Whitredge.

"It's all a farce, after all, Walter, excuse me, Mr. President, and I'm glad to see we can both still laugh."

He looked at the President.

"I thought the Attorney General was a friend. You appointed her. She owes you some loyalty."

"I thought she was at least friendly. I ignored her party affiliations. I chose her because I thought she had the best credentials. I felt free of the constraints of Party membership. She seemed pleased, and I thought she liked me, but she is a lawyer, after all. I never discussed your appointment with her, but I felt she was against the idea."

"What do you want me to do, Mr. President? First and foremost, as you must know, I am your friend and I will state publicly that I have changed my mind and do not want to be on the Supreme Court and furthermore ------."

The President put up his hand to stop him, but Brad ignored the motion.

"Furthermore, I can be completely plausible. I would say, as my reason, that I am fed up with a political system that legalizes the destruction of the Presidency because they don't like him or something he proposes. As a matter of fact, that is exactly what I should do – and at this point – I'm ready. The moment I do that, the charges against you will be dropped. It's far more important for you to continue to be President than for me to be on the Supreme Court."

"Thank-you, my friend. I have never prized loyalty more than at this moment – and what you are suggesting would almost be worth it, if only to find out if indeed your appointment was the cause of this personal attack. Since the people do not really know you yet, they would never know what they would be missing. No, Brad, we, you and I, will have to see this thing through to the end. I am convinced - more than ever - that being affiliated with a particular party is much too confining. I am paying the price for independence, but it was the people who put me in office and I still want to believe they have the power to keep me here."

"We'll soon find out."

Brad's expression was grim.

"I'm glad for Henry, by the way, Brad. He is doing his best to look out for my welfare. How are those security people looking after you?"

He looked in the direction of the two security men who were looking after Brad.

"I believe in their loyalty and expertise, but assassination is almost impossible to prevent. I am now a walking arsenal – thanks to the Prof. In view of all that has happened, I have adopted the old cowboy adage to shoot first and ask questions afterwards."

Brad suddenly grinned.

"I have an idea. Why don't you and I put on military helmets, pack visible artillery, and have grenades pinned to our armor? Of course I still wouldn't feel safe, but I would love the look on the faces of our citizens. The picture of the President of the United States and his Appointee to the United Sates Supreme Court personally armed for protection would convey a lot."

"How about a Company of Green Berets armed with machine guns and trailing guard dogs, Brad?"

"Now that would send one helluva message! Of course, Mr. President, there are other kinds of assassination that are legal."

"You don't mean impeachment?"

"Gosh! I never thought of that."

CHAPTER 45

Bradford Justice obtained a Senate Pass from NH Senator, Evan Moody.

"Want to get reacquainted with the Senate Chamber? Got a tough row to hoe, Brad."

His smile was sympathetic.

"I'm with you, Brad. It's time for some fresh air and I'm sick and tired of being surrounded by lawyers. I think lots of other folks feel the same way."

Evan paused and regarded Brad intently.

"I have faith in you, Brad. I know you're just as decent as the President who has appointed you."

Brad thanked Evan for his confidence.

"It is an awesome responsibility, not a position of arrogant power to be exercised in a vacuum. The members of that court should not be considered high priests, but understood as people subject to their own prejudices and fallibilities as are the rest of us. Above all they must believe that justice can only come from the search for truth. The Supreme Court is after all the court of last resort. There is no legal formula for justice."

The moment Brad stepped into the Senate Chamber, he felt its dignity. The Chamber was the Coliseum of Democracy. He also felt alone against such tremendous odds. He looked upward at the galleries he had been assured would be filled. The semicircular rows of desks reminded him of the main study hall at his school.

Were these members also students? There was much to learn. It was his first thought when he had been seated there.

Their purpose, as elected representatives of the people, was so noble. How could any of them allow themselves to succumb to the desire for power and financial rewards in return for their favorable votes regardless of the issues?

He had picked up a copy of the Washington Post earlier, the headline of which asked in bold black type:

WILL JUSTICE COME TO WASHINGTON?

What followed left a mixed message. Was the writer with or against Bradford Justice? Was the article tongue in cheek, or did he detect some serious message? It could be that the writer was just being clever. Brad wondered if the reporter was a lawyer.

The Chamber was empty for which Brad was grateful. He had been told the Chamber was to be used for his Hearing and it was a sellout. It was the most sought after ticket in Washington. The Senators had all staked out their seats.

Brad looked up to the high ceiling as if he might find something of comfort there. His first appearance was tomorrow.

**** **** **** **** **** ****

Brad slept or at least pretended to sleep, but he didn't fool Marilyn. Quietly she snuggled into him and when he turned away, put her arms around him. Two spooning was her favorite position. He was so big she could feel his strength – and warmth. She also felt protective in this position especially when he would tell her he was cold and needed her warmth.

He hadn't said he was cold this time but she knew he wanted her warmth. She put her arms around this bear of a man who was sometimes as vulnerable as a young boy. She liked being needed.

Normally Brad was a quiet sleeper, so quiet he invariably awakened very stiff in his knees and shoulders with cramps in his legs. The doctor had told him to change his position more often.

Tonight he was changing his position often, sometimes with grunts and deep breaths. It was also wonderful when she found herself enveloped in his big arms, her back against his chest. She always knew when he was sexually aroused in that position. He wasn't and she wondered if she should move gently to stir him.

There was so much tension in him. Maybe she should become the aggressor and let him spend himself. Possibly it would be a relief.

Marilyn was ready to be used. She began to feel aroused. This man had too much to give sexually to ever make sex a one way affair.

She turned toward Brad.

"I want you and I'm prepared to make you want me, darling."

The next morning Brad said,

"If I were a religious man, Marilyn, I would thank God for you."

"Your belief in the existence of justice is your God, my dear."

CHAPTER 46

Bradford Justice arrived at the Senate Chamber half an hour early, well aware it was a rarity when any Hearing began on time.

People were milling around talking and laughing. Brad remembered there were always jokes, frequently well told - and topical. Talking was their stock in trade.

The real trick, Brad had observed, was to talk without saying anything, sort of a non-committal commitment - conversations that could be interpreted in many ways. It was an art, and practiced particularly when in public debate or talk shows now that everything was taped and could be played back out of context. It was that old legal warning that everything you say may be used against you. Brad reflected that it was no wonder so little of consequence was generally expected.

As he stood there, behind the small table set out for him, he wished he were facing a panel solely concerned with fair play. The reality was so very different.

Like the President, Brad wanted to believe in the people, but the people he had talked to when running for the Senate, hadn't impressed him with their wisdom – even those he liked. He seemed to be gaining popularity in the Polls, but he didn't really have much faith in polls though some of his colleagues voted with the Polls in anticipation of reelection or in fear of not being reelected. It was a moot question whether legislators should or should not be guided by polls. Assuming their accuracy, did the will of the people really matter? Our democracy theoretically depended on the will of the people.

Brad Justice wasn't so sure. Unlike his father he could be sympathetic and try to understand, ready to persuade, and in the process almost always able to find something good. He found that he cared - possibly too much. Was the show of passion taboo in the United States Senate?

This was his country. He had paid his dues. Surely he had the right - and the duty - to judge it, to assess its shortcomings. He wanted it to live up to its promise as the greatest nation in the world.

The members of the Committee were taking their seats above him. Committees, like judges, were to be looked up to - at least physically. In the courts the wearing of black robes added to the forbidding atmosphere. At least our judges were no longer wearing wigs, but when a judge arrived in court, the people were ordered to stand.

Uniformed Bailiffs were now wearing guns, evidence that all judges were not respected, and in some cases, not even safe.

He had been through so much on his way to this Judiciary Committee – the trashing of his home, the destruction of years of work, threats of violence and the attempts at blackmail. It had taken the assassination of an Associate Supreme Court Justice and a President who was not a lawyer, to provide the opportunity for a seat on the Supreme Court. The memory of all that made him angry – too angry.

There were violent groups out there ready to destroy a government they believed to be evil, and now there were foreign terrorists out to destroy the US in the belief that this was an evil society.

We continue to believe that nothing is wrong, that no one, no group or national enemy, could touch us. We are too big and powerful.

Brad considered walking out of the Senate Chamber. He had become so angry he was not sure he could control it. Maybe the Prof was right. Give them Hell! Let it all hang out! He knew he was not only addressing the Committee he was addressing everyone who was listening.

"Will this Judiciary Committee come to order? Quiet please."

Chairman, Senator Joseph Callahan, Democrat of Massachusetts, looked around the Chamber and up into the packed galleries.

There was quiet – an immediate hush. Callahan observed a moment of silence.

"Thank-you."

He paused again.

"Will the Reverend Thornquist lead us in prayer?"

The Committee bowed their heads while the Reverend blessed the Senate and the Proceedings.

Chm: "The purpose of this Hearing is to consider the Appointment of former Senator Bradford Justice to the United States Supreme Court."

Callahan paused again.

"It must be pointed out that although such an appointment is Constitutional, there has never been any Justice who hasn't had training in the law on the United States Supreme Court. There is no precedent for such an appointment."

Callahan paused.

"It is our duty to consider this appointment objectively, and after hearing all evidence, to determine whether or not to approve President Whitredge's appointee.

Senator Justice, would you care to make an opening statement?"

"No, Mr. Chairman."

There was an immediate reaction from the Gallery and the Senators present.

"You do have the right to make your statement, Senator Justice."

"I am reserving that right, Mr. Chairman. I want to hear any objections to my appointment – assuming there are any, of course."

Brad did not smile.

Neither did Senator Callahan.

Callahan cleared his throat and turned to his Committee.

"Senator Morris, I believe you have some questions. You may proceed."

Senator Morris: "We have forgotten to have the Senator take his oath. Well, never mind. Are you under oath, Senator Justice?"

"I am."

SM: "Are you a lawyer?"

BJ: "No. Are you a lawyer?"

SM: "Answer my question."

BJ: " I did. Answer my question."

SM: "You are not being cooperative."

BJ: "Neither are you, Senator."

Chm: "Answer Senator Justice's question."

SM: "I am a lawyer. Do you know the law, Senator?"

BJ: "There is no such thing as *The Law*, Senator Morris. Most lawyers have a specialty, and try to keep informed in a particular area of law."

SM: "Do you believe a knowledge of law is important?"

BJ: "Yes."

SM (after waiting in vain for more) "Isn't it likely that a lawyer would have superior knowledge of the law than one who is not a lawyer?"

BJ: "Knowledge of the law is not a monopoly of lawyers. Perhaps you would like to test me on my special area of legal expertise which is the Constitution."

SM: "You're challenging me, Mr. Justice!"

BJ: "Of course. I'm not a beggar here. Our President has appointed me. If your only challenge is that I am not qualified because I don't know the law appropriate to the position to which I have been appointed, you'll have to prove that, Senator."

There was an immediate discussion behind a closed mike. The people couldn't hear, ***but they were trying***.

The question among the members was whether Bradford Justice was bluffing. They could call on renowned constitutional scholars, but of course, so could he, and some of those respected scholars ***were not lawyers***! The procedure would take forever! Senator Morris was told to proceed.

SM: "A lawyer has the benefit of legal experience – as a judge – trial attorney – defense attorney – corporate attorney. Such experiences season an attorney and make him far better able to understand the complexities of our legal system. What has been your legal experience that qualifies you for the job of Associate Justice of the United States Supreme Court?"

Senator Morris almost winced at his own question, knowing that it was far too broad. The looks of disapproval on the faces of the lawyer members confirmed it, but it was too late.

BJ: "I'm glad you asked me that question, Senator. I'm glad because it goes to the heart of the matter. My experiences with the justice system have made me realize how much in need we are of men and women operating within our courts *who are not lawyers seasoned* in the frequently deplorable ways of our lawyers and judges. Their experiences have corrupted them and the majority continue to operate without censure or punishment. This ***professional seasoning*** is what we must avoid. It has become a tragic and dangerous monopoly. It is not lawyers we need. It's more people of character with the determination to obtain the truth."

SM: (He was close to apoplexy. He nodded to the Chairman, no longer trusting himself to engage this man further. Justice's statement was an outrage.)

Chm: "The Chair recognizes the Senator from Pennsylvania."

Sen. Schneidermann: (He has the singsong Pennsylvania Dutch accent)

"You have just condemned our entire legal system! Such arrogance is unacceptable. Who are you to make such a sweeping judgment? I resent it."

BJ: "Are you a lawyer, Senator Schneidermann?"

SS: "Yes and proud of it! Answer me. Who are you? What qualifies you to make such a judgment?"

BJ: "I am a caring, thinking citizen who has served this country well and loves it deeply. I am a patriot. I have risked my life in war and served in the Senate. I have the most cherished right of every citizen – the right of protest guaranteed in the First Amendment. I have had serious experience with our legal system as defendant, Grand Juror, Petit Juror and have studied law, legal procedure, have researched settlements and judgments of corporations and friends. My criticism is sincere and well considered. Surely, Senator Schneidermann, you know our justice system needs help, that it is not equally representing all who come before it."

There were some smiles up in the Galleries. This man, Justice, was speaking up and not intimidated by those two lawyers.

"With the Chair's permission and Senator Schneidermann's, I would like to question Mr. – ah – Senator Justice."

Senator Rafter of California was having difficulty with the word. He was also an attorney and had in fact been a very successful personal injury lawyer.

Sen. Rafter: "You say the legal system is not doing its job. I can tell you that while in practice I have successfully represented people who have been severely injured emotionally as well as physically and I have done so when those injured had no money to get their day in court. There is no other legal system where that is possible. I have truly represented the people."

BJ: "For which you have been handsomely rewarded – at least 30 percent of the award – plus your expenses."

DR: "Are you against capitalism too, Senator?"

BJ: "Is money your only reason for serving a client, Senator? If you were unsure of the validity of the case and the prospect of such a rich reward, would you have taken the case? If, as in *England, contingency fees are illegal*, would you take the case without up front fees and settle for an hourly fee, if you won? Is your motivation greed instead of service to a worthy client? Where is your sense of responsibility to your society and your profession? I am unimpressed by your arguments for your representation of the poor injured souls."

There was applause from the galleries, accompanied by an order for silence from the Chairman.

Chm: (to Brad Justice) "I must warn you, Senator Justice, that your conduct is unbecoming an applicant for such an exalted position. Antagonism of the men whose good will is necessary to the success of your confirmation is counter-productive. Our members are not on trial. I must ask you to keep your comments on an objective level or I will be forced to call for an immediate vote."

BJ: "I expect no less, and so I think, does the gallery. You lawyers on this Committee should be accustomed to argument and I am here to argue that this so-called justice system is not working properly. Refute my arguments if you can, but don't simply pick up your marbles and disappear."

He stood up.

"I am angry – very angry – and I am not afraid of you in spite of the many awful tactics that have been employed against me and my appointment!"

Bradford Justice's eyes were blazing and there wasn't a sound from anyone when he finished – and then, a few seconds later - the Senate Chamber erupted!

Everybody was yelling though not exactly the same message. but the passion was clear.

Give them hell, Brad!
Sit down, Brad!
Kill the Goddamn lawyers!
Face the music, you pompous bastard!
Brad Justice is an enemy of the people.
Justice was brainwashed by the Communists.
He wants to destroy our justice system!

The strongest voices of all, however, was the insistence that the Committee hear the man out.

The Chairman called for order over and over until finally there was almost complete silence.

"This Hearing is adjourned – until tomorrow at 9:00 AM."

The members stood up as one body and left the Chamber immediately.

The Press engaged them on their way out. Callahan acted as spokesman. None of the members interrupted.

"Obviously this Hearing got out of control. Bradford Justice is a passionate man and tempers flared. We – all of us - have to take time to take a deep breath, come back and consider this matter objectively. I am not sure such a partisan would make a good Justice, but the vote is still undecided. I can promise you that. That's all, ladies and gentlemen."

The Committee made a hasty retreat to their subway.

CHAPTER 47

The Judiciary Committee Hearing, originally scheduled for the next day, was rescheduled for Monday of the next week, presumably to let matters cool down further. Senator Callahan called an interim meeting *behind closed doors.*

President Whitredge called for an informal strategy session with Chief of Staff, Cliff Sharp, the Prof, Brad and a famous trial attorney recommended by Sharp. They were invited into the President's den in the President's private quarters.

It was a pleasant room, furnished with pieces selected by President Whitredge. It was a comfortable room: green leather armchairs, a large couch, floor to ceiling bookcases on three walls filled with books none of which dealt with politics. The photographs were of the President in action – on skis in well-known resorts, a couple of tennis scenes and one showing him dressed in hiking gear at the summit of a mountain. There was one of him in his Air Force uniform and others in the pilot seats of several of the fighters he had flown. There was a picture of the Stanford championship football team and photos of his many friends, none of whom were famous.

Brad noted with pleasure a picture of himself and Whitredge as youngsters in Wentworth Harbor. There was a Bose stereo, a CD player and lots of CDs, mostly pop including the big bands and vocalists. There were a few classics. There were no photos of his former wife or any women.

All took seats as Cliff Sharp introduced Attorney Stafford Grimes, a tall angular man with big boned hands and a pleasant smile. His conservative dress and demeanor did not indicate the flamboyance displayed by some of the other famous courtroom characters.

"Well, Mr. President, what do you think of your passionate nominee?"

The President grinned.

"Brad has turned out to be a real firebrand."

"He spoke like a man who believed the game was lost and was going to have his say no matter what." Sharp frowned.

"I enjoyed it, but I winced a lot."

Sharp continued his assigned role of the loyal opposition.

"I told Brad to give them Hell, and by God, he did. I think it played well in the Galleries – and the Press. Nobody believes Brad has the chance of a snowball in Hell in front of twelve lawyers on an eighteen man committee. No possibility of prejudice there! That hearing is a bloody farce."

The Prof made his point very clear.

"I'm not so sure. With your permission?"

Stafford Grimes addressed President Whitredge.

"I would have agreed with Mr. Justice, senior, at first, but the fact that Senator Callahan did not call for a vote, which he clearly wanted to do, indicated to me that he doesn't want his Committee to be wrong footed. The reaction in the Gallery was very strong and the Press are reacting as if a bomb had struck the Capitol. I think you gave your son good advice, Professor."

"I'd sure as Hell like to think so, Staff. That's what people call you, isn't it?"

The Prof. didn't wait for confirmation.

"What kind of objectivity is it when Callahan told the Press he didn't think a passionate man would make a good judge in such an exalted body?"

"Perhaps Brad should reprimand the Chairman. The Chairman is not supposed to offer the Press any opinion before any official decision. In fact, Senator Callahan isn't supposed to talk to the Press at all." Stafford was serious.

"I don't suppose there are any legal grounds for discrediting the Senate Judiciary Committee, but what a delicious, goddamn thought, Counselor."

"Now now, Professor, you're beginning to talk like a lawyer." Sharp grinned.

"You think we have a case here, Sharp?"

"A lawyer always thinks he has a case, Dad."

Brad Justice did not smile.

"Never mind Brad, Sharp. Let's have the practicing defense lawyer's point of view. I think the lawyer members should recuse themselves on this issue Don't you love that goddamned corruption of the English language?"

"There's no doubt about that, Mr. Justice, but perhaps we should have complained at the imbalance *before* the Hearing. Still, the fact that there is definitely a preponderance of attorneys should be regarded as unacceptable in this particular case. Yes, there is a case to be made here."

"What do you think, Cliff?"

"I agree, Mr. President."

Brad got to his feet and began to pace.

"Now wait! Let's not rush to court. I realize all of you may think that, until the Hearing, I haven't shown enough force. I have waited until I thought the place and the time were right to be forceful."

Brad paused for several moments and stood up and began pacing.

"I received the reaction I had hoped for, and now the people and the Press are becoming aware not only of some of the problems inherent in the legal system, but the incredible power of this legal monopoly. Think of it. The lawyers are in possession of the legal system and actually have the power to rule on President Whitredge's Appointee of a non-lawyer to the Supreme Court."

Brad stopped pacing and regarded each one of them in turn.

"I don't need to go to court. This Hearing *is* my court. It may take some time, but I believe the majority of witnesses to what is going on will see what we in this room see. We know there is a need for someone who is not going to perform like a lawyer, whose primary standard of judgment will be made on the basis of what is right, what is fair and best for this country – a person who will look to the law as a guide not an absolute."

"Are you saying that for you to be represented by counsel is wrong?"

"I am saying, Mr. Grimes, that to go to court with counsel will reduce the dignity of my position. I do not want to lose - or win - on the basis of some legal maneuver. Everybody will know that this Hearing by a prejudiced Committee is wrong! I do not want to resort to counsel to weaken the truth of that. If that Committee refuses to accept the President's appointee solely on the basis that he is not a lawyer, it will hang itself for the world to see. If that happens and I am rejected, we will have struck one helluva blow."

"That is the first time I've heard of any person refusing counsel when offered. I'm prepared to offer my services gratis, Senator."

"While I don't want to impugn your motives, Counselor Grimes, but as my Attorney you would receive world wide attention."

Brad shook his head, and apologized immediately.

"For me to be represented by an attorney in this matter is not only inappropriate, but such a move would be welcome to that Senate Committee. I'm sure all of you can understand the ramifications of that."

"Sounds as if you've made up your mind, Brad."

"Unless you have serious objections, Mr. President."

"Nope."

"Sounds to me like you've spent too much time in Wentworth Harbor, Mr. President." Whitredge's reversion to New Hampshire speech was evident.

"Nope."

Walter Whitredge displayed his now famous grin.

"Thank you all for coming on such short notice."

The cue was understood and they all left.

All of them would love to have been a ghostly presence at Callahan's strategy session.

CHAPTER 48

When Brad Justice arrived, he had to run the gamut of the Press. It was very difficult to thread his way through an aggressive crowd yelling questions. A few attempted to stop his progress physically which they immediately discovered was a mistake. His forward movement was only momentarily impeded. He had resolved to keep any statements for the Hearing.

When he entered the Senate Chamber, the Committee was already seated and talking among themselves behind closed mikes. Brad surveyed the Senate floor.

Every seat was filled. The galleries were packed and people were standing in the aisles.

Brad looked for the cameras. Apparently there had been an attempt to prohibit all cameras, but that had not succeeded and all the major TV stations were represented by an agreement with CNN.

Once again Brad felt he had stepped into an arena. His stomach muscles tightened and he could feel the blood rushing to his head. He clenched his fists as hard as he could and then opened them and let go. He had done exactly that just before he had made contact with the enemy. He had found it an effective procedure, enabling him to focus on the target.

He admonished himself to be calm. How could he possibly stay calm when every nerve was taut? He was convinced the entire world was tuned in and assumed the pressure must be just as hard on the Committee. That thought helped a little. He was certain at least one camera would be focused on him all the time, and with advice from Marilyn, he was dressed like a banker. He was wearing what he called his Eliot Ness suit – muted dark blue pinstripe complete with vest, handkerchief in his breast pocket, white shirt with French cuffs, cordovan shoes that gleamed and a conservative blue silk tie. Marilyn had told him he was gorgeous and very very impressive.

"You'll make the Committee members look like a bunch of nobodies."

Her kiss had been both welcome and reassuring.

Brad stood by his chair at the small table. There was no other chair beside his – no counsel telling him how to answer the questions, a situation he hoped would be noted. Brad looked up at the Senate Judiciary Committee and scanned each face carefully. Several of them looked away.

He seated himself.

The Chairman immediately called for silence. He did not have to ask twice. The entire Chamber was quiet.

Chairman Callahan: "Good Morning, Senator Justice, I trust you have taken the time afforded you to comport yourself in an appropriate manner."

He waited for Brad's response.

The ensuing silence was deafening.

Brad Justice (BJ): "Good Morning, gentlemen. I trust you have taken the time, you have afforded yourselves, to comport yourselves in a manner more suited to a judicious and objective line of questioning."

The Chairman's face reddened and everyone could hear his sharp intake of breath. His opening salvo had been returned - in spades. There wasn't an inattentive person in the entire Chamber.

The hearing had begun.

Brad immediately thought of "the law case" the Chairman was continuing to build against himself.

"Do you have a statement you would like to make at this time, Senator?"

"No"

As before Callahan waited for more. When the silence had lasted for a few seconds, he invited the Senator from Connecticut, Senator Harkins, to begin the proceedings.

SH: "I am a lawyer, admitted to the Bar in both New York and Connecticut. I have separated myself from participation in my law firm during my term in the Senate.

"I liked the practice of law, but I prefer the Senate and the possibility of improving the quality of life in my state. I believe in the law, and I certainly believe that a society without law would be a disaster, Senator."

Harkins paused, for effect, and then asked Brad,

"How do you feel about that, Senator?"

BJ: "Let's begin with the second part of your question which I will answer this way."

He paused, and then he said,

"The idea that a search for truth will eliminate laws is preposterous. Your statement has been used by lawyers for years as a self-serving remark. It is irrelevant and obviously untrue.

"As for a belief in the law, everybody knows laws are frequently unreliable and unclear. Laws are what too many lawyers spend far too much time arguing about instead of the merits of a case. The law is a guide not an absolute. Laws are made by man, not God. Lawyers' often stated belief in the rule of law is because laws provide them with the tools to obtain a desired result – and not always a just one. Most damaging of all, it removes the necessity of any responsibility to society.

"No, Senator Harkins, while I realize the need for laws, I do not believe in *The Rule of Law.* We can and must do better than that. The law should never be used as a substitute for truth. As for your idea that you can do more for the people of your state as a Senator - I believe that, as a practicing attorney, you had a unique opportunity to make life better for everyone – not just your State. Lest I confuse the issue because of my stated need for the reform of our so-called justice system, I have the utmost respect for the lawyers who accept their responsibility to society when practicing their profession. I also feel that it is a very difficult line to keep."

SH: "Your inference that my allegiance is limited to my State is insulting."

BJ: "I apologize. I should have realized you were just being political, Senator. I'm sure as a United States Senator your concern is to make laws that best serve the entire nation – regardless of Party affiliation and a purely local result."

From the look of confusion on Harkins's face, it was clear he was not mollified, but he must have realized the futility of disputing Justice's picture of the ideal United States Senator. He yielded to the Senator from New Hampshire, Evan Moody.

EM:"Why do you make points at the expense of your appointment? The men on this Committee have the power to reject you. It seems the much wiser course to have your say without any unpleasant asides."

BJ: "Thank-you, Senator Moody. I'm sure, in front of a more ***balanced*** Committee your advice would be excellent, but I have to assume that most, if not all of the lawyer-members, are against my appointment."

He looked carefully at all the members of the Committee, and continued.

"I'm not here to make friends, Gentlemen. I'm here to state a fundamental flaw in our judicial system, - which I believe is *our* ***nation's most important institution***."

He paused for a moment.

"However, in future, I will try to stick strictly to the issues. I stand rebuked."

The galleries expressed a mixed reaction.

Don't give in now! Give 'em Hell! They deserve it!

That's right, show some respect!

CH: "The Chair recognizes Senator McClure."

Even seated, Senator McClure from Texas was tall. He had a big head which was bald and picked up the light from the floods. His features were strong and he had a deep resonant voice reminiscent of the legendary fictional, Senator Claghorn.

"Oh yeah, I'm a lawyer, practiced for some years in a small town. A lot a nitty gritty in that little bitty old town, ever body related to one another. Sure glad to give that up. Tell me, former Senator Bradford Justice, what do you think about the United States Supreme Court? I sure as Hell don't think much of it. That's fer danged certain."

The audience reacted to that!

BJ: "In Britain there is no Supreme Court. Perhaps the greatest use for ours is that it – most of the time – is the last legal resort. A case, which might be litigated forever as in Dickens' Bleak House, can come to a halt. Arguments as to the pros and cons of our Supreme Court and its rulings seem endless.

"The problem, it seems to me, Senator McClure, are the myriad misinterpretations of the Constitution. Our Constitution was not meant to be rigid. It does not deal with specific laws. It was created to be the framework of our government and established the separation of powers. The Preamble is particularly valuable because it sets out, in a few words, with pristine clarity, the purposes of the

Constitution, the most important of which is ***"to establish justice***" - **not under law**. Also of particular importance to every citizen is the First Amendment's guarantee of the Right of Protest. It is the right of every citizen of this nation to protest against any law or official act any citizen believes to be unjust."

Brad regarded McClure steadily.

"SMc: "Those are tall words, Bradford Justice. Unlike some of my brethren I don't think these guarantees are properly understood. I would like to hear more."

CH: (interrupting) "I don't think this Committee has time for an elaborate discussion of the Constitution. Senator Justice has not been authenticated as a Constitutional scholar who has spent his life in research. Your time is up, Senator McClure. I'm sure there are other members who would like to ask the Senator some questions."

SMc. "Ah am not awah of any time limits assigned to this impotant Hearing."

He raised his voice.

"Maybe you think our justice system is perfect, Senator Callahan, but I sure as Hell do not! Here we have the President's Appointee to the US Supreme Court who has something important to say and you want to shut him up. Well, Mr. Chairman, I am not going to let that happen. I want to hear more – much more!"

This time everybody in that Chamber agreed loudly – the Senators present included.

Senator Callahan struck the gavel repeatedly for order.

When he could be heard sufficiently he closed the Hearing. He set no date for its continuance.

Everyone who could, immediately crowded around the Committee who called the Sergeant at Arms and his police to clear their way out of the Senate Chamber and through the Press to a waiting ***special*** bus.

The newspapers were full of news of the Hearing and editorials, the gist of which said, that this was the first time any candidate for the Supreme Court had anything to say that was so controversial and important. Constitutional scholar or not the man has something to say and he was saying it extremely well. Hooray for Senator McClure, a lawyer, who recognized that our justice system is far from perfect. Our very own Senator Claghorn raised his voice for something important.

An editorial in the Washington Post made a point that was possibly on a lot of minds when the writer recalled another such hearing in the past in which the President's Appointee never answered any question that would commit him to any conviction. He hadn't refused. He had simply changed the subject.

He won without a dissenting vote. No one listening *to that* Hearing had the slightest idea what the man stood for – except possibly – the law, since he was at the time a member of his state's Supreme Court.

The Editor concluded that Bradford Justice, on the other hand, was ready to answer any question any of the members asked - without any hesitation. How very refreshing!

CHAPTER 49

The Senate Judiciary Committee Chairman ordered an Executive Session, behind closed doors. He made sure security was tight. Security Police were stationed outside at all exits and entrances. Had he been able, he would have conducted the discussion in whispers and in the dark.

Callahan drew a deep breath, searched the faces of all seventeen members of his committee, and spoke.

CH: "To begin with, I want to know where we stand."

He let his frustration show.

"Is there any member of this Committee in favor of appointing this appointee to the United States Supreme Court?" He paused. "I am going to go around this table and ask you, individually, to give me your opinions. I will begin with the lawyer/members.

Evan Moody (EM) "With your permission, Senator, I would like to begin."

Callahan nodded his assent, with obvious regret.

EM: "I am not a lawyer and for most of you that puts me at a disadvantage, possibly a crippling disadvantage."

He cleared his throat.

"For the first time in our legal history a President has appointed an educated citizen who has served our country well but is not a member of the legal fraternity. To some of you, I think, that amounts to heresy.

Do you, any of you, really believe only a lawyer can understand the truth or have the wisdom to make fair judgments? If any of you do, then all branches of government must be headed by lawyers. I wonder if, even lawyers, would really want that. We're certainly headed that way. Lawyers are everywhere. Our Presidents have been lawyers, but according to the Constitution being a lawyer is not a requirement for the Presidency. In my opinion that was not an oversight. The Framers did not trust the sovereignty of the law certainly not to a King who was the law. If they could see our justice system and government monopolized by lawyers and the power they exercise, I think they would be horrified.

Can any of you lawyers really believe that legal ethics have anything whatever to do with genuine ethics outside the law? I know there are Bar Associations which want to improve the ethical standards to be more in keeping with what most of us laymen believe are true ethical standards, but like so many movements for reform they stall because of the opposition by the majority of lawyers.

I believe the appointment of an educated, obviously intelligent person is just what our justice system desperately needs. We need the non-lawyer perspective. We need people who will question the law - especially the practices, though presently legal, which informed citizens deplore."

Moody paused again.

"The law is not sacred. That's what the man said, and he is right!"

None of Moody's fellow Senators had ever heard Evan Moody speak so passionately and articulately.

Senator Scott (SC): "Evan, you are attacking our most important institution. We lawyers are sworn to uphold the Constitution, which is far more than most of the citizens have to do. We are all Officers of the Court. Ours is a trust conveyed by the people, and most of us try to live up to those standards and have studied the law and try to operate within the law. An attack on our most cherished institution is not warranted."

EV: "Cherished? There are more derisive, demeaning jokes about our legal system and lawyers than any other - with the possible exception of politicians. The American people do not like or respect lawyers, and are finally becoming aware that no one is minding their store. There are almost no effective penalties for lawyers who misbehave. A lot of the mean tactics employed by lawyers in pursuing a case are accepted as the customary procedure and as such legal. That is deplorable and must be questioned. Litigation must not be the only way to register a complaint or settle a dispute.

"There are so many wrongs done within our system and the men and women who operate in it that it is impossible to catalog them all. What Bradford Justice wants is to refocus the Justice System on what, in his opinion, and my opinion too, is the delivery of justice for every American. We have put the law above the discovery of truth. It has been a tragic mistake. This nation owes President Whitredge gratitude for such forward thinking and Bradford Justice for his courage and willingness to accept the challenge.

"This is the first time in our history that our legal system - the law per se - is being challenged as being neither wise nor fair. Ours is not only a great responsibility it is a wonderful and heretofore unavailable opportunity.

"The law must never be used as an excuse for disgraceful behavior."

He regarded each of his colleagues carefully.

"The people want Bradford Justice to be on that court. If any of you want to be reelected, you should vote in the affirmative."

Sen. McClure: "I'm not thinking of reelection. Whichever way we vote we'll be damned if we do and damned if we don't. We do need some fresh air in our legal system, and for my money, Bradford Justice will provide the right amount of fresh air. I will vote to accept the President's appointee! I hope some of the lawyers on this committee will wake up and hear the birdies sing.

"We're not improving our system from within, anyway not nearly fast enough, and we've had donkey's years to make some very important changes. It will take a Bradford Justice – a non-lawyer - to do it, and you all know it. Hell, we might even be popular for a change. Wouldn't that be pleasant."

Chair: (now clearly alarmed) "I am shocked, Senator McClure. You are being a traitor to the legal profession."

McC: "The legal system stinks! It is filled with greedy, socially irresponsible people who will litigate anything for anyone if there's the slightest possibility for gain. They will do anything, no matter how unethical, to win. It can and should be a noble profession made up of people who care about the society that depends on them, and when you, who know the truth of what I have just said, refuse to take the first chance for establishing dignity and respect, you're either too thick to understand or afraid of a system based on truth because it will interfere with your practice. And that, my friends is my honest opinion."

Ch. (Callahan): "Is there any other lawyer on this Committee who is ready to approve the President's appointee?"

A stony silence ensued as everyone looked at each other waiting for someone to speak up. When nobody did, Callahan rephrased the question.

"Are all the other lawyers on this Committee going to deny the President's Appointee?"

When another silence followed, Callahan threw up his hands.

Callahan: "Does anybody else want to say anything? Any questions?"

Evan Moody: "OK, I'll ask a question, Joe. How are you prepared to vote?"

Callahan: "Well, Evan, I'm not sure."

Evan Moody: "You waitin' for God to tell you?"

Callahan (nodding slowly) "That's not such a bad idea, Ev."

There was one lawyer/member, who had for a long time, tried not to let a conversation with his friend, Alvah Trickey, continue to trouble him. Alvah had thought he had fallen asleep – passed out – when Trickey had suggested the possibility of assassination as the ultimate solution. This Senator now wondered whether Trickey had hired an assassin! He tried to reject the idea as incredible, but Alvah Trickey was an incredible man and absolutely ruthless. There was no doubt what motivated Alvah Trickey.

This Senator now felt compelled to find out, but he was suddenly afraid. He shrugged. Trickey would never tell him. Alvah Trickey would never tell anyone. And then the Senator wondered what effect that would have on the Committee's vote, if those who were opposed to confirmation learned that Bradford Justice would never serve.

The Senator shook his head. It was too much to deal with.

As the members left the room, Callahan asked Senator Hamilton Harkness to wait up.

Callahan: "I guess I know how you're going to vote, Hamilton."

Hamilton: (startled) "Well, I know a non-lawyer should never serve on that court, but," he hesitated "there may be another way to prevent that."

Hamilton cursed himself, but he couldn't help it. Keeping his mouth shut had never been his strong point. Assassination would be the ultimate solution. The committee could appear attentive to the idea of justice and look good knowing that there was --- Hamilton stopped dead – but they couldn't know! Conspiracy to murder was too much knowledge - even for lawyers.

Senator Hamilton Harkness resolved to have a meeting with Trickey. Only this time he would control his drinking and stay awake.

CHAPTER 50

Alvah Trickey led Senator Hamilton Harkness up to the soundproof conference room in the penthouse suite of Trickey, Slye and Diddle. It was an inner room. He had never been there before. There were no windows, no telephones and only one door and that was soundproof. It was 10:00 PM and the place was deserted. This was probably the most secure room in Boston – if not the entire world.

It made Senator Harkness nervous which the absence of alcohol didn't help.

He looked around him and felt trapped. It was almost like entering a vault.

"You could plan the destruction of the world here." His voice was almost a whisper.

Hamilton thought he saw Alvah's eyes gleam.

"Yes, Hammie," the paunchy little man hated the nickname. "Yes, Hammie," Alvah repeated. "This room has hatched a great many schemes, some of them very successful. I call it the Room of Denials because it is a place in which to make deniable statements."

Alvah made no attempt to hide his pride in his Room of Denials. For him it was as sacred as a temple.

"You don't have a recorder on you, Hammie?"

Alvah regarded the Senator suspiciously.

"Of course not!"

"I don't tolerate any recorders in this room."

"What happens when one of your partners has the temerity to disagree with you here?"

"They're not invited again."

"Does anyone ever disagree with you?"

"Occasionally."

"Really?"

"Not that it matters. Nothing is official here so I don't need a quorum. What did you want to see me about, Hammie?"

"Nothing important, really. I just thought you would appreciate an update on our Committee's thinking."

Senator Hamilton was afraid. He was sorry he had come and especially to this inner sanctum. The place was obscene.

"Well, what's your impression? Your esteemed colleagues are not going to support the President?"

"I'm not entirely sure. Senator McClure has declared himself in favor of the man. Evan Moody and his fellow laymen seem inclined that way too."

"Cowards! Turncoats!"

Senator Harkness cleared his throat.

"I'm leaning towards approval myself, Alvah."

He had to force the words.

"I wish you were a man of influence instead of a damn lush."

"How unkind of you, Alvah, but I expect no more of you."

"Well, I expect more of you – a lot more. I want you to convince your fellow committee members to vote *for* Bradford Justice."

Trickey ***had hired an assassin***!

Hamilton Harkness wanted to get out of that room – now! He did not want to hear any more. He looked at his watch.

"Gosh, Alvah, it's later than I thought. I've got to go. I have another appointment."

Hamilton stood up and turned toward the door. Alvah, with agility surprising in such a big man, inserted himself between Hamilton and the door.

"You don't have an appointment, you little son of a bitch! You're not important to anyone but me. Sit down and listen to what I'm going to tell you."

Alvah backed the man down and into a chair.

"I don't want to hear you! What I don't know, I can never be responsible for. Please, Alvah, for old time's sake, don't involve me in any scheme of yours!"

"You didn't really pass out, did you? You know I was considering hiring an assassin. I'm not telling you something you didn't suspect."

Trickey began pacing.

"I've been hanging on to this business for some time now. I can't put it out of my mind. Above all, I was convinced I could never tell anyone what I had done. Never!"

Trickey was talking to himself as if Hamilton weren't there. Abruptly he faced the man. Trickey's eyes were wild.

"Yes, Goddammit, I have hired an assassin! I paid him fifty thousand dollars as a non refundable deposit with a guarantee that in the event of Justice's approval by the Committee, I would give him another one hundred thousand to kill the son of a bitch."

Alvah's face was suddenly a mask of fear.

"There is no way I can turn the assassin off! I hate Bradford Justice! I have never hated anyone so much! I hate him because he probably believes in this twaddle about justice."

"Don't pay your assassin the hundred thousand and he'll go away."

Hamilton was pleading.

"I don't believe that's possible. I think the guy wants to kill – that he will - even if I don't pay him. I think there's a possibility he'll kill me too. He certainly will, if I don't give him a hundred thousand dollars."

Hamilton let his mind wander, unbidden. If he could be sure, he would be willing to put up the hundred thousand to the assassin to kill Alvah Trickey. The man was certifiably insane. Hamilton did not believe anyone would mourn Trickey's departure. Hamilton was almost in a trance just thinking about a world without Trickey.

"Maybe, *you,* Hammie, should tell the lawyers that Justice will never serve – to go ahead and approve him. *You* could do it, Hammie."

Trickey was rapidly warming up to the idea.

"You could tell them you know there's a contract out on Justice, but only if he is approved. You'll get an affirmative vote just like that!"

Alvah clapped the poor little bent over man on the back and almost knocked him down.

"I'm not going to tell anyone anything! I don't want to have any part in this. That hurt, Alvah! You're much too big to go around hitting people!"

Hamilton tried to stand up straight and winced with pain at what turned out to be an unsuccessful maneuver. He would give his soul for a drink.

"You're going to do it, Hammie. For once in your life you're going to do something worthwhile. You will be the savior of the Justice System. You'll go down in the secret annals of American legal history! You will have earned the respect and gratitude of lawyers everywhere! I envy you, Hammie!"

Hamilton managed to move just fast enough to avoid another smashing blow of congratulation from the now ebullient Alvah Trickey.

"I won't do it. You can't make me do it!"

"You'll do it, Hammie or I'll make it two for one. That guy will kill anyone I tell him to! The man's a fucking lunatic. I've bought plenty of witnesses in my time, but this guy takes the cake. He makes me feel pious, for Christ's sake. What a deal! Everybody looks good. The Judiciary Committee can bathe in its welcome of Justice, get credit for being open-minded and my man bumps Justice off never to be a pimple on the legal behind. You've got to do it – to convince the legal diehards to vote their approval!"

Trickey's voice was suddenly conspiratorial. His thick lips began to moisten, savoring his delicious strategy.

"You haven't got much time and you've got to talk to them one at a time. I mean you can't simply call a meeting and convince them all to become a conspiracy. Even they don't have big enough balls for that!"

Trickey paused at that thought because he wasn't entirely convinced. In his professional experience even the pious seemed to have balls enough for everything --- still, he shook his head – it would be better to go at each one of the them singly.

Senator Hamilton Harkness shook himself and finally managed to stand upright. He had nothing to lose so he steeled himself and faced Trickey.

"It simply will not work, Alvah."

Hamilton tried to keep his voice steady.

"Of course it will work. It is the way out for them."

"I'll tell you why it won't work. You will be putting each man you tell this to in the position of an executioner, directly responsible for Justice's death. If you breathe one word about your assassin, they will never vote Justice's approval. They'll be looking at each other convinced that any affirmative vote by any fellow lawyer means he is an assassin! I don't think most of us even like each other. I know we don't really trust one another. Your plan will guarantee Justice's rejection."

He paused.

"Now that I know, Alvah, I cannot vote for Justice either."

Alvah looked dejected for the first time. He shrugged.

"Hate to let such a wonderful opportunity go by." He looked thoughtful.

"I could have the assassin murder the President. No."

He shook his head.

"Too late now. The President couldn't withdraw his support for Justice, if he were dead."

Alvah Trickey's disappointment was palpable.

Hamilton discovered he had to go to the toilet, and convinced Alvah to let him out.

Hamilton fled.

CHAPTER 51

Senator Joseph Callahan raised the gavel to begin the Hearing. The gesture was unnecessary. Everyone who had a seat was already in it. All conversation had ceased. Once again, Bradford Justice was standing alone in the well of the Senate.

Outside the building, crowds had assembled. They were also silent. Some were displaying placards pleading for “Justice First”, “Justice in ***Our*** Courts” and “Justice for ***All***.” They were quiet – tense and listening.

Every Bar in the city had its TV tuned to the Hearing.

George Justice’s living room in Wentworth Harbor was crowded with his special people all of whom, even the Prof, were quiet. Laura Peniman had set up the bar, but no one was making a move in that direction. Laura seated herself on the arm of George’s leather chair. Her hand was on his shoulder. She had been giving him a much-needed massage trying to loosen up back and neck muscles that were much too tight.

Had the accommodations been large enough, the entire adult population of Wentworth Harbor would have crowded into the Prof’s home.

Every public building was filled with well wishers. The Wentworth Harbor Inn had offered their public rooms and provided tea, coffee and doughnuts. Most of the rest of the residents of Wentworth Harbor invited friends and neighbors to their homes. The few who didn’t have TV listened to New Hampshire Public Radio. Even those who had taken no interest in the proceedings suddenly wanted to hear Brad Justice’s last argument. Their attention was similar to the interest, even among the initiated, in the last game of the World Series or the final Bowl Game. They did not want to be left out of something so obviously of vital interest to so many people. The whole world wanted to know the official ruling on the role of justice in the legal system of the United States of America, the most powerful nation in the world. President Whitredge and Bradford Justice had struck a deep chord. Never in history had their been such a forum for Justice.

President Whitredge was seated in the Oval Office, surrounded by most of his personal staff including Cliff Sharp, whose expression showed his disbelief in what he had been convinced was the impossible. Whitredge was watching his little legal eagle and realized with regret that Sharp had still not gotten the message, and wondered how many lawyers still refused to understand.

Cameramen had been permitted to stand by outside the Oval Office ready to get the President's reactions.

**** **** **** ****

Chairman Callahan: "Are you ready to make a statement, Senator Justice?"

"I am."

"You can take your seat, Senator."

"I prefer to stand, Senator."

The Chairman's face reddened. The man had not asked for permission. Callahan briefly considered a sarcastic invitation to come up to the dais, but was afraid the man would accept.

"You may proceed."

"Thank-you."

Brad turned first to his left and then to his right. He looked upward to the Galleries. He turned briefly to the Senators seated behind him.

"I feel the presence of all of you even those I cannot see."

Bradford regarded the Committee members carefully.

"I'm reminded of a previous occasion at which I was asked to speak. I had asked the Chairman what he wanted me to speak about. His reply was, "About five minutes."

There was laughter - to everyone's momentary relief.

"Having spoken in every media available to us, I'm sure our President and I have left no doubt of our belief in the need of people not trained in the law, to have a place on our Supreme Court. And you now know why."

Brad lifted the glass of water from his small desk. His voice was about to become hoarse. Occasionally his asthma could affect his voice especially when he felt pressured.

"There is an important difference between the training of lawyers and that of the rest of us. Lawyers are trained in the art of argument and arguing to win – whatever the side of the dispute, regardless of its fairness, their client's character, the alleged crime or uncivil action. Their tools are the myriad of laws created by legislation, trials and sometimes by the rulings of the Supreme Court. Their playing fields are their courts. It has become a game of win or lose and winning is always their goal. Their opponents and judges, with very few exceptions, are also lawyers – players in *the game*. Their reputations – and fees are dependent on the number of wins. It is for them a game in which legality - not right or wrong - is the standard for performance. Moreover this procedure can be extremely profitable. To consider anything that might cause them to lose a case or minimize their access to our courts is not acceptable.

"There really is little motivation to change anything even in the interest of fairness or even handed procedure. Truth is too easily legally maneuvered and even concealed. Their primary responsibility is solely to their clients - not to society.

"And now we come to judges, now required in most states to have had legal training – the same training as practicing attorneys.

"What is their mission? To follow and adhere to the appropriate laws – regardless of any other consideration. To be legally correct will considerably reduce the possibility of their rulings being overturned – a black mark against their professional reputation. There was a time when citizens could be elected or appointed judges without having had any legal accreditation. Was it their poor performance that has mandated a change or was it accomplished by the various Bar Associations to maximize their power?

"Doesn't that sound like a monopoly to you? Only selected lawyers can appear before the Supreme Court. Who engineered that? Are their qualifications rigid adherence to the laws pertaining to the Supreme Court? Doesn't that sound prohibitively rigid to you? Where are the people in all this rigidity? What happens to those who require change – who wish to exercise our most fundamental right – our right of protest – right to appeal? What happens to fairness and the search for truth? Is it any wonder that our present system is in such ill repute, subject to ridicule and contempt – here - and abroad.

"Surely judges should be able to recognize when legal performance has not produced a verdict most people can respect. They are on salary – without hope for a minimum of thirty percent of a huge settlement. Judges can afford to be fair in their judgments. The drawback is that they are trained to the law.

"The only chance, and it is certainly a slim one, is to bring in an outsider – a layman – whose primary interest is to secure fair play for every American citizen who applies to our Courts.

"There is no punishment for ignoring that."

He paused to let that thought be digested..

"No, I am not a lawyer. I am not trained to win a questionable dispute by purely legal argument. I am not ashamed to use the words truth, fairness and justice. I do not need to adopt the lawyer substitute for those qualities expressed in their word 'proportionality'. I have not been trained to dissimulate. To dissimulate means to deceive. I care deeply about my country and accept my responsibility to society.

"Not only is the average citizen confused about the function of our courts and the law, many are afraid of the law and the courts. It is a procedure that is intimidating, very costly and with uncertain result. Many an official – within the system - has advised – actually warned – people not to go to court expecting to find justice.

"What other legitimate reason is there to go to court?

"The most meaningful writing in our so-called Justice system is the Preamble to the Constitution. It is short and wonderfully clear."

He observed a moment of silence in which he was joined by everyone.

"It is quite wonderful, and easy to remember. Our Constitution establishes our form of government to carry out those aims.

"The first purpose is to **ESTABLISH JUSTICE.** ***There are no conditions.***

"The preamble does not agree with the engraving in marble on our Supreme Court building. **EQUAL JUSTICE UNDER LAW.**

"Justice ***is*** equal. It cannot be anything else. The word equal is redundant.

"Laws are subject to change, created by man not by God, frequently confusing and poorly written not to be considered rigidly as superior to justice. Enforcement of laws must always be subject to the circumstances under which their transgressions have been made."

He waited a moment before continuing.

"What else does any thinking person need to know?

"The law cannot think! The law does not care. Only a lawyer could insist on putting the rule of laws above justice?"

Again he paused.

"Think of all the propaganda one hears almost every day. A nation without law is chaos. A man who defends himself has a fool for a client. Don't you wonder who thought that one up?

"Who wants a nation without rules and regulations? Some would have you believe I do. We want, and you have the right to expect, rules and regulations to be clearly written so as to be readily understood. Why, if a person's cause is just, and the rules clear, is one in danger if not represented by a lawyer? Are the tricks of the trade more important than a legitimate position? Should they be?"

He now addressed the Committee.

"What are you so afraid of, gentlemen? Certainly not me. I am only one man, one vote on a Court with eight lawyers!

"We have been misinformed, gentlemen.

"The law ***will not - cannot - by itself - tell the judge what is right or wrong nor should it compel a judge to make a judgment he knows is wrong.*** The law doesn't have a social or moral conscience. The ***Game*** has become far more important than its purpose. And that ***Game*** is not the game the people can afford and should be obliged to play."

Brad was out of breath. He began again but softer.

"People's lives can hang in the balance. Fortunes can be lost or won. Freedom can be removed forever. Everything can hang on legal technicalities that may have no real bearing on the actual facts.

"I know there is a middle ground of professionals who respect their profession, assume their responsibility to society and care about being of service to those who need their help. They are there and I have the greatest respect for them. Given the carte blanche available to lawyers' legal behavior and the potential for great reward, I know it must be extremely difficult not to succumb. Unfortunately the voices for reform have not been strong enough. Time has proven that the necessary improvement will not come about from within.

"We cannot continue to muddle along and fail to bring about a just society unless we finally realize that the major problem **is *the legal system itself and some of its practitioners*.**

"Former Associate Justice, Oliver Wendell Holmes, one of our most quoted Justices, when told, hopefully, "Now that we have you on the Supreme Court we can expect justice." He replied, "I don't do justice. I do the law."

"I want you, the Senators on this committee who have been trained in the law, to ask yourselves the following questions:

"Is our legal system fair to all regardless of race or economics?

"Should lawyer ethics be less than those of the people?

"Are changes in the law needed such as the elimination of contingency fees, the primary motivation for which is greater access to the courts, the awarding of all legal costs to the defendant in the event of a summary judgment in his favor? Shouldn't there be fines and disbarment of lawyers who bring frivolous or malicious suits? Should laws be written without unnecessary outmoded legal vocabulary confusing to laymen? Since ignorance of the law is no excuse, should the law be kept a secret? Shouldn't the present code of legal ethics be expanded to include ethics most Americans understand?

"Don't we need the perspective of the non-professional to better represent the point of view of the people so we can have the respect for our system essential to the well being of our society?

"Isn't the woeful lack of respect for lawyers and judges degrading the legal system and the society that tolerates it?

"We are a truly polyglot nation representing many religions – many of which are divisive – an increasingly real threat to our nation's survival, Our legal/justice system can and must represent everyone – the one institution we all can respect that will bind us together.

"It is after all in our Pledge ---- with liberty and JUSTICE FOR ALL.

"Yes, gentlemen, I want the opportunity to serve on the United States Supreme Court where my first consideration will be to reestablish justice as our first consideration.

"Thank-you."

The entire chamber went up. It was Bedlam. Justice was the cry. The few doubters were quiet. If at that moment, there had been a negative vote, the Judiciary Committee might have been in personal danger. There could be absolutely no doubt about what the people wanted. And they would not be denied.

It was the fundamental of a Democracy not to resist the will of a people who could be led but never forced to accept what they did not want.

Senator Callahan searched the faces of the members of the Committee and the answer was unmistakable. He pounded his gavel for order. It took quite awhile. He spread out his hands as if in a welcoming embrace. He spoke to his Committee.

"Do I hear a vote in the affirmative, gentleman? Is it unanimous?

It was!

Callahan stood and waited until order was resumed.

"This Committee has voted - unanimously - to confirm President Walter Whitredge's Appointee, Bradford Justice, Associate Justice to the United States Supreme Court. This hearing is adjourned."

Bradford Justice solemnly accepted the hand of congratulation from every member of the Committee as the people cheered and began swarming around the newest member of ***their*** Supreme Court.

CHAPTER 52

Two weeks after the confirmation of Bradford Justice Associate Justice to the United States Supreme Court, the following story appeared on page three of the Boston Globe.

Alvah Trickey, senior partner of Trickey Slye and Diddle, was found shot to death in the study of his home in Weston, an upscale suburb of Boston. There was nothing reported stolen or any known motive for his killing. Weston Chief of Police has volunteered the opinion that the crime seems to have been committed by someone the deceased knew as there was no sign of forced entry. The motive appears personal. The investigation is continuing.

A brief editorial in the same paper offered the following comments on the Trickey murder.

Alvah Trickey was a member of the Massachusetts Bar, a substantial contributor to civic causes, and a strong advocate of the Rule of Law with strict adherence to the Constitution. As an advocate of a well known member of Organized Crime it is possible that he had made enemies within that organization – even though his body was not found in the trunk of his car or at the bottom of the Harbor his feet encased in cement shoes.

Whoever said it was possible to do business with the Devil as long as you know it is the Devil was wrong – dead wrong.

Bradford Justice's induction was performed in the United States Supreme Court..

The oath was administered by the Chief Justice and witnessed by the Associate Justices and the President of the United States, Walter Whitredge. The courtroom was filled to capacity in the front row of which were Marilyn Justice and their two sons.

The vast marble lobby was crowded and the guard, doubled in force, were on special alert, but the people were relatively quiet and very well behaved..

The broad marble steps were also covered, and the street below as well.

It was, after all, a solemn moment, never before witnessed in American history.

Author's Note:

This book was first written 11 years ago. Since the Legal Monopoly continues to grow ever stronger, I saw no need to bring it up to date.

Henry S. Maxfield

Printed in the United States
80204LV00002B/151-186

9 780966 628913